EYE FOR AN EYE

Kerry Wilkinson has been busy since turning thirty.

His first Jessica Daniel novel, *Locked In*, was a number one ebook bestseller, while the series as a whole has sold a million copies.

He has written a fantasy-adventure trilogy for young adults, a second crime series featuring private investigator Andrew Hunter, plus the standalone thrillers *Down Among Dead Men* and *No Place Like Home*.

Originally from the county of Somerset, Kerry has spent too long living in the north of England, picking up words like 'barm' and 'ginnel'.

When he's short of ideas, he rides his bike or bakes cakes. When he's not, he writes it all down.

For more information about Kerry and his books visit:

www.kerrywilkinson.com or www.panmacmillan.com

www.twitter.com/kerrywk

www.facebook.com/kerrywilkinsonbooks

Or you can email Kerry at kerrywilkinson@live.com

Also by Kerry Wilkinson

KERRY WILKINSON

EYE FOR AN EYE

PAN BOOKS

First published 2018 by Pan Books
an imprint of Pan Macmillan
20 New Wharf Road, London N1 9RR
Associated companies throughout the world
www.panmacmillan.com

ISBN 978-1-5098-0665-2

1 3 5 7 9 8 6 4 2

A CIP catalogue record for this book is available from the British Library.

Typeset by Ellipsis, Glasgow
Printed and bound by CPI Group (UK) Ltd, Croydon, CR0 4YY

Visit www.panmacmillan.com to read more about all our books
and to buy them. You will also find features, author interviews and
news of any author events, and you can sign up for e-newsletters
so that you're always first to hear about our new releases.

EYE FOR AN EYE

SEVENTEEN YEARS AGO

Alice was annoyed.

Not just 'Oops, I forgot to put the bins out'-annoyed; more 'I could stop the car right now and make my idiotic husband walk the rest of the way home'-annoyed. She glanced away from the road towards said idiotic husband, Dylan. He was slumped against the window on the passenger's side of their Micra, asleep with a thin slime of drool slinking across his chin. Attractive. Very sexy.

It was after midnight, the intermittent street lights along the deserted A road cutting through the darkness, and Alice was ready for bed. It had been her work's party, yet she was the designated driver and Dylan had launched himself at the free bar like a desperate singleton hunting down a thrown bouquet.

She took another glance at him and then allowed the car to gently drift across the central line, before wrenching the steering wheel back into place and straightening up. The tyres squeaked across the surface as Dylan's head flopped away from the window and then bounced back into it with a solid clunk. He gasped and coughed as he awoke, sending a splutter of saliva onto the dashboard.

'Whuh . . . where are we?'

Alice focused on the road, unable to bring herself to look at him. 'Earth.'

He sounded groggy. 'Where?'

'Never mind.'

Dylan snorted up what sounded like a thick glob of snot and then continued sniffing, before launching into a flurry of tongue clucks. 'That was a decent night.'

Alice clamped her teeth together, not trusting herself to reply.

'Allie?'

'What?'

'Decent night, yeah?'

'It was until some dickhead spoiled it.'

'That guy with the glasses who was dancing? Yeah, I thought he was a bit much.'

'I meant you.'

There was a pause as Dylan tried to swallow, before succumbing to another round of coughing. The alcohol had unsurprisingly dried out his throat. His voice was scratchy but outraged: '*I* spoiled it?'

'The free bar was a reward because we've worked so hard this year, not a challenge for you to drink everything they had.'

'The barman talked me into doing those whisky shots.'

'It didn't take much convincing – then what happened with dessert?'

'What about it?'

'You had four! It was supposed to be a classy three-course meal but you had your own pudding, then finished off Deborah from accounting's—'

'She said she didn't want it.'

'Then you had half of mine and took an extra one off the waitress. If that wasn't enough, you ate most of that block of cheese afterwards.'

'So what?'

'So you looked like a pig. I've got to go back to the office next week and now everyone's seen you troughing like a rabid pig.'

'*I* was embarrassing?'

'Are you saying you weren't?'

'What about your boss? Coming around telling jokes that weren't funny. Everyone was laughing like he was the reincarnation of Bill Hicks.'

'That's because *he's* the boss. When he tells a joke, you laugh. You were sat there with four empty pints of Stella in front of you, an empty bottle of wine and four dessert bowls. He'd paid for all of that. The least you could do was smile.'

Dylan strained against his seatbelt, twisting, ready for an argument. 'He wasn't funny.'

'I don't care. You're not coming next year.'

'I wouldn't want to. What were those company awards all about? They did a *This Is Your Life* for some bloke who packs boxes. I thought it was a gag but some woman at the front started crying and I realised everyone was taking it seriously.'

'That's because Frank's worked there for twenty-five years and he's retiring. It was a nice gesture. You spoiled the whole thing by laughing.'

'They were playing *Wind Beneath My Wings* and he was singing along. I thought it was a joke.'

'*You* were the only joke.'

'Oh, whatever.'

The windows were beginning to steam up, so Alice reached down and turned the heating on, knowing it was going to be a long week. She'd get the sideways smirks from her colleagues, who would gossip among themselves about who had the most embarrassing partner. There was little doubt it was her. She knew this had always been likely to happen but there was only so long she could get away with hiding her husband. She was surprised he'd worn the required suit instead of one of his collection of Manchester City shirts. At least nobody had got him onto the subject of football.

After taking the turn onto Eccles Old Road, Alice accelerated, heading towards the hospital. The road was empty but the traffic lights were glowing crimson anyway.

Typical.

She rolled to a stop, leaving the engine growling as she continued to face forward, refusing to engage with Dylan, who was leaning on the window again. After what seemed like an age, the amber light appeared. Alice was about to pull away when the shadow of a figure stumbled off the pavement on the far side of the junction. Her first thought was that it was a drunk, faltering their way home after a night on the lash, but there was something about the shape that didn't seem right. As the silhouette staggered underneath a street light, the features became clearer. It was a woman, her dark hair a tangled mess piled on her head, her top ripped and halfway down her arm, jeans loose and unbuttoned, feet bare.

Alice pulled the car to the side, leaving the hazard lights blinking. She opened the door and leant out, the chill bristling across her skin. 'Hey, are you all right?'

The young woman turned to face Alice, her skin pale, eyes wide. She was shaking, hugging her arms across her stomach. For a moment, they made eye contact, then the girl turned away and started to move more quickly, spinning on the spot and hurrying along the road. Alice held onto the car door, wondering if she should follow. They were a mile from home and it was late. Stopping anywhere at this time could be dangerous . . . but there was something chilling about the girl's gaze: she wasn't drunk or lost, she was terrified.

Dylan opened his door and climbed out, peering into the distance. He sounded calm and clear, no longer after an argument, not even drunk. 'Is she all right?'

'I don't know.'

Before Alice could say anything else, Dylan had stepped onto the pavement and was crossing the junction. Alice locked the car and followed, quickening her pace to pass him. The girl glanced back over her shoulder towards them and tripped, her bare feet scraping across the gravelly tarmac as she bumped into a lamppost.

'Do you need help? I can give you a lift somewhere.'

Alice's voice echoed through the darkness without reply. The girl tried to run but there was no strength in her legs and she was off-balance. She lurched sideways, entangling herself in a hedge. As Alice approached, she saw the blood smeared across the girl's midriff, the red seeping in all directions across her white top like a macabre Rorschach image. The girl kept one hand on her stomach, using the other to try to push herself out of the raking greenery.

'Are you okay?'

The girl opened her mouth to answer just as Dylan arrived at Alice's shoulder. Her eyes flickered towards him and then she screamed. Alice winced as the banshee shrill pierced her ears. She pushed her hand across her husband's chest and forced him away, pointing towards the other side of the road, not needing to say anything as he did as he'd silently been told. The girl was out of breath, panting as her shriek dissipated to a whimper.

'What happened?' Alice asked.

The girl continued gasping, watching Dylan cross the road as she allowed Alice to lift her out of the hedge. Her hands were covered in blood, leaving a palm print on Alice's coat as she leant on her for support. She continued glancing nervously across the road.

'He's my husband,' Alice whispered. 'You're safe. There's a hospital down the road – I'll drive you. What's your name?'

The girl nodded, teeth chattering in the cold, one hand still pressed into her blood-drenched stomach. Her voice was soft, barely there, a tickle on the breeze that chilled Alice to the bone. 'I'm Anne . . . He had a knife.'

1

MONDAY

Detective Inspector Jessica Daniel suppressed a shiver, refusing to admit she was cold despite the gale howling through the gaping window. From her experience, hotel windows could usually be opened an inch or two at most, which proved utterly useless in the middle of summer. Still, she was more of a Premier Inn type of person and had never rented the entire floor at the top of a five-star hotel.

Blaine Banner sat on the corner of the super-duper king-size mega-bed, picking at something between his teeth. He was wearing skin-tight jeans that brought a new meaning to the phrase 'skinny fit' and left Jessica in no doubt on which side he dressed. Not that she was thinking about that as she tried to focus on her notepad, not him. There was a magnetism that was hard to ignore. He was in his late forties, tanned and topless, long blond hair hanging down his back. His left side was tattooed with an enormous sun, orangey stencilled rays creeping around his back and torso, arms slim yet muscled.

'You cold, darlin'?' The gravelly tones scratched from his throat and even his voice held a charm, despite the casual sexism.

'It's fine,' Jessica replied.

The hotel room was enormous – bigger than the ground floor of Jessica's house – with luxurious carpets, fresh flowers and a tray in the corner piled high with food.

Banner nodded at the window. 'Fresh air's good for the mind.'

Given the faint odour, she suspected it was more to do with giving him somewhere to smoke, despite the row of 'no smoking' signs next to the lift.

'I was wondering if you still had the note, Mr Banner.'

'Call me Blaine, hon.'

Jessica gritted her teeth. 'The note?'

'What note?'

'You called the police to say that someone had threatened to kill you by leaving a message in your room.'

He stared at her with the air of someone who didn't speak English. 'Right.'

'And you've already had officers come out to you this morning . . . ?'

'Right.'

'But your management *insisted* they wanted someone more senior.'

He stared at her blankly, bottom lip pouting. 'I might've told them I wanted someone *prettier*.' He winked and broke into a crooked smile, showing a flash of Hollywood teeth. Jessica wanted to be offended but it was hard not to be taken in.

'So . . . do you have the note?'

He shook his head. 'There wasn't a note.'

Jessica put down her pad. 'I don't understand why I'm here then.'

'It was all on the mirror, plain as day.'

'What was?'

'The message. As soon as I went in for a shower, it all got a bit steamy' – another wink – 'and then it appeared.'

'Did you show the, er, *message* to the officers this morning?'

'Nah – rubbed it away.'

It took a lot of effort but Jessica managed not to roll her eyes. She'd known this visit was going to be a waste of time from the moment Detective Chief Inspector Lewis Topper asked her to go. Everything concerning Blaine Banner had been front-page news in the area since he'd announced his two-week residency at the Manchester Arena. He'd not performed in his home town for a decade, despite being one of the biggest rock draws on the planet. Tickets had sold out in under an hour and, now the gigs were upon them, a permanent phalanx of paparazzi had bunkered down across the road from the hotel in which he was staying.

'Can you remember what the message said?' Jessica asked.

'It just said, "Dead man". I wasn't that mithered but Sledge told the boss and she called you lot.'

Jessica glanced at her notes. 'And "Sledge" is your guitarist, right?'

'Aye, Sledge the Ledge. I s'pose I should tell you about the other message.'

'What other message?'

He nodded at the A4 pad on the desk behind her. 'Someone left me a note on there.'

'I thought you said there wasn't a note.'

'This happened the other day.'

Jessica wrote the word 'DELUSIONAL?' on her pad.

'What did that say?'

'I dunno, "wanker", or something like that. I thought it was one of the lads having a laugh.'

'What did you do with the note?'

Banner shrugged. 'Ate it, dint I?'

Jessica looked up. She wasn't sure what she'd expected as a reply but it definitely wasn't that. 'You *ate* it?'

Another shrug. 'Aye – I spent some time in Tibet and this monk bloke told me about facing my fears. Some grandmaster something-or-other. Big fan of the band. I signed his pet tortoise.'

Jessica crossed out the question mark on her pad and flipped it closed, moving across to the desk. She perched on the edge and started to leaf through the A4 sheets.

'You coming along?' Banner asked.

'Where?'

'To see the band.'

Jessica didn't have the heart to tell him that she'd never been a fan. 'I couldn't get tickets.'

Banner was now scratching his crotch, which, given the tightness of his trousers, was borderline pornographic. 'Aah, don't worry about that. I'll talk to Steph – she's the boss. She'll stick you on the list.'

'Sorry, I've got to work.'

Jessica scratched the side of her pencil lightly across the top of Banner's pad. At first there was nothing but as she moved towards the centre of the paper, the indented white etchings began to appear in the middle. Whoever had written the note had pressed a little too hard on the paper. Banner was a renowned boozer, the type of rock star whose drinking spells were celebrated by the red-tops and became legendary. According to the tabloids, he'd once got so drunk that he'd been escorted from San Francisco's Golden Gate Bridge while clutching a rubber dinghy after telling passers-by he was going to jump. It was no suicide attempt, more an inflated belief that he fancied a bit of sailing around the bay. True or not, Jessica got the sense that his powers of recollection weren't what they might be – though his memory of what was written on the pad was along the right lines. The word 'TWAT' appeared in the centre of Jessica's scribbling.

She held up the pad for Banner to see. 'Is this the note you're talking about?'

He squinted, still scratching his crotch. 'Aye, summat like that.'

Jessica put the hotel pad in a bag, wondering if their fingerprinting budget would stretch to having it examined. Almost certainly not – it was enough hassle getting it authorised for a burglary half the time. Besides, there was every chance Banner had done it himself.

'What's your name?' Banner asked, typing on a mobile phone.

'Er . . .'

'I'll stick you on the guest list anyway.'

'Right, I, er . . .' Jessica didn't know how to tell him that she didn't like his music. 'I'm not very good at gigs,' she managed to say. 'There's always someone who's

11

six-foot stupid that decides to stand in front of me, then I can't see anything.' Banner grinned at her, the gentle wrinkles of his skin folding in on themselves. He looked like he'd spent a lifetime on a sunbed, yet his smile was intoxicating. He gave her another wink and before Jessica could stop herself, she was off, as if chatting to her mates. 'They should bring in a height limit at gigs – if you're over six foot, you either stand at the back, or you're not coming in.'

Banner started to laugh. 'Aye, we could put up one of those boards like they have in front of rollercoasters. If you can't pass under a certain height, then you're at the back.' His gaze lingered on her a fraction too long. He was definitely giving her the eye, though Jessica was in no doubt that this was probably how he looked at anyone female or, indeed, anyone with a pulse. 'So, what's your name?' he added.

'Jessica Daniel.'

He tapped away on his phone. 'Right, and your number?'

'You can call 999 if there's a problem.'

'What if there's no problem?'

He smirked mischievously and, much as she wanted to ignore it, Jessica felt a tingle in her stomach. It was definitely because she hadn't eaten that morning. *Definitely.* She rolled her eyes a little too theatrically, taking out a business card from inside her jacket and handing it over.

'*Don't* call unless you really need to,' she said. 'If it's an emergency, dial 999.'

He scanned the card and then dropped it on the bed. 'Will do, hon.'

Jessica took a step towards the door, ready to leave. The uniformed officers had already visited to do the job properly, she was only there to shut up Banner's management.

'You leaving already?' Banner asked.

'I've got to get to work.'

Banner's expression had changed. His lips were pursed, eyes narrower. 'You've lost someone, ain'tcha?'

Jessica felt glued to the spot, one foot a little in the air. She leant against the wall, held in his gaze as he waited for an answer.

'I, um . . .'

Banner stood and Jessica realised how tall he was – at least six foot and even more imposing because of his sculpted arms. His eyes shone a bright blue, drilling straight through her. She felt tiny.

'Was he a boyfriend or something? Husband?'

Jessica wanted to look away but was transfixed. Banner crossed the room and rested a hand on her shoulder. He smelled rugged, of hours-old smoked cigarettes and alcohol from the night before, like her dad in the old, old days. The two names of those she had lost rested on the tip of her tongue – Adam and Bex, different people, different circumstances but each with one crushing thing in common: Jessica.

One was in a coma; one had vanished without a word. Would each of their lives have been better if they'd never met her? That was the question that kept Jessica awake at night, yet she didn't want to know the answer. All she could do was carry on with her life and pretend it wasn't happening.

'It's complicated,' Jessica whispered, finally able to edge towards the door.

Banner nodded slowly, the moment lost. 'I'll put you on the guest list anyway,' he said, back to his previous self. 'There's a private box with your name on it. Any time you fancy coming along, just turn up at the door and tell them who you are. They'll whisk you straight through – free drinks, food, the lot. Bring your friends.'

Jessica nodded appreciatively. 'Right.'

She finally it made it through the door, taking a large gasp, the claustrophobia clearing. She wondered how he'd known. Did she wear the hurt so obviously that anyone could tell?

Jessica hadn't even reached the lift when her phone started to ring. The display showed an unknown mobile number but the gravelly voice was distinctively obvious the moment she said hello.

'Hey,' Banner said.

'I told you to only call in emergencies.'

'Yeah, but I wanted to hear your voice.'

Jessica hung up.

2

As she stepped out of the lift, Jessica was accosted by the hotel manager who wanted assurances that things were 'in hand', before insisting three times that, in his view, there was no need for the media to be told anything. Jessica gave him some gumpf about press office-this and media relations-that before he ushered her out of a side door, away from the watching paparazzi.

Back in her car, Jessica sorted through her notes, glanced at the scribble-covered 'TWAT' and then dumped everything on her passenger seat. This was not how she'd expected to spend the morning. She wasn't sure if there was anything in what Banner had been saying and, given it wasn't his idea to call the police and that he didn't seem bothered by the apparent death threat, Jessica wasn't sure what else she or her colleagues could do. Sometimes the job meant acting as a glorified babysitter and she had the sense she'd been appointed as Banner's.

Jessica took out her phone and called DCI Topper. He answered on the second ring, the thunder of his fingers hammering at a computer keyboard punctuating his greeting. 'Hello.'

'It's Jess.'

'How's our rock star?'

'Do you want the official version?'

'No.'

'He smells like he's still hungover and I'm not sure these death threats are anything other than someone playing a joke, or in his own mind. He said someone had left a message on the mirror, but that he rubbed it away; then he ate another note.'

'He *ate* it?'

'Don't ask.'

'What did the hotel manager say?'

'Not much, other than worrying if things were going to get into the media. Our officers checked the CCTV but there wasn't much to see, plus Banner himself doesn't seem to know when it happened.'

There was a pause in the typing. 'What do you think?'

'Keep quiet and see what happens. Banner and his band have the entire top floor to themselves. You can't get there without a keycard and Banner's refusing security. There's probably nothing in it.'

Thump-thump-thump. It sounded like Topper was hammering in a nail. He must go through keyboards like an infant through rusks. 'Fair enough. When will you be back?'

Jessica glanced at the clock on her dashboard – twenty to ten. 'Ten minutes?' she replied. 'Fifteen? Depends on traffic.'

'Good, there's a briefing at ten and you need to be here.'

'Why?'

There was a pause and then: 'Best put the radio on.'

*

Jessica pulled into the queuing traffic, scrolling through the radio stations until she found someone talking about how bad the day's traffic congestion was . . . as if it was ever any different. The travel bulletin ended and one voice handed over to another, the radio presenter thanking her colleague in a stony hard news voice. Jessica wondered if broadcasters ever mixed things up, introducing a story about murder in jaunty tones, before banging on about a duck who'd befriended a Shetland pony in the harshest accent. Probably not.

'A quick recap,' the presenter said. 'We're talking about the imminent release of the serial killer known as "Jaws". We've learned this morning that the murderer, real name Damian Walker, will be released from a secure hospital in the coming days under a new identity. Seventeen years ago, Walker abducted five young women over the course of three summer months. All of the attacks occurred in Salford, Greater Manchester, and, if you'll excuse the graphic nature of the details, he bit his victims, leaving teeth marks on their shoulders.'

The presenter gulped, perhaps understandably. Jessica knew little about the specific details of the case, although it was semi-familiar because of how big it had been in the news at the time. It was before she'd become an officer, before she'd even thought about the Force as a career.

'Four of the women died from their injuries,' the presenter continued, 'but the fifth survived and gave the police a description of her attacker. Damian Walker was arrested the following day and didn't deny the murders, telling officers that the voices in his head told him to do it. The survivor of those attacks, Anne Atkinson, is with me today. Good morning, Anne.'

There was a scratch of microphone and then a much quieter female voice, racked with understandable nerves. 'Hi . . .'

'Thanks for being with us today, Anne. Your attacker has spent these last years in a secure hospital. How do you feel about his release?'

Jessica sighed, knowing exactly how the interview was going to go. As if anyone needed to ask that question. What did the presenter think the answer was going to be? That Anne was going to break out the balloons and streamers?

Anne's voice quivered as she replied, her terror far more evident in her hesitations than in her words. 'I've not really left the house. We were told today that he's already been released and it could have happened over the weekend. My husband and I . . .'

She tailed off, a sob catching in her throat as the presenter offered comforting words. It was always quite the trick to make someone cry and then put a hand on the person's shoulder.

Jessica's row of traffic was finally moving but she stuck to the inside lane, continuing across the city on autopilot as she listened.

'He's got a new identity, hasn't he?' the presenter cooed.

Anne was tearful, struggling through her reply. 'That's what they told us but they said they can't reveal any more. We don't know where he's living – he could be down the road for all we know.'

'Do you think you'd recognise him today?'

Jessica felt a chill. She'd been attacked in the past, felt fingers and needles pressing into her. She'd never forget the faces of those who'd hurt her.

'I don't know . . . I just . . . We were in the supermarket last night but I had to go home because I couldn't stop looking at people, thinking they might be him. It was really scary.'

'Do you think he's reformed?'

Jessica's fingers tightened on the steering wheel, knowing what a loaded question it was. When she'd been attacked, been hurt, she'd wanted vengeance but there was a point at which she had to let go. As sorry as Jessica felt for Anne Atkinson, she knew the victim was the worst person to judge something like that, especially when it came to mental health issues.

Anne faltered and didn't avoid the questioner's trap. 'All I can say is that he abducted me. He cut me, tried to bite me. What sort of person does that?'

'Do you have a message for the authorities?'

'I'd beg them to lock him away again.'

'What about a message for the community into which he's been released?'

'My husband and I are going on holiday to get away from this. I don't know who his new neighbours are, let alone where he's living, but I can only tell them to be afraid. He did this to me and he can do it to you.'

The presenter thanked Anne and then said they'd be back after the weather. Jessica turned the radio off. She didn't necessarily disagree with anything Anne Atkinson had said but knew that a large proportion of people assumed 'the authorities' meant the police. In their minds, it would be the police who'd released Jaws.

It was going to be a long week.

Jessica continued following the route along Stockport Road until she reached the series of turns that would take her back to Longsight Police Station. Her heart sank as she reached the entrance. Outside the gates was a woman dressed in fluorescent pink athletic gear holding a large placard. As soon as Jessica indicated to turn into the car park, the human beetroot waggled the card up and down in an effort to get Jessica's attention. Jessica offered a weak apologetic smile, unsure what else she could do as the words 'WHERE'S LIAM?' bounced into her eye line.

It was going to be a *very* long week.

3

After parking her car, Jessica walked through the front door of the station into the almost empty reception area. Fat Pat was standing behind the desk, not eating for once. He was the heart of the station, knowing everyone's business and able to gossip like a divorcee at a mother's meeting. As much as Jessica wouldn't want to admit it in front of him, Pat was a more than competent sergeant who was perfectly suited to dealing with the scroats who turned up at their door, not to mention keeping an eye on what went on around the place.

He was watching the wall-mounted television and didn't bother to look in her direction. 'Everyone's upstairs,' he said.

Jessica peered at him, wondering if he'd lost weight. His face didn't seem as round as it usually did.

'What?' he asked, finally focusing on her.

'Nothing.'

'You not going to compliment me?'

'On what?'

His eyebrows formed a bushy V. 'Lost six pounds this week.'

'In the chocolate machine? That's always nicking pound coins off me.'

Pat's eyes narrowed, before he continued as if she'd said nothing. 'That's sixteen pounds in total.'

'Er, well done,' she managed. At some point, he'd have passed a medical to get into the Force, which was a frightening thought. Jessica tried to blink away the vision of him sweating on a treadmill.

Pat nodded at the door. 'That nutter still outside?'

She had started towards the stairs but stopped. 'Don't be a dick, Pat. She's lost someone close to her and wants to know where he is.'

She couldn't tell if Pat was chastened or hungry. Either way, he nodded towards the stairs. Jessica knew that it wouldn't have been too long ago that she'd have joined in, calling the placard woman a nutter too. It was worrying how much she'd changed, how much the direction of her life had made her grow up.

Upstairs, DCI Topper's office was empty but there was the sound of clinking teacups from along the hallway. The recently installed incident rooms were an architectural stroke of genius in that the heating worked, there was no water leaking from the roof, and basics such as pens and whiteboards were present. It was a far cry from the shambles with which they'd been lumbered for the past few years. The rooms were also very white, possibly for hygiene purposes, but more likely to catch out anyone with a hangover.

Jessica was met by the smell of instant coffee. DCI Topper was sitting next to Detective Superintendent Jenkinson, each sipping from mugs sporting the Greater Manchester Police logo. As she looked around the room,

Jessica realised everyone was holding a new mug. Someone, somewhere, must've found a few quid in the budget. There was even a plate of custard creams plonked next to a bowl of sugar. In the league table of biscuits, custard creams were undoubtedly near the bottom but it was a step up from the usual nothing.

Jessica poured herself a coffee and took a seat. Her presence had barely been noticed as the men continued to talk around her. Detective Inspector Franks – her nemesis and accident waiting to happen – was standing tall, boring the arse off Acting Chief Constable Aylesbury about who knew what, though it was almost certainly related to himself. Narcissist didn't go far enough in describing the inspector: he was the type who couldn't walk past a mirror, or else he'd lose a morning.

Aylesbury was peering away from Franks, looking for an escape, when he spotted Jessica. Years before, he'd been her DCI, prior to sliding his way up the greasy pole of promotion. He was surely destined for the chief constable's job at some point, being one of those who rarely left his office but always looked good for the cameras with swept-back hair that hadn't gone completely grey.

'Aaah, Jessica, you're here,' he said, extricating himself from Franks in one slick movement and shaking her hand. They weren't exactly friends but cordial would just about cover it and he certainly wasn't on first-name terms with the other officers present.

'Sir,' Jessica replied with a nod as Aylesbury took his spot at the front of the room, the whiteboard behind him. The ripples of small talk evaporated as the assorted officers took their seats. Pinned on the wall above Aylesbury was a flatscreen television that was turned off. It was part of the refit, though no one seemed to know from whose budget it had come. They never had money for anything, so there was every chance it had been repatriated from unclaimed stolen goods.

Aylesbury nodded at the blank screen. 'Morning, everyone. It falls to me to tell you that the story about Damian Walker – Jaws – being released is true. First, I should make it clear that everything said within these walls must remain here. I'm sure you realise that anyway, but . . .' He tailed off, not finishing the sentence. Jenkinson, Topper and Franks were all sitting in front of him, backs straight and knees crossed in perfect alignment, like an ageing boyband on a comeback tour about to hit a key change. Jessica wondered why she was there.

'If you're unfamiliar with the case, Walker had thirteen and a half years at Ashworth High Security Hospital, before spending another three and a bit in a medium-to-low facility just outside of Greater Manchester. He is now considered safe for release. I only know this because it came to the attention of the management team last night that Ms Atkinson was going to appear in the media today. She's already been on television and radio and I believe there are more appearances lined up. We're not sure of the full details but it does appear as if someone has tipped off Ms Atkinson about Walker's release—'

DI Franks opened his mouth before his brain kicked in. 'Is that leak something we should be investigating?'

Aylesbury, ever the pro, kept his calm, eyes unrolled.

'No one believes it would look very good if we were to launch such an investigation, especially if we were to bring in Ms Atkinson for questioning. For now, it's being treated as an internal matter at the hospital.'

Which was surely something Franks could've worked out for himself. It was that type of attention-seeking stupidity that had earned him a series of nicknames that started with 'Funtime Frankie' at one end of the scale and 'Wanky Frankie' at the other.

Aylesbury continued with barely a breath: 'Walker's new identity is known only to a handful of people, and that type of information usually goes too high for me. Walker's release was supposed to be low-key and confidential but obviously that's not now the case. Someone from the Force tried to contact Ms Atkinson but she's not interested in talking to the police and, according to the radio, off on holiday anyway.'

He paused for a sip of coffee as Franks shuffled on his seat, leaning forward with his fingers cathedralled together like a praying mantis.

'What I must impart to you,' Aylesbury added, throwing in a bit of corporate speak for good measure, 'is that we need a coordinated line from everyone who works for GMP. The other assistant chiefs are touring the local stations today passing this message on to your colleagues. If anybody asks you anything to do with Walker then your reply must be "no comment". It doesn't matter if it's journalists, friends, some bloke in a pub, whoever. "No comment" at all times. Everyone needs to be on message. The last thing we need is some flappy-mouthed inspector telling someone in a pub that Walker should've been locked up for good, then it turns out that person talked to a journalist.' He puffed out loudly. 'God knows GMP has had enough bad publicity recently.'

He was right about that – ever since the Pratley report had accused the Force of being 'institutionally corrupt' in the past, everyone who worked for Greater Manchester Police had felt the greater level of scrutiny. Still, it was typical that the management were on a trip around the stations reminding everyone to keep away from talking to the media. It was a shame they weren't so quick to muck in when there was actual work to do.

'Everyone has to stay on message,' Aylesbury concluded. 'If you could make sure that's passed on to officers at all levels, it would be strongly appreciated.' He nodded towards Jessica and then Topper. 'If you two could remain, there's another matter we need to discuss.'

Franks took the hint and stumbled his way to the door, glaring over his shoulder towards Jessica, no doubt outraged that her presence was requested and his wasn't. DSI Jenkinson was even more confused. As superintendent, he would have expected to be a part of whatever was going on but Aylesbury assured him all was in hand. Reluctantly, the two men left, inching along the corridor and peering back towards the incident room in case they were called back.

They weren't.

Aylesbury continued to sip his coffee, offering a thin smile and lowering his voice slightly. 'I've not been entirely honest with you . . .'

He crossed the room, poked his head out of the door to ensure the corridor was clear, and then beckoned them after him as he continued in the opposite direction of the stairs. In the old days, he would have been leading them towards a series of rooms filled with boxes and who knew what. Currently, the station was undergoing a refit that never seemed to end. All Jessica knew was that her office had received no attention, although it would probably need a deep clean before any builders started knocking through walls.

They passed a second incident room before Aylesbury directed them through the next door. A suited man and woman were waiting, perched uncomfortably on plastic chairs with an open packet of custard creams on the floor.

Aylesbury stood between them. 'Clayton Gordon, Millie Evans, this is Detective Chief Inspector Lewis Topper and Detective Inspector Jessica Daniel.'

The four of them shook hands and exchanged niceties before they all sat around the packet of biscuits. Topper seemed confused, which was unusual for him. He'd migrated to Manchester to take the job of chief inspector almost a year before, having previously worked in Scotland. Gradually the job was getting to him, the hair starting to grey around his ears, wrinkles deepening around his eyes. It got to all of the chief inspectors in the end. Most officers wanted to get out and do some real work but a DCI position was the death knell of that, leaving capable policemen jammed behind a desk. For some, like Aylesbury, it was exactly what they wanted; for others, like Topper, it was a slippery slope to retirement.

Aylesbury pointed towards Clayton and Millie. Clayton was black, in his thirties with a chunky gold bracelet and not much muscle; Millie was a similar age, white, with blonde hair tied into a ponytail. Clayton was wearing glasses and fidgeting in his seat.

'Mr Gordon and Ms Evans both work for the witness protection programme,' Aylesbury went on. 'As acting chief constable, I've been informed of Mr Walker's new identity for reasons that will become apparent.'

He nodded and Millie took up the story. She glanced between Jessica and Topper, apparently unconcerned by rank, nor easing them into the secret. 'Mr Walker has been given the name of Eric Seasmith. He is currently living in the south of the city, close to the M60.'

She turned back to Aylesbury and there was a pause, in which Jessica and Topper exchanged a glance acknowledging that either or both of them were about to be stitched up.

Aylesbury nodded appreciatively, turning back to Jessica and Topper. 'So far, none of the assistant chief constables knows this information, only me and now you. None of your colleagues is aware, nor can they be. With the information of Walker's . . . Seasmith's release now in the public domain, there is a risk of a possible threat to him. Things have moved quickly but after much discussion last night, it's been decided that CID will offer a pair of officers to support witness protection in their work around Mr, er, Seasmith.'

He paused, apparently finished. Jessica turned to Clayton and Millie. 'You said he's currently here – so how long has he been back in the area?'

The newcomers glanced at each other but Millie answered, pushing a thread of hair behind her ear. 'Mr Seasmith was actually released two weeks ago. He's a Salford native, but with the history he has there, it was considered too high risk for him to return to that exact area.'

Jessica thought that 'history' was one way of putting it. Also, his new location was only a handful of miles from Salford.

Millie continued: 'That said, his crimes occurred seventeen years ago and the chances of him being recognised in the locality are considered to be slim – he's a very changed man. We offered other spots around the country but Mr Seasmith was reluctant and his doctors felt he would integrate into society better by having familiar things around him. He has no family or friends, so this allows him to start again.'

Clayton cut in, his bracelet clinking on the table: 'It's been hard for him, too. He's been in secure facilities for seventeen years and now he's suddenly in the real world and has to fend for himself. That was before any of this media furore.' He nodded to Jessica and Topper. 'Our bosses are hoping – *we're* hoping – that your involvement won't be necessary but we need people who know what the situation is, not officers who might read things the wrong way, or call handlers out of the loop. What we really need is someone, or pair of people, on call who can act in a police capacity if anything goes wrong.'

'Like what?' Topper asked.

'Say, for instance, if his identity is discovered. Assuming

there are no objections, we'd like to take your details and then, if necessary, we'll be in contact.'

Topper looked to Jessica, eyebrows raised. He was clearly in but it was her decision. She took a breath and shrugged. 'What could possibly go wrong?'

4

Jessica sat in her office deleting emails. Did she want to go on a training course? No. Management course? No. Penis enlargement? No, though she forwarded it to Detective Constable Rowlands, along with half a dozen others relating to 'blue pills'. Was she interested in taking part in some amateur dramatic shite the constables were knocking together for Christmas? Not a sodding chance.

As well as the usual, she'd won the Canadian lottery, was being offered an exciting investment opportunity in Burundi and had almost a dozen emails relating to weight loss. She'd long suspected Rowlands had signed her up to a variety of dodgy mailing lists, so found a website that offered a free sanitary product sample and entered his name and address. That'd teach him.

She was about to start doing some actual work when there was a tap on the door. Detective Sergeant Isobel Diamond entered, two cups of machine-made tea clasped between her fingers.

'Morning,' she said.

'I wondered when you'd show up.'

Izzy mimed outrage but with acting that bad, she'd have been better off with the constables in their amateur dramatic thingamabob. She was in her thirties, a little younger than Jessica, slim with long dark hair and probably Jessica's best friend, certainly around the station.

'What?' Izzy said, passing across one of the teas and taking a seat at the spare desk. Despite space for two inspectors, DI Franks preferred to work in another area of the station, which was fine with Jessica. Somehow, nobody else had been thrust upon her, leaving her working in a tip partly of her own making. Boxes and files littered the room, most of which had been there when she moved in, though Jessica had made no effort to clear them.

'You can ask,' she said.

'Ask what?' Izzy replied, still feigning innocence.

'I'm not telling you anything until you ask.'

Izzy broke into a grin. 'Fine – what was he like?'

'What was *who* like?'

'Tell meeeeeeee.'

Jessica rolled her eyes. 'Aren't you married?'

Izzy huffed, apparently unbothered by such a spurious thing as having a husband and child. 'Yeah, but . . . y'know . . . ?'

'I know what?'

'He's Blaine Banner! I had posters of him on my wall. Me and my mates used to have his music on loud when we were getting ready to go out.'

'You lurrrrrrrrrrrrrve him.'

Izzy nodded. 'I actually do.'

'He was topless.'

'Oooooooh. Tell me more.'

'He was wearing tight trousers. Very tight.'

'Oooooooh. You lucky cow.'

'Can you stop making those noises? I feel dirty just listening to you. People are going to think I'm watching a porno in here.'

'Wouldn't be the first time.'

Jessica frowned at her. 'That was for work purposes.'

Izzy winked. 'I believe you.' She took a sip of her tea and then let out a long breath. 'So . . . what was he like?'

'You *do* know his real name is Graham?'

'Oh, stop it. His name's Blaine.'

'Fine – your boyfriend's a nutcase. He thinks someone's trying to kill him.'

'Are they?'

'I doubt it. He looks like he's spent the past twenty years drinking and snorting.'

Izzy flapped a hand. 'Stop spoiling it! Isobel Banner-Diamond's got an amazing ring to it.'

'What does your husband think?'

'Oh, balls to that. I can dream.'

'Would you give it all up for a night with Blaine Banner? The husband, your daughter, the house, suburbia?'

Izzy chewed on her cheek. 'Hmm . . .' Jessica hadn't expected an instant 'no', but the reply took at least ten seconds. 'Probably not *a* night. Maybe if I got to go on tour with him or something. I'd probably dye my hair red again.' She peered at Jessica, shrugging. '*What?*'

'Are you one of those couples with a list of celebrities you can sleep with?'

She batted another hand. 'Noooooooo . . . well, no. Definitely not. I reckon Mal would understand, though. He could look after Amber for a few months while I go on tour with Blaine.' She started twiddling a strand of her hair. 'Maybe we should make a list? He'd go for young actresses he'd have no chance with. I reckon I could pull a rock star if I really tried.'

'I suppose sleeping with famous people is the bedrock of any successful marriage.'

'You're such a spoilsport.'

Izzy continued drinking her tea as Jessica hammered the delete key a few more times, getting rid of more weight-loss emails. This, above anything else, was why she loved spending time with Izzy. Other people could be edgy around her after what had happened with Adam and Bex, but Izzy understood Jessica needed normality. When the time came, they'd talk about the other stuff.

'Did you hear the news about Jaws?' Izzy asked.

Jessica continued to focus on her screen. She could tell Izzy what was going on and be confident it would stay confidential but Aylesbury's warnings about things not leaving the upstairs room were still fresh.

'Only what's been on the radio,' Jessica replied. 'Anyway, when you're not dreaming of illicit flings with rock stars, our "Where's Liam?" woman is out front again.'

Izzy sighed. *Really?* Not again.'

'Is Funtime still keeping his head down?'

'Course he is. I still don't know how it ended up on my desk. He should be running that investigation, not making me clear up his mess.'

'Not found him yet, then?'

'Obviously not.'

Liam McGregor had gone to his stag party almost a month previously and hadn't been seen since.

'Do you know it's supposed to be the wedding on Saturday?' Izzy said.

Jessica checked the date in the top corner of her monitor. It was Monday, easy to forget given her shift pattern. 'Really?'

'I suppose that's why she's outside again. Her name's Ellie Scanlon. I don't know what else we can do. We spoke to everyone at the stag party, plus other people in the area and we've gone through the CCTV and so on. No witnesses have come forward and Liam disappeared into thin air for all we know.' She paused, making eye contact. 'Sorry, I didn't mean . . .'

Jessica shrugged, thinking of Bex. Two months previously, Jessica had gone to work one morning, said cheerio, and not seen her housemate since. Bex had left all of her belongings, including her phone and shoes. None of the neighbours had seen anything and she was now officially a missing person. No note, no clue, no anything. As Izzy said: disappeared into thin air. It had taken that for Jessica to realise that a quarter of a million people went missing in the United Kingdom every year. The number was astonishing given the lack of coverage. Bex was now another statistic.

'No ransom yet?' Jessica asked, trying to move on.

Izzy shook her head. 'Nothing: no demands, no phone calls, no cash withdrawals. His phone's either off or discarded. Ellie emails me every day but I don't know what to tell her. Her fiancé's an adult. As far as we know, no laws have been broken.' She stopped again, judging the mood. 'Is there any sign of . . . Bex?'

Jessica shook her head. 'I submitted hairs to the DNA people in case anyone finds . . . *something*, but y'know . . .' She couldn't bring herself to say the word 'body'.

Izzy nodded shortly. 'Have I shown you Ellie's blog? She writes two or three entries every day, either asking Liam to come home or begging witnesses to come forward. She wrote one this morning saying she's going to put on her wedding dress and go to the church regardless on Saturday.'

'What's the web address?'

Izzy grabbed a Post-it note pad from Jessica's desk and wrote down the details. Jessica skimmed it.

'She writes a love letter every other day,' Izzy added. 'It's quite sad really. I feel sorry for her but there's so much going on.'

Jessica nodded at her monitor. 'You don't have to tell me.'

'I'm still on that robbery thing but every time I read her blog, I find myself wondering what happened to Liam. It'd be nice to know. If Funtime would pull his finger out, he could get on it himself. He never has anything to do.' She finished off her tea and expertly threw the cup across the room into the bin. It didn't even rattle around the rim, let alone bounce off the wall.

'Show-off,' Jessica said.

Izzy smiled. 'If he wasn't such a dick, I might feel sorry for Franks.'

'*Sorry* for him?'

'With Dave seeing his daughter, all the constables are getting stuck in. One of them asked Dave if he'd been up all night because he looked exhausted. When Dave stretched the other day, someone said he had to be careful because he was going to put his back out with all the late-night activity he's getting.'

Jessica didn't know whether or not she found it funny. DC Rowlands had started seeing DI Franks's daughter, Katherine, without realising who she was. Somehow the relationship was still going a couple of months on.

'Is Funtime still dumping all the shite jobs on Dave?' Jessica asked.

'Yep, he was given that pickpocketing thing last week and then got stuck babysitting that PCSO complaint.'

'I hope Katherine's worth it.' Jessica slipped open her bottom drawer, revealing the super-secret stash of chocolate digestives. 'Want one?'

Izzy shook her head and patted her stomach. 'I'm in training, remember? Which reminds me – are you ever going to sponsor me?'

'Er . . . when is it?'

'Don't you ever read your emails? I messaged everyone. I'm doing the Liverpool Marathon next month.'

Jessica gazed at her screen and the avalanche of deleted, largely unread, emails in the trash folder. She huffed unconvincingly. 'I think there's some problem with the system. Emails not making it through, that sort of thing.'

'So it's not that you've deleted it?'

'Definitely not.'

Izzy reached across and typed a web address into the

browser, loading a fundraising page. 'I'm running for breast cancer,' she said.

'For or against? Nobody's ever in favour of diseases nowadays.'

Izzy shook her head and rolled her eyes. 'Hilarious.'

'How much are people sponsoring you?'

'Check the list.'

Jessica scrolled down the page, taking in the names. 'Dave's sponsoring you a fiver? The tight sod. What's that? Thirty pence a mile?'

'Nineteen point zero seven . . . or so.'

'Not bitter, then? Hang about, the guv's in for fifty quid? That's like . . .' Jessica counted on her fingers, 'two quid a mile . . . ish. He must be loaded.'

'It's not that much considering the hours of training.'

'Yeah but he's Scottish. Fifty quid for him's like five hundred for the rest of us.'

Izzy nodded at the screen. 'So . . .'

Jessica patted her pockets. 'I don't carry cash.'

'That's why it's online. Stick in your card details and away you go.'

'Yeah but it's all fraud-this and scam-that nowadays. You can't trust anyone with your details – especially when Funtime's supposed to be finding out who's been skimming cards in the city centre.'

Izzy didn't reply, her raised eyebrows saying it all.

'Fine!' Jessica said. 'How much should I put in?'

'That depends on if you want to be a tight arse, plus whether you support cancer. The less you sponsor me, the more you're in favour of it. Anything under twenty quid looks stingy.'

Jessica looked at the screen and the list of donors, scrolling up and down. DC Archie Davey had chipped in thirty quid, which was a night on the lash for him. In total, Izzy so far had pledges for over a thousand pounds – miraculous considering the tightness of their colleagues. 'Twenty-five?'

Izzy pulled a face. 'Constables have chucked in more than that. The new girl, DC Evesham – Ruth, she put in forty quid and we've barely spoken to each other.'

'For God's sake. This is a shakedown. Old-school extortion.'

'Just sponsor me.'

'How much training have you done?'

'I've been building up, running for two to three hours a day before or after shift.'

'Two or three hours?'

'Four or five on my days off.'

'Are you mental? I was hoping you'd not bothered. If you collapse halfway round, I could've at least claimed my money back. It sounds like you're going to make it.'

'Thanks for your faith,' Izzy smiled as Jessica swivelled back to the screen and started typing. Izzy peered over her shoulder, eyeing the amount. 'Fifty quid and one pence?'

'I couldn't let the guv take all the glory, could I? But if you don't finish, I'm having my money back.'

5

Jessica unlocked her front door and stepped inside. She clicked it closed behind her and waited in the hallway, listening to the silence. It was part of her routine in case Bex had returned. They'd lived together for less than a year in an indefinable relationship that definitely wasn't mother-daughter, despite Bex only turning eighteen the previous summer. Given the two-decade age difference, it was difficult to describe it as pure friendship, either. Bex had been living on the street when Jessica invited her to stay and things had simply worked, regardless of how others might want to label whatever relationship it was they had. That had been a different time, before Adam's *accident*. Then it had been the three of them, now it was just Jessica.

'Hello?'

Jessica's word echoed around the empty house, un-answered.

She dropped her bag and made her way up the stairs, heading into the bathroom, which was opposite Bex's bedroom door. Jessica sat on the toilet and listened with the door open. The nights were drawing in with the clocks soon due to go forward or back, whatever it was they did at this time of year. Either way, it meant months of cold and dark. Somewhere at the rear of the house, kids were laughing but that was the only sound Jessica could hear.

The house had been a place in which she and Adam had intended to grow old together, now it was an expensive trap that was far too big, too empty, too quiet. Jessica was never sure who the real her was: the outgoing, confident person at work, or the introspective silent shadow that ghosted around the void she called home. As the kids at the back of the house disappeared towards their houses, it left only the low rumble of traffic somewhere in the distance.

Jessica crossed the hallway into Bex's room and stood in the doorway, as she had done so many times. It didn't feel right going through the teenager's things, so, after the official search that had to happen, she'd tried her best to return everything to as it was. Because she'd lived on the street, Bex owned very little but she'd 'borrowed' clothes from Jessica and then raided charity shops with her meagre part-time wages. The bed was made, clothes hanging in the wardrobe and a neat row of shoes underneath the radiator. On top of the dresser was a stack of textbooks that had been bought in preparation for Bex beginning her college courses. The teenager had been looking forward to it, thinking about university beyond and a future that she might never have had. Now she was somewhere else, a number on a database.

The stairs creaked as Jessica returned downstairs. She plucked her phone from her bag, willing it to ring. As much as she'd told Blaine Banner not to call her, not to mention the witness protection pair, a call from any of them would mean something was happening. Something that would take her away from these four walls. She checked the screen but there was nothing, not even a text message with a discount for the local takeaway or a spam email.

She thought about going into the kitchen to make something but didn't fancy cooking for only herself. There were ready meals in the freezer that she'd have a look at later if she was hungry . . . which she probably wouldn't be.

In the living room, Jessica switched on the laptop, waited for the temperamental Wi-Fi to kick in, and then loaded Ellie Scanlon's blog. The most recent entry had been written barely an hour before, posted alongside a photograph of Ellie outside the police station with her 'WHERE'S LIAM?' banner.

Liam, oh Liam
My hurt could fill a museum
I lie awake at night
Hoping you are all right
Please come back to me
My love for you could fill the sea

It was hardly a rival to Kipling but Jessica couldn't help but feel Ellie's hurt. The next entry, from that morning, was even worse.

6.12 a.m.
I've been lying in bed for hours but have hardly slept at all. Every time I drop off, I wake with a shudder wondering where my Liam is. I'm supposed to be getting married on Saturday but have no idea where he is. Mum (hi!) keeps telling me that I should call

it off but what if Liam (hi?) arrives at the church and I'm not there? (I will be, Babe. X.)

Nathan was the last person to see him at the stag do in the Lake District but the area is so vast that he could be anywhere – well, that's what the police say. Fat lot of good they are. Nathan reckons Liam wasn't that drunk but what if he fell into one of the lakes? Or if he wandered into the woods for some reason and couldn't find his way out? Or if he fell down a hole? Or went off hiking and got lost?

Mum reckons I'm being silly (I'm not, Mum) but she doesn't know what it's like. I know Liam was looking forward to getting married (weren't you, Babe. X), so why would he disappear? Something must've happened to him but the police aren't listening to me. I told them about my theory that he might've gone walking but they don't want to know. I read this thing about bears but they said there are no bears in the Lake District. If that's not true then how do they explain that picture that's on the Internet? I told them it's too big to be a dog and they didn't have an answer for that. They keep saying things like there's nothing else they can do, that they're monitoring his bank cards and so on, but what good is that if he's living in a cave halfway up a mountain hiding from a bear? (I hope you're not, Babe. X.) They say they don't have the resources to check every lake or every mountain but what do I pay my taxes for if not that? (You paid your taxes too, didn't you, Babe? X.)

I don't know if I should be up there myself trying to find him, or if I should be spending my time outside of the police station trying to get them to do something. (What do you reckon, Babe? X.) I'm not even sure who (whom?) I should be contacting. The *police up there started looking into things but when they couldn't find him, the Manchester lot got involved. No one's answering my emails or phone calls and I don't really know what to do.*

I was thinking about emailing a band – Coldplay or U2, something like that – to see if they'd be interested in doing one of those charity single things. They're always doing stuff for African kids and that lot don't even live here, so why not Liam? Blaine Banner's in Manchester at the moment, so I could try to get a message to him. Anything for awareness, really. I tried going to the newspapers with my idea about putting Liam on the front page but they said they don't do that sort of thing because they'd have to do it for everyone. It's rubbish really. I mean, who's interested in politics and all that boring stuff? Or football? I reckon people would be interested in finding my Liam (Wouldn't they, Babe? X) rather than the president going on about the economy or whatever. When I told them that, some bloke told me we don't have a president, so I know he was just trying to fob me off. I keep hitting brick walls wherever I go.

Yesterday, my friend Sharon came over and she was telling me how brave I was (thanks, hon). I just want the wedding to go well. I've (we've) been planning it for ages. After the church, we're all off to the Hilton for a massive party. All our mates are supposed to be there and there's going to be a free bar for a bit. Liam would love that (wouldn't you, Babe? X). We've got this massive seven-tier cake. I've been so good for so long so I can fit in my dress and this was supposed to be my reward.

I just want him to come home. (Please, Babe. X.) The flat's so empty without you. Love you. Love, love, love you. X X X X X X X X.

Jessica scanned through the previous few entries that were all along the same lines. It was easy to sneer but she knew how Ellie was feeling. Well, not the charity single thing, or the British 'president', but she knew the rest. She continued skimming through the site until she found a set of links at the bottom. She was about to close the page when she settled on the Greater Manchester Missing People support group. She clicked through to their site and read the details. They met every Tuesday evening in the Club Academy on Oxford Road, which was part of the university. It was more or less on Jessica's journey home. She stared at the time for a moment before emailing the link to herself and closing the laptop lid. Jessica stared at the blank television screen wondering what she should do with her evening. As with so many others, she had no idea.

Jessica was sitting on the side of a hill when the boulder started rolling. It bumped and bounded over a craggy outlook, sending a scatter of smaller stones cascading down the rock face. She glanced up too late, realising the boulder was almost upon her, looming tall, its speed increasing. Jessica started to run, hearing the thump-thump-thump that soon became a higher-pitched beep-beep-beep. She tried to up her pace when she realised the rock was gone, that she was in bed, lying in darkness as something flashed through the black.

Her phone was ringing.

Jessica grabbed the device from the floor, her sleepy eyes wanting to remain closed as she swiped to answer. 'Hello?'

It was Topper. 'You awake?'

'I am now. What time is it?'

'Just after three.'

'Brilliant.'

'You're needed.'

The chief inspector didn't realise how much Jessica wanted to hear that.

6

Rain was teeming as Jessica drove along the near-deserted East Lancs Road towards Buile Hill Park in Salford. It was pouring so hard that the drops of water were bouncing from the surface of the road, leaping onto her car as if it was raining upwards. The orange glow of street lights made little impact on the deluge, with visibility minuscule and the sound of any other traffic drowned out by the roaring thunder of water on tarmac. Jessica drove slowly until she took the turn into the car park and was met by a solitary spinning blue light on top of a police car stopped among a unit of other vehicles, some marked, others not.

Jessica parked her car at the back and ran towards the collection of officers who were huddling under the overhang at the front of the historic hall on the edge of the grassy area. It was only a short distance but, by the time she reached the shelter, her hair was plastered to her cheek, errant drips of water slinking along her back, making her shiver. A uniformed officer she didn't recognise handed her one of the huge coats that were usually kept under lock and key at the station. They were waterproof, windproof and probably bombproof given how heavy each coat was. Jessica slipped into it, doubling her body weight, before somebody thrust a polystyrene cup of tea into her hand. She could get used to this level of service.

DCI Topper was leaning against one of the stone pillars, staring into the darkened distance. Jessica sidled alongside him as best she could, fighting for balance in the Michelin man get-up. Beyond the trees, almost lost through the torrent, was a pair of white tents lit by beaming white lights.

Topper glanced at her and then away towards the tents. 'Did you swim here?'

'Doggy-paddled.'

'This bloody city. I've never seen rain like this and I come from Scotland.'

'Is it as bad as you thought on the phone?'

'Worse.'

'Shite.'

'From what we can tell, it's an eighteen-year-old girl who was cutting through the park after an evening out. Two lads found her on their way home. Her wallet was at her side with name, age and details. Her stomach's been sliced open and her innards left, well, out.'

Jessica took a sip from her steaming tea, feeling the liquid burning its way down to her stomach. The situation was bad in so many ways.

'Is this the park where . . . ?'

She tailed off, not wanting to finish the sentence. They each knew it was true. This was where Anne Atkinson had been attacked seventeen years previously, before staggering onto the road and surviving in order to identify Damian Walker as the person who'd sliced her open. He'd barely been released from a secure hospital and another attack had taken place on the same spot.

'Have you seen what's under the tents?' Jessica asked.

'You don't want to see it.' He nodded towards a copse of bushes between them and the tents. 'Two of the lads were sick. It's everything you can imagine but worse.'

Jessica gazed towards the bushes and the tents, knowing she'd seen enough gore for one lifetime. The extreme stuff made a person more desensitised to the lower levels of crime. What was someone with a broken nose when you'd witnessed someone else sliced to pieces with a machete?

'Teeth marks?' Jessica asked.

'Not that were obvious.'

'Where's Walker?' she whispered.

Topper glanced over his shoulder and beckoned Jessica away from the overhang. The rain thumped onto her – thankfully waterproof – hood as they strode towards a nearby tree. By the time they arrived, her tea was a write-off, overflowing with rainwater. She tipped it onto the grass as they huddled together, peering back towards the other officers.

Topper spoke softly, his words almost lost to the clatter of the elements. 'Someone woke up the chief constable and that was the first call he made before getting me out of bed. I spoke to our witness protection friends too. Walker, Seasmith, Jaws – whatever you want to call him – is tucked up in bed.'

'How long's he been there?'

'All night, apparently.'

'Has someone been with him?'

'Not as far as I could tell – there's no obligation for him to have anyone nearby. He's as free as you or me.'

'There must be some terms to his release.'

Topper dropped his hood, sending a waterfall of water to the ground behind him. He ran a hand through his sodden hair and breathed out, a plume of steam disappearing into the air. Jessica hadn't realised how cold it was but suddenly her hands were freezing.

'I suppose we'll find out,' Topper replied. 'The media's going to go apeshit.'

They stood together, watching and listening to the rattle of the rain, contemplating what came next. Whatever it was, it wouldn't be good.

7

The sun rose, or at least tried to, masked by the clouds. Jessica left her car at the station and sat in the passenger seat of DCI Topper's 4×4. It had too much money written all over it, especially as he didn't seem the type to drive anywhere other than roads. At least he didn't own a BMW – that was the point at which Jessica would have lost all respect for him.

They said little on the journey towards the south of the city, instead listening to the radio. Jessica wanted to turn it off but there was a morbid fascination in getting a verbal kicking.

A phone-in caller was off on one: '. . . I just don't understand why we let him out. I'd've brought back hanging if it were me.'

The presenter interjected, reminding listeners that the identity of the young woman killed in the park was unknown, as was the identity of the attacker and the exact details. The press office had released no official particulars but that didn't stop the speculation. People lived nearby and as soon as one person knew, so did the rest of the street – not to mention the number of officers who'd received early morning phone calls, or others who'd limped home after a night shift to tell their other half where they'd been. By the time the city was in the process of waking up, everyone knew what had happened – or thought they did. Regardless of what had *actually* occurred, 'Jaws' was back in the minds of too many people.

'We're too soft in this country,' the caller continued. 'They should line 'em up against the wall and set the dogs on 'em. They'd have never settled for this in Nazi Germany.'

The presenter cut the caller off just in time. There were plenty of other things that also weren't tolerated in Nazi Germany and it probably wouldn't be good for ratings if she were to let the caller list them.

Topper continued driving, showing an impressive knowledge of the back streets. He drove past a newsagent with a sandwich board outside proclaiming the simple but devastating 'Jaws 2'. If it wasn't so serious, it would be almost amusing how fast misinformation spread. Jessica scrolled through the missed calls on her phone, seeing the two from Garry Ashford at the *Manchester Morning Herald*. They'd be crying out for information given their deadlines.

Not this time, she thought.

Topper continued through Fallowfield and Withington, the properties becoming larger and nicer, the streets cleaner, until they reached Didsbury. The area was affluent, full of either couples who had money, or younger people who were house sharing after clubbing together to stay somewhere half-decent. Buy-to-rent merchants were prevalent all over the district. After leaving her first flat which had been close to the universities, Jessica had rented an apartment in the area and always felt she was dragging down the house prices by parking her skip-worthy Punto on the road.

Good.

Topper didn't need directions, turning onto a housing estate, taking a pair of right turns and then ambling along a road wide enough for four lanes. Tall trees were placed intermittently along the kerbs, swaying in the breeze. Thankfully the rain had slowed from an outright monsoon to its usual drizzly mistiness but there were still puddles pooled along the edges of the road, struggling to seep through the mash of fallen leaves that were quilting the drains. Topper took one final turn onto a sleepy cul-de-sac lined with pretty grass verges and more trees. Away from the road was a semicircle of identical cream properties, decent-sized family houses, with a garage at the side. There were no cars on the road, no news crews, no satellite trucks. It was perfect unassuming suburbia.

And home to a man who'd killed four people seventeen years previously.

Topper parked next to a black Vauxhall on one of the driveways and they both climbed out. Jessica glanced backwards towards the crescent of houses but there was nobody in any of the windows, no one paying them the slightest bit of attention.

Before Topper could knock, Millie opened the front door. She was wearing a similar suit to the previous day, hair again tied into a ponytail, with the weary look of someone else who'd been woken up at an unearthly hour. She failed to block the yawn as she nodded them inside, peering past towards the street and closing the door.

Millie lowered her voice as Jessica and Topper turned towards her. 'Don't take this the wrong way but I was hoping we'd never have to see one another again.' She took their coats and then nodded towards a door at the back of the hall. 'He's in there.'

The house was clean and appeared new, with crisp carpets on the floor and clear magnolia walls. Topper led the way into what turned out to be a kitchen. The edges were lined with heavy black worktops and appliances but the rest was white, aside from a large wooden dining table in the centre. An open box of Coco Pops was in the middle, almost hiding the man sitting on the far side who was shovelling a spoon into a bowl that was sloshing with chocolaty milk. He only glanced briefly away from his breakfast but it was enough of an angle for Jessica to see the similarity. He was older, greyer, more wrinkled, but unmistakeably Damian Walker. Jessica had been looking through photographs of him the previous day and the shape of his nose was the same, plus there was something about the squished ears that matched her memory. There was every chance he wouldn't be recognised in public but if a person saw the front-page photographs that had adorned yesterday's news and looked – *really* looked – they'd see it too. Once it was spotted, the similarity was impossible to forget.

Jessica shivered as she stared at him: the monster in plain sight, eating Coco Pops as if he hadn't murdered four young women and tried to kill a fifth.

Clayton was leaning on a washing machine at the back of the kitchen and reached out to shake Topper and Jessica's hands. He looked even more tired than Millie, his eyelids drooping, the haunted gaze of a man whose worst fears were coming true.

Topper extended his hand towards Walker: 'Mr Seasmith . . .'

Jessica had already forgotten the man's new identity. He was always going to be Damian Walker.

Walker hovered his spoon over the bowl, staring crookedly up towards the chief inspector but not motioning to shake his hand. His teeth – *those* teeth – were yellow and crooked.

'That ain't my name.'

Topper and Clayton exchanged a confused look, before Clayton answered. 'Eric's not too fond of the identity change.'

'No, I bloody ain't. My name's Damian Walker.'

Clayton sounded firm. 'People have been through this with you, Eric. You know you can't use that name – it's for your own safety.'

Walker huffed before diving into the bowl for another spoonful of mushy cereal. He swallowed and then jabbed the spoon towards Millie in the doorway. 'What's wrong with some proper milk? I can't stand this semi-skimmed shite. I want proper milk. Christ's sake . . .'

Topper moved in between Walker and Millie. 'You do know why we're here, Mr Seasmith.'

'If you have to use that name, at least call me bloody Eric.'

'Where were you between the hours of midnight and one o'clock this morning?'

'Sleeping.' Walker thrust his leg out from under the

table and rolled up his trousers, revealing a plastic and metal ring clamped around his ankle. 'This bloody thing stops me going anywhere.' He nodded towards Millie. 'Ask her.'

As he grabbed the box and poured more cereal into the bowl, Millie led Jessica and Topper into the living room, closing the door behind them. The brown carpet smelled fresh and new, with a leather three-piece suite arranged around a large flatscreen television. The walls were clear of photos and pictures, the curtains pulled back, allowing the grey murk to seep through the thin net curtains. Millie sank into one of the armchairs and rubbed her eyes as Jessica and Topper took the sofa.

'Sorry,' Millie said. 'He's not usually so, erm . . .'

'Who owns this place?' Topper asked.

'I don't know – it's being rented through a letting agency.'

Topper nodded at the kitchen. 'Is he paying?'

'As far as I know. I think he's got money from before all of this. The programme would have sorted out moving the money into accounts with his new name and so on.' She waved towards the kitchen, lowering her voice. 'A lot are like this. It's called "witness protection" but that's a general term. *Actual* witnesses want new identities, of course, but some like Eric don't understand that it's for their own protection. In his mind, he did the crime, he did the time and now he's better. He even asked about moving into his old house. It was one of the conditions of his release that he maintains the new identity. I think it's only with us that he tries to push his luck. He was lucky to be allowed back to the Manchester area. Most people would be shunted to another area of the country. I guess it's only because the city's so big that they allowed it. It's not my job to be part of the decision.'

Topper shuffled to the edge of the sofa, maintaining the whispered conversation. 'I gather neither of you stayed here last night.'

She shook her head. 'There's no reason for us to. This is the end of the process and Eric's been preparing for his release for months. At first he was allowed out by himself during the day but had to be back at the hospital in the evenings, then it was weekends, then he was allowed nights away in agreed places. Some of that would be escorted but those days are gone now he's been released.' She pointed to the small black box above the window at the back of the room. 'The electronic tag is only temporary and then he's free to come and go as he pleases. He'll have semi-regular meetings with a psychologist for the rest of his life but that's all.'

'What are the terms for the electronic tagging?' Topper asked.

'He has to be inside between ten at night and six in the morning. If he's not, an alarm goes off. If he's inside and leaves then an alarm sounds.'

'And everything's working fine?'

'It was double-checked half an hour ago. Everything's working perfectly.'

'There were no alarms last night?'

'Nothing. As far as everyone's concerned he never left the house.'

'I know it sounds stupid,' Jessica said, already knowing the answer, 'but is there any way he could have removed the tag?'

Millie shook her head. 'The security company checked that this morning. It's not been tampered with. Eric resented having it checked and wasn't happy that you were coming round.'

'What time did you get here?' Jessica asked.

'About five. Clayton was already here. I think someone from the police contacted our bosses. I don't really know.' She covered her mouth as another yawn erupted. 'Sorry.' She waved her hand as a tear squidged along her cheek. 'What happens now?'

'We'll have to talk to Walk . . . Seasmith,' Topper said.

'He'll tell you what he told us – that he was asleep.'

'I know.'

'Either Clayton or myself will be staying here from now on. It's not ideal and we've made it clear to Eric that it's not to keep an eye on him, it's for his own protection. Outside of the restricted hours, he can come and go as he wants – not that he wants. I did his shopping yesterday because he didn't want to leave the house.'

'Is that part of the job description?'

She yawned again. 'Let's just say it's not in my contract. It's not that sort of job. Neither of us was supposed to be here today. We were only around yesterday because of the media leak. I've got loads of paperwork.' Another yawn. 'Sorry, you don't need to know any of that.'

The three of them smiled at each other, all thinking

the same thing. No matter what the job, it was usually the paperwork that got a person in the end.

There was a clatter from the kitchen, which sounded like a spoon being flung into a metal sink. Millie offered a weak smile. 'I guess you're up.'

Topper switched on his engine and instantly turned off the radio. He pulled away from the cul-de-sac onto the adjacent street and started to weave his way back towards the main road.

'Well, that was fun,' he said.

'I particularly liked the bit where he called you an effing-bleeping-c-word,' Jessica replied.

'I lived in Glasgow for a while, that's an affectionate hello up there.'

'What do they say if they don't like you?'

'You don't want to know.'

Jessica allowed herself a smile, stretching out her hands for the heaters to gust a torrent of warm air onto her chilled fingers. It was raining hard again. 'What do you reckon?'

Topper edged onto the main road and checked his mirror. 'He says he didn't leave the house and the monitoring equipment backs that up. We can ask the security company to recheck everything but this is what happens when it's all privatised. We can hardly keep pushing them, accusing them of having dodgy kit, else we'll end up getting sued. Aside from the similarity in the park attack, there's nothing to indicate he was there. Buile Hill's about eight miles from here and he doesn't have a car. We can

59

ask the taxi companies if they accepted a fare from this house but I doubt much will come back.'

'Who's investigating what?'

Topper shook his head and sighed. 'You'd think that was a simple question but they're back at base deciding things right now. It'll be the afternoon by the time the assistant chiefs have stopped bickering over who does what. If we're ruling out Walker – which we are for now – there'll have to be an investigation from scratch. Not only that, there's no way they're going to bring more officers into the circle of knowing who Walker is and where he lives. The investigating team will have to take our word for it – via the chief constable – that Walker's clear. I got a message from Aylesbury to sit tight. Everyone's so paranoid about making a mistake that we've not even made a start. They can hide behind forensics for now but everyone knows we've got no chance with that, not after all this rain.'

'This is a shambles.'

'You're telling me. I'm the one who has to report to headquarters later.'

'If we stick someone on Walker to watch him around the clock, we're going to have to make sure we don't get caught.'

Topper didn't reply but from the aggressive way he snapped down the indicator stick, it was clear he already knew that.

8

Jessica and DCI Topper were led through the winding corridors of Livingstone low-security hospital. It sat on the border of Merseyside and Cheshire, a smart wooden panel and glass structure that must have cost a fortune, with no fences or obvious security measures on the outside. The inside was more like a modern hotel than a hospital – echoing wooden floors, pale blue walls decorated with an assortment of prints, and individually numbered rooms.

They eventually ended up in a recreation room with brown leather sofas scattered around the edges and dining tables with orange plastic chairs at the far end. Bookshelves were pushed against one wall with a collection of paperbacks and magazines in neat lines and there were two flatscreen televisions fixed to the walls at either end. The receptionist pointed them towards one of the sofas and the two officers sat as she left.

'Not bad, is it?' Jessica said.

'I can probably arrange for you to be booked in for a few weeks.' Topper winked at her, which Jessica replied to with a smile. This was the most time she'd ever spent alone with the DCI. He was usually so office-bound at the station that nobody saw much of him.

Jessica gazed around the room, trying to come up with some sort of acceptable small talk: 'wow, isn't the floor squeaky?', 'my house is nowhere near this clean', 'I wonder if they've got cable?' all flitted through her mind before she was saved by a man entering. He was in his fifties, wearing dark trousers and a blue shirt with the sleeves rolled up, and introduced himself as Doctor Marwick. He didn't seem very *doctory* to Jessica, though it might have been because he wasn't wearing a white coat. Marwick already knew about the discovery of the body from the morning – he'd have to have been a cave-dwelling hermit to miss it. Topper assured him they weren't there because Walker was under any specific suspicion, more because they were looking for background. It was nonsense, of course. Walker was most certainly under suspicion given someone had been murdered by the same method in the same place as his final attack.

Marwick nodded slowly throughout the explanation and then squeezed the bridge of his nose. 'You have to understand about patient confidentiality,' he said, talking to Topper and largely ignoring Jessica.

'Absolutely,' Topper replied, though Jessica had the sense he was going to put on as much pressure as he could. It had taken her a while but she realised he played up the accent when he wanted to. She still wasn't sure if it was Scottish or Irish but it became far more growly when he wanted his own way. As he spoke, each syllable sounded as if it was being scratched across a blackboard.

'Was it you who made the decision to release Mr Walker?' Topper asked.

'Not by myself but, collectively, yes. Mr Walker had a mental breakdown seventeen years ago that was largely brought on by a cocktail of drugs and alcohol. He was thirty-four at the time and had been abusing his body for most of his life. This is all on record.'

Topper ignored the dig at the end. 'Was the breakdown entirely down to the drugs?'

'It's hard to tell. There were underlying aspects in Mr Walker's past I'm not going to reveal unless you have a warrant.'

Topper held both palms up. 'This is supposed to be a friendly chat, Mr Marwick.'

'*Doctor* Marwick.'

'Sorry, *Doctor* Marwick. We're not fishing for information, more looking for background.'

Marwick eyed them both, no doubt wondering if the hospital – and possibly he himself – was about to get savaged for releasing someone who'd murdered within a week. His defensiveness was perhaps understandable.

'I'll put it in as simple terms as I can manage,' Marwick said, turning his attention back to Topper. 'Walker had a break with reality. He didn't see his victims as people. In his mind, he was being terrorised by demons. He thought his victims were devils trying to drag him into hell. Despite what's happened overnight, there's no reason to think Mr Walker would attack anyone now. He's recovered and realises the enormity of what he did. I spoke to him on the phone this morning and there's a face-to-face session due later in the month. I see no reason to bring that forward – and if any of your superiors want to tell me how to do my job—'

'We're not here for that, *Doctor*.'

Topper's Celtic growl was so severe that it left Marwick with his mouth hanging open. 'Right . . . fine,' he replied.

There was a moment of silence before Jessica spoke: 'Does this mean that Walker confessed?'

Marwick examined her, eyes narrow, lips pursed, before the reply came. 'You're thinking about your world, Inspector.'

'Huh?'

'I have to be careful about what I say . . . patient conf—'

'Confidentiality. We get it.'

Marwick frowned at her as he started drumming a pen on the edge of the clipboard he was carrying. He snorted through his nose and then finally replied. '"Confession" is the wrong word. Mr Walker doesn't remember the attacks as such. He sees them as dreams, a blur between the real world and the demon-infested one in which he lived at the time. As I said, he doesn't occupy that world any longer. In layman's terms, he's as sane as *you* or me.'

Jessica couldn't help but feel the stress on the word 'you'. Topper interjected into the conversation: 'We met with Mr Walker in his new guise earlier today and he seemed a little, well, anxious.'

The doctor nodded, apparently in agreement. 'That's likely because of the incredible upheaval. It's the same not just for Mr Walker, but for anyone who leaves a secure hospital or a prison facility. These men and women spend years having every facet of their lives decided, from when they're allowed to wake up, to what they eat, what they wear and when the lights are turned off. Their schedules are fitted into tidy boxes – an hour of this, half an hour of that. It's easy to get used to and then, all of a sudden, these men and women have to sort their own meals, do their own shopping, make decisions for themselves. Even something simple such as when they should go to sleep can cause great confusion. One of the reasons reoffending can be so high among prisoners – not here, I should add – is that the support for those being released isn't what it could be.' He leant back into his seat, holding both hands up. 'It's always about funding. Men and women who spend years, perhaps a decade, having everything done for them are suddenly thrust back into the world without the support they need. Things are a little different for Mr Walker because he has the protection people around him. This is the end of a very long process of rehabilitation.' He nodded at Topper. 'You may as well just ask it. It's clearly why you're here.'

Topper hesitated anyway: 'You understand why I have to ask.'

'I don't, actually – how many of *your* decisions are questioned daily?'

'Most of them.'

The two men stared at each other, even though there was nothing for them to be arguing about. Both men were doing their jobs.

Topper eventually broke the impasse. 'Is Mr Walker a threat to the public?'

Marwick shook his head. 'Absolutely not. If anything, the overnight events could affect him as much as anyone else as it will bring back memories—'

'I suspect the victim's family will be affected the worst.'

Jessica had blurted out the comment without thinking, unable to shut herself up: an old character trait that was increasingly finding its way back into her repertoire.

Surprisingly, Marwick nodded slowly. 'You're right – but you're the ones who came here asking about Mr Walker and it's to him I'm referring. In my opinion – and plenty of other people's, incidentally – Mr Walker is no threat. If he was, he never would have been released.' He started to stand. 'Now, unless there's anything else, I'm a very busy man.'

9

Jessica held her hands to the heating vents as DCI Topper pulled out of the hospital's car park. It was still raining, still cold, but the peace of being away from the station was lovely.

'Everyone's being nice and friendly this morning,' Jessica said.

'It must be you,' Topper replied, not turning away from the road. His voice sounded more like his own, the harsh edge no longer there. 'Everyone's normally fine with me.'

'Who's next?'

Topper's gaze flashed to the small clock built into the dashboard. 'We've got an hour to get back to Longsight. They're doing a media briefing at headquarters for eleven, then the chief constable's coming to visit.'

'Twice in two days? Aren't we privileged?'

Topper reached forward and turned on the radio, most likely to shut her up.

Acting Chief Constable Aylesbury was back in the same incident room as the previous day but the wind and rain had got to him. Usually so well turned out, he looked as if he'd been down a water flume fully clothed. His hair was limp and flopped to the side, his eyebrows were like a pair of small bottlebrushes super-glued to his head. He was trussed up in the full uniform, with a row of medals above his breast pocket, meaning he'd probably been in front of the cameras at some point during the morning. Hopefully before he was baptised with his clothes on.

DCI Topper and Jessica were sitting next to each other a metre or so away. Thankfully, there was no sign of DI Franks. It was almost lunchtime, so he was probably sniffing around a set of public toilets somewhere.

Aylesbury leant back into the leather swivel chair, which hadn't been in the room the previous day. 'HQ's under siege,' he said, sounding as serious as if he'd announced the loss of a few hundred lives, not the fact that he'd had a few problems getting out of the car park. 'It's a media storm over there. Thankfully you've only got that woman with the placard outside of here.' He clicked his fingers in Topper's direction, his manners apparently deserting him. 'What's going on with her?'

Jessica answered for him. 'Her name's Eleanor – Ellie. Her fiancé went on a stag do last month and disappeared. We've done what we can but there's no trace.'

The chief constable shook his head. 'We could really do without that sort of distraction at a time like this.'

Jessica opened her mouth but just about hung onto 'Shall I go out and tell her to stop being so inconvenient?' What did he expect? If he wanted to redirect the entire budget into looking for one person, he could do that. They might even find Ellie's husband-to-be in the process. If he wanted the crime figures to look nice and ship-shape for the annual statistics release, then he could leave things as they were. It was disheartening how quickly the high-ups forgot what it was like to do actual work.

'Anyway,' Aylesbury continued, 'you probably know already but last night's victim has been identified – well, as much as she can be. Someone named Casey Graves, eighteen and a Salford local. The murder is going to be investigated by a large team working from Bootle Street. They've got their own incident room and it's going to be headed by Superintendent Deacon from the Northern district. They're pulling in officers from the North, South, East, West and Central divisions.'

Topper was nodding, expecting the news. 'Where does that leave us?'

Aylesbury suddenly couldn't make eye contact, peering past them towards the door. 'It's not your job to investigate Ms Graves's murder *as such*, more to keep an eye on Mr Walker. The forensics from the park are a mess – not that we told the press that. The rain's washed anything obvious away, plus there's already a backlog. If – and that's a big *if* – they get anything, it's going to take a while. We'll be lucky if it's this week.'

'Were there teeth marks on Ms Graves's shoulder?' Topper asked.

Aylesbury shook his head. 'It seems not. We're going to need old-fashioned policing, the way it used to be.'

He chuckled, leaning forward and patting Topper on the shoulder as if they were old friends. The best the DCI could manage was a thin smile. He wasn't amused.

Aylesbury took the hint, angling away and interlocking his fingers, then twiddling his thumbs. 'I'm the liaison between anything you discover here and the main investigation at Bootle Street. They don't know – *can't* know – about Walker's identity so there needs to be a lot of trust.' He turned to face Jessica, raising his eyebrows. 'There's no time for heroes.'

Sod off, she thought, though for the second time, managed to keep herself quiet. She didn't respond, not even with a nod. If he wanted to tell her something, he could bloody well say it.

After a moment, Aylesbury continued: 'The reason you've been entrusted with Walker's identity and allowed to meet him is that you have to have the freedom to look into other angles regarding this killing. Just bear in mind that Mr Walker is *not* under arrest, nor under suspicion.' He glanced between them. 'Unless you can say otherwise.' Neither of them did, so he went on: 'As long as you don't trample on Superintendent Deacon's main investigation, and as long as you go through me for anything major, you should feel free to show initiative and not feel obliged to run every small thing past me. Okay?'

Topper squeaked back into his chair, shoulders tense. If he wasn't going to say it, then Jessica would. 'So we *shouldn't* be heroes and *should* run things through you, but we *should* show initiative and *not* bring everything to you.'

Aylesbury nodded. 'Precisely. All clear?'

Topper answered before Jessica could: 'One hundred per cent, Sir.'

They all shook hands and then Aylesbury blustered into the corridor carrying a hand towel and rubbing his hair. It'd take him a good hour to get himself back into pristine condition and there was bound to be another press conference later.

Jessica waited until she heard the sound of the door at the end of the corridor closing and then turned to face the chief inspector. He was scratching the back of his head, sending a flurry of dandruff to the floor.

'What the hell was that all about?' she hissed. 'He told us two contradictory things. He can't tell us to show initiative and then say there's no time for heroes.'

Topper yawned wearily, ageing in front of her. They'd been working together for almost nine hours and there was no sign of going home for the day yet. 'It's internal politics, Jess. Someone high up thinks Walker's involved. Because the radio, TV and papers are banging on about it, someone like the Home Secretary has put a phone call in, wanting to make sure Greater Manchester Police have everything in hand. Aylesbury's only standing in as chief constable while Pomeroy's off on the sick, so he's got to say we're examining all possibilities. He and the other assistant chiefs will be unhappy that Walker's out and that we're getting it in the neck even though it's nothing to do with us. Doctors have made that decision but the police get blamed. Basically, Aylesbury's telling us to do what we can to either prove it *is* Walker who killed that poor girl, or to make sure it's definitely *not* him.'

He stopped for another yawn, not bothering to hide how tired he was. 'The problem is that Walker's a free man with a new identity. If we get caught sticking our noses in somewhere they're not wanted, or Walker gets unmasked, HQ will deny all knowledge because the Bootle Street investigation is the official one. They'll say we were acting off our own backs.' Topper nodded towards the door. 'Aylesbury's told us conflicting things because if things go wrong, he can turn to whichever viewpoint fits best. If we get caught out doing something off our own backs, he'll say we were supposed to run everything past him; if we tell him everything we do and it *is* Walker who killed that girl, he'll take the credit. Either way, he wins and we lose.'

Jessica took a few moments to think it through. She'd been stitched up before but never quite so comprehensively. Topper was right – there was no glory to be had here. If they were *really* lucky, Walker would have nothing to do with the killing and the Bootle Street lot would pull their fingers out and find the actual murderer before someone else was killed. The price of being unlucky wasn't worth thinking about.

'What are we going to do?' Jessica asked.

Topper stood, straightening his blazer and pacing the room. The walls were relatively clear aside from a selection of Blu-tack marks. On the whiteboard at the front, someone had drawn a large question mark in the centre.

'We're going to treat it like it's our own investigation,' Topper replied, spinning and stopping close to the door. 'Sod everyone else – especially Aylesbury. He's not even got the job yet and he's playing politics. They forget that I'm not from here. I can go back to Scotland any time I choose. If any of them try to take me down, I'll bring the entire senior management team down with me.' His eyes glinted ferociously, his voice gruff and hard again. Jessica really liked this version of him. 'Who do you trust downstairs?' he asked.

'DS Diamond . . . Izzy.'

'Who else?'

'Rowlands and Davey.'

He nodded slowly. 'Rowlands is assigned to Franks, isn't he?'

'Yes.'

'I don't want to rock the boat here. How are things between you and Davey? Anything I need to be aware of?'

By asking the question, it was clear he already knew. Jessica and DC Archie Davey had had a relationship of sorts. Nothing serious, little more than a physical thing, but it had all come out a couple of months previously in the most embarrassing way possible. It was all the worse because of what had happened to Adam.

Jessica shook her head. 'No, Sir.'

'Good – if you bring Davey and Diamond up to my office, we can get cracking on finding out whether or not Walker's our man.'

10

Jessica could feel the adrenaline flowing as she, Izzy and Archie waited on the opposite side of Topper's desk. The chief inspector struck his keyboard as if it had wronged him, thick fingers slamming away on the defenceless keys, before he looked up. He nodded at Izzy and then Archie.

'Jessica's vouched for the pair of you, which is enough for me. Before anything else, I'll say that this is going to impact on both of your workloads. If you're desperately concerned about your to-do piles, then I suppose you've already realised that you're in the wrong career.' He shrugged. 'If either of you has a problem, you can return downstairs, no harm done.' He paused but neither of them moved and he broke into a smile. 'Good, let's get to work.'

Topper spent the next couple of minutes explaining the dual investigations. There was the official one looking for whoever had killed Casey Graves, which had already excluded Damian Walker as a suspect. Then there was the unofficial, unacknowledged side investigation – theirs – that was supposed to be focusing solely on Walker under the guise of offering him protection. He told Izzy and Archie that, for now, they had to remain in the dark as to Walker's new identity and location.

'We're covering our own backs,' Topper said. 'There's no way we're going to be able to prove or disprove that

Walker killed this young woman last night unless we look beyond him. We'll let Superintendent Deacon do his thing and we'll do ours.'

Jessica, Izzy and Archie all nodded. A young woman might have died but it was hard to fight the feeling of excitement that they were part of something illicit, like being alone in the school halls, allowed to roam free.

Topper continued: 'Let's assume for now that Walker didn't kill Casey Graves. If he didn't, who did?'

Archie was the same bundle of energy as always, his leg twitching. His hair was greased into tight curls, body angled forward, ready for action. 'Copycat? Someone who saw the news yesterday about Jaws and thought they'd have a go?'

Topper nodded but was scratching his chin, unconvinced. 'Is this really the type of thing you'd copy? If you wanted to kill someone – even a stranger – wouldn't you just do it? This poor girl had her stomach sliced open.'

'Does she have a boyfriend?' Archie asked.

Topper shook his head. 'That's the type of thing we have to keep our noses out of. Superintendent Deacon will be looking into relatives and things like that. We can't talk to the same people he does. We're focusing on Walker and people connected to him.'

'Does Walker have any relatives?'

Topper continued shaking his head. 'His parents had already died when he killed seventeen years ago.'

'Hmmmm . . .' Archie leant back into his chair. He wasn't unintelligent but sometimes he thought a bit too directly.

Izzy wrote something on her notepad and looked up. 'How about someone who wants to frame Walker?'

'Like who?'

'The family of one of his old victims? Someone who wanted to prove a point.'

Topper nodded. 'We'll have to be careful if that's where we look but it's a fair suggestion.'

Izzy continued writing, already ahead. 'There were four previous victims, plus Anne Atkinson herself. There's bound to be a few family members of the other victims floating around the area. I'll get on it.'

Archie nodded. 'Anne Atkinson and her husband Mark are already on holiday. They went yesterday.'

'How do you know they've already gone?' Jessica asked.

'He put a photo on Twitter last night. It was of a bunch of rocks and said something like, "No more interviews, please respect our privacy".'

Topper typed something on his keyboard and then looked up. 'Any idea where?'

Izzy replied: 'Somewhere on the coast in West Wales. Chalets, caravans, food poisoning, the lot.'

'How'd you know that?'

She shrugged. 'I saw the picture too and recognised the shoreline. I was interested. It wasn't too hard to narrow down the possible caravan park from that. It could be one of two or three but they're all close to each other. We can easily visit to see where their car's parked.'

Jessica suspected it would have been hard for most people to find out where the couple had gone given that all there was to go on was 'a bunch of rocks' but Izzy was in a class of her own.

If Topper was impressed, it didn't show. 'What's the distance there and back?'

'A hundred and a bit miles each way. Three hours on the A roads if you're lucky.' She answered the unasked question. 'They could have made it here and back in time.'

Topper stared at his screen for a few moments, sucking on his bottom lip. Jessica felt she could read his thoughts, hearing Aylesbury's words bouncing around his mind.

'You should feel free to show initiative . . .'

The chief inspector took a deep breath. He opened his palms towards Izzy. 'Are you sure you know where they're staying?'

'I don't know the exact caravan park but I'm pretty sure about the resort. I can do some Googling. Mark Atkinson put up two pictures last night. It shouldn't be too hard to track them down.'

'We can't be seen to be checking up on them, especially after Anne Atkinson spent yesterday morning on television and radio.' Topper paused, taking another breath, seeming unsure of his own mind. 'We're *not* checking up on them, just examining other possibilities that Deacon and co. won't be able to. That's what Aylesbury told us to do.' He stopped again, scratching his head and sending another small flurry of dandruff onto his lap. It looked as if he was trying to convince himself. 'Why would they announce they're going on holiday rather than just go? If they wanted to get away from what's going on here, if they were after anonymity, why wouldn't they just disappear for a few days? Not only that, it's October – are caravan parks still open?'

Izzy replied: 'Some of my friends go away when it's half-term. Places like that are open more or less all year round. They're just quiet.'

'So why not just go?'

Topper was met by blank faces but he had a point. If Anne Atkinson wanted to be left alone, the worst thing to do was tell the media she was going away and then have her husband post a picture. They'd have been better off going to ground and turning their phones off. Still, it was difficult to judge someone's motivation, especially when she'd just been notified that the person who tried to kill her had been released from a secure hospital.

Topper slapped a palm on his desk, mind made up. 'Right, this is what we're going to do. Before anything, first-name terms. None of this "guv" or "DC-this", "DS-that" stuff. We're a small team who are looking out for one another. I'm Lewis, so that's what you should call me. Isobel: double check the location of where Anne Atkinson and her husband have gone. If you can narrow it down to a handful of caravan parks, that's good enough. Archie: we need a list of suspects. We're looking at Anne Atkinson because she's the local victim we know about. Who are the surviving relatives of Walker's other victims? Parents, siblings, kids if there are any. Get a full list and cross off everyone who has an obvious alibi – the dead, the emigrated and so on. There shouldn't be too many names left.'

'Gotcha.'

'Between the pair of you, see what you can find out

about Walker's past seventeen years. Were there other people in hospital with whom he might have had a feud? Be discreet.'

Izzy's pen was flashing across her pad and didn't stop as she replied. 'With all the negative publicity from yesterday, anyone could have it in for him.'

'I'm aware – but we can't examine the sixty-five million people who live in the country. We've got to start somewhere.'

'Understood.'

Topper turned to Jessica. 'You and me are going to stick on Walker himself.'

'What about Anne Atkinson?' she asked.

The chief inspector sucked in his cheeks again. 'It's probably nothing, but . . . A hundred miles isn't that far. We could ask the local force to poke their noses in but that'll get leaked.' He looked across at the three of them and muttered something about not being able to spare anyone, then picked up the phone and asked for Franks. Jessica exchanged a momentary glance with Izzy, hoping the imbecilic inspector wasn't about to be called upstairs but the conversation was very one-sided.

'I need two people you can spare,' Topper said. 'It doesn't matter what for. They're going to need to spend some time on a job together . . . Yes, together . . . I'm not at liberty to say . . . Yes, they'll be together . . . Fine.'

From what she overheard, Jessica had no doubt about the identity of one of those who had been suggested. Topper put down the phone and turned to her. 'Rowlands and Evesham – what do you think?'

'Dave's fine,' Jessica replied. 'I don't know much about Ruth. She's new and seems keen.' She was also pretty. Very pretty. Exactly the sort of person DI Franks might want to send away with the man who was going out with his daughter.

Topper nodded shortly, taking a deep breath. Jessica had the sense he was regretting his own decision before he'd even made it completely. 'That's settled then. We'll send DCs Rowlands and Evesham off to Western Wales to keep a watch on the Atkinsons. If another body shows up, we'll have eyes to say they've not left wherever they're staying. I'm sure it's nothing but better safe than sorry.'

Aylesbury had told them to show initiative but this was going beyond anything even Jessica could have thought of. Spying on the victim? If anyone found out, Topper would face some serious questions.

Topper nodded at the door. 'Okay, let's get going.'

Izzy and Archie stood but Jessica didn't move, asking them to wait for her by the stairs and then remaining quiet until the door had closed and they were out of sight.

'Can I ask you something, Sir?'

'Lewis.'

'Fine, can I ask you something?'

'I'm under the impression that you already are.'

'Why are we going this far?'

For a moment, she didn't think he was going to answer. He took a breath through his nose. He had a long black hair poking out from his nostril that vibrated as he puffed. She could tell he was angry, a seething silent fury that he was doing well to contain. He spoke through clenched teeth. 'Honestly? Because I'm already sick of the politics here. A girl died last night and those pricks across the city have spent the entire morning fussing over who gets to go on TV, wondering about how they're going to spin things. I don't know if Walker did it but this is no way to run an investigation. We shouldn't be doing this, Deacon and his men should – but that's too simple because, if there's any shit to be thrown, it'd end up all over the management team. Instead, they do this. They want us to investigate Walker without investigating him. If he's guilty, the wrath of the public will be hurled at the establishment for releasing him. If it's not him, then there was no investigation in the first place. Typical double-play. If Aylesbury wants us to look into Walker's background without putting ripples in the water, then fine – we'll do it my way.'

Jessica was beginning to *really* like him.

'I was wondering if you remember . . .'

He nodded. 'I know what tomorrow is. You don't have to come in . . . you shouldn't come in.'

'I want to. That's not why I wanted a word, I just didn't want . . .'

'I won't disturb you. Do things in your own time. If that means you have a day or two off, then so be it.'

Jessica stood slowly, relieved, even though she had suspected he'd say that. 'Thank you, er, Lewis.'

Topper stood unnecessarily. For a moment, she thought he was going to stretch across and touch her arm, perhaps even hug her or something else slightly inappropriate. Instead, he did nothing, arms hanging awkwardly by his side. He didn't know what to say, but who did? She'd not told many people about what the following day held, largely because she didn't want moments like this.

'I should go,' Jessica said.

'Of course.'

Jessica hurried through the door and clicked it closed behind her. Archie and Izzy were waiting at the top of the stairs, having a mini argument. Archie was so easy to wind up – say something derogatory about Manchester United and he was drawn in every time.

'. . . that's absolute bollocks,' Archie said, flapping his hands around. 'Wembley? Have you ever bloody been? It's in London for Christ's sake. *Wembley?*'

'What about Twickenham?' Izzy said, offering Jessica a barely perceptible wink.

'Egg-chasing? Are you joking?' He jabbed a thumb in Jessica's direction. 'Have you 'eard this? She reckons Twickenham's a better ground than the Theatre of Dreams.'

'Someone told me they were renaming it the Theatre of Penalties.'

He shook his head ferociously, like a dog trying to dry itself. When he was angry, he forgot to stand on the tips of his toes, making himself appear even shorter than usual. 'Oh ha-bloody-ha. I've always reckoned you were a City fan.'

'I've told you a hundred times, Arch, I couldn't care less about football. All I know about the sport is that the greatest stadium in the world is Anfield.'

He looked like he was going to pop, cheeks puffing and reddening, eyes widening. 'Anfield? Anfield! You do know where that is, don't you? *Anfield?!*'

Izzy cut him off before he spontaneously combusted. 'You all right?' she asked Jessica.

Jessica nodded. 'I just wanted to check a few things. Are you both all right? You can work from my office. There's a free terminal and I'll tell Fat Pat I'm signing out a laptop. If I bribe him with a chocolate digestive he won't even kick up a fuss.'

'Isn't he on a diet?' Izzy asked.

'So he says but I can hardly bung him an apple.'

'Fair point.'

Archie stomped off towards the stairs, still shaking his head. *'Anfield!'*

11

Under usual circumstances, after almost twelve hours at work, Jessica would either be on her way home, or trying to catch a quick snooze in her office. Unfortunately, and entirely down to her own stupidity, her office was being used. Izzy was at the spare desk, beavering away on the computer terminal like a woman possessed, while Archie had set himself up with a laptop in the corner, perched on a chair with a tea tray stolen from the canteen. He was still shaking his head and muttering under his breath, unable to let the Anfield jibe go. When it came to football, he didn't appreciate jokes about his beloved United, especially if they'd lost within the past week. He was two different people – if they'd won at the weekend, he'd bounce into the station like a four-year-old hopped up on sugar at a birthday party. If they'd lost, it was as if his entire family had been wiped out in a coach accident. There was little middle ground, even when they drew. It was win or nothing in DC Davey's mind.

'*Anfield*,' he muttered for approximately the fortieth time.

Jessica had endured enough, spinning in her chair to face him. 'Give it a rest, Arch.'

'You've never even been to the ground, have you?'

'Have you actually been doing work over there, or just Googling facts about football stadiums?'

'It's stad*ia*, actually.'

'Yeah, well, you can do some work, *actually*. Now what have you found?'

Jessica ignored Izzy's snort, which she unsuccessfully tried to disguise as a cough. She could tell from the glint in Archie's eye that he was well on with what he was doing. The annoyance was an act. 'Anne Atkinson's parents died a year or two after she was attacked and she has no brothers or sisters. Aside from her husband, it's just her. Walker had four other victims. One had a sister but I can't trace her. Two of his victims were students, so their families lived elsewhere anyway. The closest I can find is a brother of one of Walker's victims who lives in Middlesbrough.'

Jessica grinned at him. 'What's Middlesbrough's stadium like?'

'The Riverside? It's—'

'All right, I don't care. Learn to let things go, Arch. Iz?'

Izzy had been in and out of the office all afternoon, seemingly managing a dozen tasks at the same time. Jessica sometimes wondered if she was a twin, with two of her floating around the station, never seen in the same place at the same time.

'I put in a few calls,' Izzy said. 'I managed to get through to someone at Ashworth. That's where Walker was based for most of his sentence. I'm waiting on a call back to find out if he pissed off any of the other patients but was told not to hold my breath.'

So far, so little.

'I know what the guv told us,' Jessica said, 'but I've had a quick peep at what Deacon and his mob are up to. Apparently last night's victim – Casey – has no boyfriend, no jilted lover, nothing like that. Her parents were having a long weekend away in Edinburgh so they've rushed home. It looks like a random attack.' Jessica could sense Archie watching her, wanting to say something. 'Spit it out then,' she added.

He shrugged. 'Aren't we overthinking this whole thing? We've got two investigations, a pair of constables heading off to the middle of nowhere, TV cameras parked outside of HQ . . . why can't it just be Walker? I know what the guv said upstairs but what if Walker found a way of ditching his tag and off he went?'

Jessica understood where Archie was coming from and, to an extent, agreed with him. The most likely option was probably the truest. 'He lives a fair distance away,' she said. 'You know I can't tell you where but he couldn't walk it. He doesn't own a car.'

'But he could've rented one and parked it somewhere else. Or cycled, or any number of things. Just because he doesn't live next to the park, it doesn't mean it's not him. Maybe he knows someone who fits the ankle tags who sorted him out with a new one? Maybe the system's faulty?'

'They checked all of that.'

'But it's not foolproof – you know how useless the security lot are. It was only the other month they lost three prisoners in rush hour in the city centre.'

'I know.'

'If we're really thinking outside the box, all that shite, did Walker actually admit to the attacks? Could it be someone from the past and we had the wrong person all along? Now they're attacking again because Walker's a scapegoat?'

It was something that hadn't occurred to Jessica and, as unlikely as it seemed, it was good somebody was coming up with those sorts of ideas. 'I asked Walker's doctor and he says Walker sees the attacks as dreams, as if the real world combined with the demons in his mind. He thought he was fighting devils.'

Archie raised his eyebrows, tilting his head. 'Oh . . .'

'What's that for?'

'Does that mean he confessed or not?'

'I don't know, Arch. The file says he was found with the victims' blood on his clothes. He never denied it and the break with reality – whatever you want to call it – is documented.'

'Okay.' His eyebrow flickered higher.

'Stop looking at me like that. I'm only telling you what I've been told. It was seventeen years ago. None of us worked here then. There's no way anyone's reopening an investigation from that long ago, not after the bloke they convicted has done his time in a secure hospital.'

'All right, all right, I'm just saying . . .'

Izzy's phone started to ring and she held it in the air before hurrying into the corridor, closing the door behind her. Archie and Jessica were left watching each other until she caved first. 'Sorry, I know we're supposed to be going over these things but there's only four of us and the guv's got way too much on to get his hands too dirty . . .'

'It's all right. I'm more pissed off by the Anfield thing. I don't know how anyone could think it's better than Old Trafford.'

'We're winding you up, Arch. Let it go.' He eyed her suspiciously, unconvinced that it was a joke. Jessica couldn't hold his gaze, unable to bear him watching her as she asked the next question. She glanced towards the door instead, making sure Izzy wasn't anywhere near. 'Anyway, later on, are we . . . ?'

There was a pause that lasted far too long, giving Jessica her answer. 'I'm busy tonight,' Archie said.

Jessica tried to sound breezy, unconcerned. 'Doing what?'

'Just, er . . . stuff.'

'You can tell me.'

'I'm sort of seeing someone.'

'Oh.'

'I met this girl at the weekend. We started chatting and—'

'I don't need a commentary. It's fine, we're not together.'

That was the line they'd been sticking to if anyone around the station asked outright. Those who wanted to were busy gossiping anyway, drawing their own conclusions after what had happened a couple of months previously. Jessica and Archie could never stop the wagging tongues regardless of what they said but Archie had at least been someone with whom she could spend a few evenings a week. Someone to stop her feeling so alone when it was time to go home.

'Are you really all right?' he asked.

Jessica swivelled back to her monitor, not wanting him to see her face. 'Of course, no worries. Have a good evening.'

For the third time that day, she managed not to say what she was really thinking.

12

The Club Academy was an oddly named basement room underneath the university's students' union in the centre of the city. The actual Academy was an adjacent building that could hold a couple of thousand people for music gigs. Jessica had been there in the old days, dancing and drinking with her friend Caroline. Then, they were young and had no cares, other than whether they'd have enough money to get through the evening. It was before Caroline's divorce, before Adam, when their lives were simple. She hadn't been there in years, unsure of who most of the bands were and, even when there was someone she might have wanted to see, worried that she'd end up being *that* person. There was always some old weirdo who turned up at student gigs that everyone pointed at, wondering how they'd got a ticket.

Inside the students' union itself, the Academy Two was on the middle floor, another music venue that could hold a thousand or so people. The Academy Three was an even smaller room on the top floor, which held music and comedy gigs. Underneath all of that was the Club Academy.

Jessica was feeling her age as she walked into the reception of the students' union. There were orange and black decorations looped around the doors, ready for Halloween, and armies of students hurrying back and forth looking, well, young. There were short skirts, ripped tights, protest T-shirts, band T-shirts, long hair, short hair, ridiculous make-up and someone paying for a coffee with pennies. Despite the signs about free Wi-Fi, Jessica couldn't help but feel that the more things changed, the more they stayed the same. Twenty years previously, the exact same types of people would have been hanging around in the same places. The subjects which they protested against might now be different, as were the bands – and definitely the price of a coffee – but the general atmosphere was identical.

Jessica's work suit suddenly felt like a burden, as if she was drastically overdressed for the venue. She followed the signs towards the back of the building, heading down numerous flights of stairs until she arrived at an open door. A gaggle of intermingling voices seeped onto the steps as Jessica crept inside. Metal shutters were pulled in front of the bar on one side, with tall stacks of metal chairs lined up along the wall. Jessica followed the sound of voices, peering nervously around a wooden divider towards the stage. An abandoned microphone stand was in the centre, but the performing area was otherwise clear. Instead, on what would be the dance floor, a circle of chairs had been arranged. Thirteen or fourteen people were sitting and mumbling quietly to one another while sipping from glass mugs of tea. An urn was set up on the edge of the stage, next to a tray of fairy cakes decorated with baby blue icing and silver sugar balls.

As the floor creaked underneath her feet, Jessica felt

the group turn to look at her. A man squeaked his chair backwards and stood, stretching out a hand.

'Hi, are you here for the meeting?'

He was around Jessica's age and had a shaved head. He was wearing jeans and a white shirt with the sleeves rolled up. He smiled widely, making an effort to instigate eye contact that Jessica couldn't match.

'I saw something on the Internet about a support group . . .' Jessica stumbled over her words, nervous about the number of people watching her.

He stretched his hand out further and Jessica took the hint, shaking it. 'That's right, I'm Steve.'

'Erm . . . hi.'

Jessica realised he'd stopped shaking but she was still holding his hand. She snatched her fingers away, wrapping her arm behind her back as if trying to forget it had happened.

Steve leant in, still smiling, his voice a whisper. 'We're a friendly lot.'

'Right.'

'Do you want to sit? We'll give it a few minutes more to see if anyone else turns up, then we'll start.'

'Do I have to do anything?'

'It's up to you. Some of the group find it comforting to tell stories about those they've lost, others prefer to listen. We only have one rule – that you shouldn't talk over others. This isn't supposed to be a stuffy formal affair, just something that will hopefully help.'

'Okay.'

He nodded towards the stage. 'Get yourself a brew.

Pam's made a tray of cakes for everyone, too. They're delicious.'

Jessica edged around the circle. She was neither hungry nor thirsty but didn't want to stand out, so did as Steve suggested, pumping a torrent of tea into a mug, adding a splash of milk and then picking the smallest cake and finding an empty seat where there was no one on either side of her. A few of the group offered sympathetic knowing nods and smiles but everyone else seemed to know one another, talking quietly among themselves. Jessica nibbled on the corner of the cake, trying not to be noticed as she peered around the circle. It felt like a cross between an Alcoholics Anonymous meeting and a church coffee morning.

After a few minutes, Steve stood and closed the door, then returned to his seat and leant forward, fingers interlocked. They went around the circle, everyone giving their names, though Jessica knew she'd never remember any of them. What struck her was the mix. There was a girl who must have still been a teenager, all the way up to an old man wearing a suit. A young Asian girl was sitting next to an older black man, showing a near full cross section of the city's cultural diversity. Although Jessica had found the group's website via Ellie Scanlon's blog there was no sign of Ellie herself. She'd spent the day picketing outside the police station in the rain, so was hopefully now somewhere warm and dry.

After the introductions, Steve asked if anyone wanted to speak. Jessica kept her arms firmly crossed, eyes down, just in case he glanced in her direction. A woman three seats away from Jessica put her hand up. She was in her forties with long straight black hair. She would have been pretty but it was hard to see past the puffy eyes and reddened nose. Before she'd said a word, the woman was dabbing at her face with a tissue.

'My husband's called Jim . . . James, really, but everyone called him Jim. We've been married for thirteen years next month. He, um . . .' She stopped and blew her nose. The rest of the circle was silent, most of its members watching the woman, though a few were gazing at the floor. '. . . he worked in the Co-op building over by the Printworks. One morning six weeks ago, he went to work and never came home. His colleagues said he never arrived and the police say he didn't get onto the tram he usually takes. He's not touched our bank account or used his credit card, he didn't take the car . . . he just disappeared.'

There was a sob on the opposite side of the circle from the young Asian girl, who was hunched forward, face buried in a handkerchief.

Now she'd started, the woman barely paused for breath, desperate to get her story out in one go, probably knowing that if she stopped she'd not start again. 'We've got two kids – four and six – and I have no idea what to tell them. At first it was that Daddy's gone away for a few days, then a week. Then that he was on holiday. But what do I tell them now? He's just . . . gone. I don't know if he's alive and isn't coming home for some reason, or if there was some sort of accident and he's yet to be found. I don't know if I should be angry or upset. We'd argued the day before, some stupid thing about the fence panels at the back of our house and whether they should be painted orange or brown. It was so ridiculous, so . . . nothing, but I'm always thinking about that. Did that tip him over the edge? Is that why he left? Are there two kids without a father because of stupid fence panels?'

She wiped the tears away from her eyes, gazing at the floor and leaning back in her chair. Jessica glanced at her quickly and then peered away, feeling like she was intruding on a moment that should be private.

In her effort to turn away from the woman who'd been speaking, Jessica accidentally caught Steve's gaze. He raised his eyebrow, asking the silent question of whether she wanted to speak. Before Jessica knew what she was doing, she was croaking out a sentence: 'Hi, I'm Jessica and things have been hard for me recently.' Her voice cracked but she continued speaking through it. 'My fiancé's in a coma and the doctors say there's no chance of him waking up. I know it sounds horrible but I've sort of developed this way of coping that allows me to live two lives. There's the time I spend with him – an hour here or there, talking and reading, telling him what's going on in the world. Then there's everything else, my job, my friends, where I don't allow myself to think about him at all. I have to lock him away because I'd never be able to do anything otherwise. It's the evenings where I feel it the most, in bed by myself. Not only am I without him, I'm stuck with the guilt of pretending he's not around.'

Jessica took a breath to compose herself, feeling the eyes of the others upon her, hoping none of them knew she was a police officer. She wanted to be anonymous.

'I'd more or less got that under control but then . . . I've been living with a friend. She'd had a lot of problems in her past but there was a lot going for her. She'd just had her birthday, she was off to college, but I went to work one morning and then she was gone by the evening. As far as I could tell, she'd taken none of her possessions. Her phone, her shoes, her clothes – everything was left. She'd left the stove on and the front door unlocked. None of her friends had heard from her, neither had her mum or tutors. The neighbours saw nothing. She just went. It's hard to describe but, with my fiancé, it's something I can get my head around.'

She faltered, almost telling the truth about what was to happen, before correcting herself.

'I know where he is and, for the most part, understand why he's there. With my friend, I don't know what to think. Did she leave by herself? Was she snatched? Did she have a secret life I didn't know about?'

Jessica stopped for another breath, managing another sip of tea to soothe her throat. Someone was sobbing on the far side of the circle but Jessica didn't dare look up for fear she'd break down too. This was why missing people were one of the worst things to understand. With a body, there was closure. It might be brutal but at least the dead person's friends and family knew. When someone disappeared, there was only a hole in the lives of the people around him or her. Those who remained were left running through the minutiae of stupid events like arguments over paint and fence panels because they were desperate to find a reason – any reason – why their loved one had gone.

'My friend helped me a lot with what happened to my fiancé but they've both gone for different reasons and I can't understand it. I just want to know she's safe – even if she left because of me.'

Jessica took another mouthful of tea, directing a quick glance towards Steve to let him know she was done. There was a lot more she could say but this wasn't the place. Before disappearing, Bex had been in contact with her mother for the first time in four years. Was it a coincidence that the girl had disappeared days later? Bex's mother claimed she'd not heard or seen anything of her daughter but they'd had a fractious, abusive relationship in years gone by that had led to Bex living on the street. Jessica wanted to believe her mother knew nothing but it was easier to believe *she* was the reason than to think that Jessica herself might be at fault. Then there was the issue of Jessica having worked on a case involving many of the city's crime bosses. She'd felt followed at the time but it was difficult to know if that was paranoia or truth. Over her career, she'd annoyed and banged up a long list of people. Could someone have taken their revenge by snatching Bex?

In so many ways, it was almost comforting to think that was what had happened because it detracted from the even worse scenario that Bex had left because of something Jessica said or did. For someone whose job it was to find answers, Jessica had precious few of her own.

As the next person started to speak, Jessica pecked

around the edge of the cake. She'd hoped that sharing would make her feel better but, if anything, running through the thoughts and emotions she'd spent the past few months shoving deep down within herself had made her feel worse.

Jessica stood inside her front door listening to the silence.

'Hello?'

Nobody answered.

She left the lights off and held her arm out, feeling her way into the living room and finding a spot on the sofa. Jessica curled her legs under herself and took out her phone, scrolling through the list of contacts. There were so many people that she hadn't spoken to in a long time. Caroline had once been her best friend, yet they'd only shared a few text messages in the past year or so. Caroline had found out what had happened to Adam via Jessica's mother, which left a feeling of confusion on all sides. Who was a friend with whom? Jessica hovered over Caroline's name and then continued scrolling, flicking all the way to the bottom of the list and then thumbing her way up again. She eventually settled on the name 'Dave' and pressed to dial.

DC Rowlands answered on the second ring. 'What's up?'

Jessica was taken aback by the question but gulped away the thoughts of her evening, sounding as confident as she could manage. 'Nothing's wrong, I'm just making sure you're doing your job properly.'

Rowlands blew a soft raspberry. 'Man alive, Jess, you

should see this place. I didn't know we had internment camps in the UK.'

'Enjoying West Wales, then?'

'I've been to cheerier funerals. It's like the end of the earth. I've never known anywhere so windy. I was all up for getting away from Wanky Frankie for a bit, then I realised he'd set me up.'

'What's the problem? I'm sure DC Evesham can keep her hands off you.'

Rowlands lowered his voice. 'I know – but Wanky's going to be telling Katherine that I'm off in a caravan with some other woman.'

'I'm sure she's not going to worry, unless you give her reason to. Anyway, what's going on?'

There was a scuffing and then a quiet bang. 'Sorry, the curtain rail's as frail as a pensioner with a double hip replacement. We're in a caravan across the way from where Anne and Mark Atkinson are staying. They're in this chalet thing that looks like a Ukrainian bomb shelter. Their car's parked out the front and there's no chance of them leaving without being noticed.' He coughed quietly. 'Well, assuming neither me or Ruth fall asleep.'

'Oh, Ruth is it? Does Katherine know you're on first-name terms?'

'Oh, sod off.'

'I'm messing with you. Anyway, you've not been spotted, have you?'

'Not really – we've got the car outside but we're just a pair of holidaymakers at some tatty park in the middle of nowhere. There are a couple of other cars dotted around but the place is basically empty.' There was a pause in which Jessica heard Rowlands gulp, before he added: 'Do you think we're doing the right thing?'

'It's not up to me.'

'But I'm asking if *you* think we're doing the right thing. This woman was attacked years ago and has nipped away for a few days to get away from the media. Now we're sat around spying on her.'

'I don't know what to tell you, Dave. It's not my decision but, whatever you do, don't get bloody caught, else we're all in the shite.'

13

Detective Constable Ruth Evesham peeped through the caravan curtains towards the building opposite. Most of Evergreen Caravan Park was covered by rows of near-identical caravans but the area at the front close to the road had a wide one-storey concrete block that housed half-a-dozen units. With its flat roof, rickety gutters and pebble-dashed exterior, it wasn't the type of place in which she might choose to spend a week away. Not that the caravan was much better. Or, indeed, *any* better. Plus the park definitely wasn't evergreen. The trees were more of a mawkish yellowy brown and most of the grass was coated with mud.

Only one of the flats appeared to be occupied, its inner lights turned on but with no sign of movement. Since they'd arrived a few hours before and identified the Atkinsons' hatchback outside the block, she and Rowlands had seen very little. Mark Atkinson had been out to the car and taken something from the boot and then they'd spotted Anne pulling the curtains from inside the chalet. As surveillances went, it was low-rent at best. It wouldn't have been quite so bad if they were in a caravan in which it was fit for humans to stay but there were dark black spots of damp in all four corners, plus mould in the gap where the pitiful excuse for a sofa met the wall. Worse still, because this most definitely was *not* a police operation, Ruth had paid for a week's stay on her credit card. She'd probably get expenses back at some point but wasn't going to hold her breath that it would happen any time soon. She was new to CID and didn't want to say no to anything that would make her seem useful to those who worked above her.

Ruth nudged the curtain aside and nearly brought the entire rail down. She stretched up, perching the horizontal plastic bar on top of the nail sticking out of the wall. As that balanced precariously, Ruth settled back on the sofa. She'd been so bored that she'd taken to counting the cupboard doors. Around the single room, there were eighteen hiding various compartments but, of those, eight were missing either one hinge or both. After counting cupboard doors, she'd moved on to hooks, then nails or screws that were sticking out, then potential health and safety traps. Still, it was better than spending a day working with DI Franks. There was something worryingly weird about the way he looked at her, like a starving orphan asking for more food. When she'd first heard the rumours that he hung around public toilets, Ruth had assumed it was office banter; now she wasn't so sure. There was something unsettling about him.

'Call Me Dave' Rowlands was nice enough and she wouldn't mind having to spend a few days in this hellhole with him if it wasn't for the fact that he was so determined to show that he wasn't coming on to her, that he'd gone too far the other way. Instead of sitting next to her, he would settle as far away as possible, plus he'd brought up his girlfriend so many times under the guise of 'have I told you about?' that Ruth was on the brink of shouting back that yes, he bloody had told her. More than once.

He was on the phone in one of the bedrooms talking to the other detective inspector, the female one who Ruth couldn't read. It was hard to get a grasp on who DI Daniel was because opinions around the station were so mixed. To some, she was a liability who somehow got away with doing more or less what she wanted; to others she was the second coming, destined for big things. The truth was probably somewhere in the middle.

Ruth took out her phone and checked for emails before realising that she only had a single bar of reception. One by one messages dropped into her inbox but the symbol at the top continued spinning furiously as it struggled to connect. She gave up quickly, repocketing the device and starting to rescan the inside of the caravan. It was the type of place that had 'died by carbon monoxide poisoning' written all over it. Ruth stood on the sofa, peering through the dust-caked gaps in the vent, hoping that it would be enough to keep her alive if there was a dodgy gas canister seeping poison into the caravan.

She gazed across the tarmac towards the chalet. A shadow flicked across the window and then the door opened. The silhouette of Mark Atkinson was looking over his shoulder, saying something to the person inside, presumably his wife. He walked to the boot of the car, unlocked it, and took out a cool box before carrying it back inside. The gust from the closing door sent the curtain fluttering, leaving a small gap that was wide enough for Ruth to see the television. The flickering bright images were hard to make out at first but the red bars across the bottom made it clear enough that they were watching the news, specifically the coverage about the attack on the young girl in Salford. Was that normal? Probably. Ruth wasn't sure. In truth, she felt uncomfortable being here. When she'd found out the nature of the task, she'd wondered if she should speak up but she was at the bottom of the pecking order and could hardly question those above her. Part of the job was trusting that other people knew what they were doing.

There was a click of the bedroom door and then Dave appeared, smiling awkwardly, not wanting her to think it was anything other than a signal of companionship given they were stuck in a potential deathtrap in the middle of nowhere.

'Much going on?' Dave asked. 'I saw Mark going to the car and back.'

'That's all I saw, too.'

Dave started searching through the cupboards, opening the doors and catching them before they fell off the hinges. He looked up with a shrug. 'If they're going to pack us off to the middle of nowhere, they could've at least bunged us a few Tesco vouchers.'

'There's some Shake n' Vac under the sink but that's it.'

'I didn't know they still made that. You hungry?'

'I've not really thought about it but yes.'

'Shall I go on a chip run? I'll get some bread, milk and bottled water, too. There's no way I'm drinking from the taps. We'll end up with Legionnaires'.'

'Chips sound amazing. I hope they do gravy round here.'

'I'll see what I can do.' Dave nodded across the tarmac. 'What are they up to?'

'Watching the news on a loop.'

'They could've done that at home. I don't get why they're here. It's bloody October, I'd be off trying to find sun in the Canaries or somewhere.'

'It's nice and remote here, plus they might not have the money. Who knows? At least we don't have to spend the week with Funtime Frankie. Imagine being related to him.' Dave's face creased into a grimace before she realised what she'd said. 'Oops, sorry. I didn't mean anything about your girlfriend, or whatever. I'm sure she's fine.'

Dave shrugged. 'Two large chips it is. See ya in a bit.'

14

The rolling boulder was chasing Jessica down the cliff face again. No matter how much she speeded up or slowed, the distance between her and the looming rock remained the same. She was stuck in its shadow, unable to escape. Outside of the circular gloom, there was bright sunshine illuminating the rest of the ground. She tried weaving from side to side, but the boulder followed, tracking her movements and staying close behind until the rumble of rock again became a buzzing sound.

Jessica rolled over, fumbling towards the floor for her phone. The back of her hand clattered into the side table and then the wall before her fingers finally wrapped around the vibrating device. Without opening her eyes, she clamped it to her ear.

'Hello?'

The man's voice whooped a joyous: 'Wa-hey!'

'Who is this?'

'What do you mean, "Who is this?" It's Blaine, darlin'.'

'Bane?'

'Blaine.'

The delusional fog of sleep was slowly clearing, leaving

Jessica with the realisation that the rock singer was calling her.

'What time is it?' she mumbled.

'Dunno. It's dark.'

Jessica's eyelids felt heavy but she opened them just enough to squint through the black towards the illuminated red digits of the alarm clock. It was four minutes to five. Ugh.

'What do you want?'

'Someone tried to kill me again.'

'Did you call the police?'

'I'm calling you.'

Jessica sat up in bed, sighing. He didn't sound like a man who'd just had an attempt on his life. 'How did they try to kill you?'

'It's complicated. Are you coming over?'

'I've got a busy day. This better not be a hoax, else I'll do you for wasting police time and drag you out past the paps.'

'Don't be like that, hon. I could've died. I'm in trauma here.'

'You better not be messing around.'

'I'm not. Scout's honour. Are you on your way?'

Jessica kicked the covers away, putting her feet onto the floor and feeling the chilly breeze. It was sodding freezing. 'Fine.'

15

Jessica tapped gently on Blaine Banner's hotel door. She waited ten seconds without hearing anything, so tried again, slightly louder the second time. The corridor was empty, with the other doors closed, each with a 'Do Not Disturb' sign hanging over the handles. Banner, or perhaps his management company, had rented the entire floor for his bandmates and various hangers-on. The uniformed officers had already spoken to the others in previous days to try to validate the apparent 'death threat', though nobody had seen anything. If it was anyone but Blaine Banner, this would've been treated as a nuisance call.

After a third knock with no answer, Jessica took out her phone and called back the number that had woken her up. Banner answered with a hissed whisper: 'Who is it?'

'It's Jessica – y'know, the person you woke up because you were in the process of being murdered.'

'Where are you?'

'Outside your door.'

'Why didn't you call?'

'I bloody did!'

Jessica realised she was shouting, so repeated herself more quietly. There was no need as the line was dead anyway. Moments later, the door clicked open a couple of centimetres and Banner's bright blue eye appeared. He peeped both ways and then flung the door open.

'Oh, for God's sake . . .' Jessica turned away but it was already too late. Banner was completely naked.

'What?' he said, arms out.

'Will you put some clothes on?'

Banner peered down, apparently noticing for the first time that he was on show. 'Oh, right . . . yeah. Good idea.'

Jessica followed him into the room, looking anywhere except at him. As it was, that wasn't difficult. The room looked like a hidden alcove in a rubbish tip. A tray of food had been turned over, its dribbly brown contents adding a unique pattern to the previously clean walls. Scattered at regular intervals around the carpet were champagne bottles and lager cans. There were clothes, shoes, a guitar and at least a dozen Curly Wurly wrappers.

Banner was on the bed, fighting with a pair of boxer shorts that he ended up putting on the wrong way around. Jessica thought about taking out her phone and snapping a picture. She could make a fortune from *OK!* magazine, even if it burst a few of Izzy's illusions. Banner's hair was greasy, straggled down his back into a loose ponytail. Aside from that, he was completely hairless, a fact Jessica wished she hadn't discovered. As he continued twisting, Jessica thought he was messing around, before she realised he was having a panic attack. He flopped onto his back, hands over his face, breathing so quickly that it sounded as if he had whooping cough.

Jessica moved quickly, taking a spot next to him on the bed and grabbing his hand. She hovered over him, gazing into his glazed eyes.

'Hey, Blaine, look at me. Hey.'

He continued to pant, small flecks of saliva dripping from his lips and dribbling along his chin. Jessica took his other hand, sitting astride him but not pressing on his chest. She leant forward so he could see only her.

'Hey, look at me. Breathe, okay? Slowly. Breathe with me. In and hold it.'

Banner didn't exactly do as he was told, though the pace of his gasps began to slow and his eyes started to focus again. Jessica continued to breathe in and out, telling him to follow her lead until, eventually, he seemed himself again. She let go of his hands and manoeuvred herself until she was perched on the edge of the bed, then spun back to face him.

'I suppose it's a stupid question to ask if you've taken something? I was ten seconds away from calling an ambulance.'

She expected a cocky answer but Banner had lost his confidence. He shuffled into a sitting position and counted his breaths in and out. When he replied, his words were a slurred whisper. 'You're the only one I trust.'

'Don't be silly.'

'I'm not. They're all in on it.'

'Who's in on what?'

'Who? The government, the police. Everyone. They're all at it.'

Jessica rolled her eyes. 'Right they are. Shall I go searching through your drawers for an illicit substance or have you snorted it all?'

Banner shifted on the bed, accidentally – or perhaps

purposefully – allowing his back-to-front underwear to ride up too high. Jessica turned away again, covering her eyes. 'Can you put some proper clothes on?'

'I don't know where they are.'

'They're all around the room.'

'Hang on.'

Jessica gave it thirty seconds and then spun around, only to see that Banner had tied a pair of pillowcases around his waist, like a low-rent Roman centurion.

'Better?' he asked.

'Can we get on with this? You called because someone tried to kill you.'

Banner tugged his makeshift skirt to the side, tightening the knot in the pillowcase, and then sitting back on the bed. 'Right – I did my gig but we've got a curfew of eleven. If we go past that, they turn the speakers off.'

'Was this last night?'

'Aye. Me and the lads hung around for a couple of beers—'

'Just a couple?'

'Well, I've never been good with maths. I can't remember, like.'

'What do you remember?'

'After we'd had a few beers backstage, we went out back. There were a few people hanging around, so we signed some things. This one girl, she had a cracking pair of . . .' He tailed off after spotting Jessica's disapproving look. 'Right, well, I signed them for her, then this limo brought us back here. Some of the lads came in for a beer or two, then everyone went off to bed.'

'When was that?'

'Dunno, it was dark.'

Jessica checked the time on her phone – it was quarter to six, so it couldn't have been earlier than two or three in the morning. No wonder Banner was so wired, he'd barely slept. Couple that with the amount he'd drunk and it was a surprise he was standing.

'Was it only your bandmates in here?' Jessica asked.

'There were a couple of girls but they went. It was just me in the end. I went straight to sleep, out like a light. I've always been a good sleeper. You ask Sledge, I once fell asleep on top of the bus. They spent an hour searching for me, calling my name. I didn't hear a thing.'

'So you were asleep. What happened?'

'There was someone there, man.'

'Where?'

'Over me, like a sort of demon thing.'

Jessica didn't like the choice of word – it sounded too much like Damian Walker's 'demons' for her liking. 'What did the demon look like?'

'Sort of ghost-like. All flappy arms and "wooooooooooo".'

'You're not giving me a lot to go on. There's no way I'm filing a report saying there was a ghost in your room.'

'It was there, man. I swear.'

'What did it do?'

'Just sort of hovered over the bed, going "wooooooooo".'

Jessica leant back, gazing around the room and settling on the television. 'Are you sure you weren't watching *Scooby-Doo*?'

'No way. The ghost was all like, "wooooooooooo . . . tell them what you did".'

'It spoke?'

'Yeah, all sort of ghosty.'

'And it told you to tell people what you did.'

'Right.'

'What did you do?'

'I don't know. All sorts – there was those three girls in Utah that time. It might've been talking about that.'

'I really doubt it.' Jessica sighed. Two visits, two wastes of time. 'Did this "ghost"' – she couldn't stop herself making bunny ears – 'actually threaten to kill you?'

'Sort of.'

'How "sort of"?'

'It was like, "wooooooooooo . . . if you don't tell them what you did, I'll be back".'

'Right, so it didn't threaten to kill you, then?'

'It was a ghost, man.'

'Stop calling me "man".'

'Okay, hon.'

'Right – no "man", "babe", "baby", "hon", "darlin'", "sugar", "sweetie" or any such variations, all right?'

Banner reached underneath his skirt, scratching and thinking. Perhaps the two went hand in hand? '"Love"?'

'No.' Jessica stood, angling towards the front door. 'Who was the last person you saw last night?'

'Dunno, m . . . Ms Police Woman. Prob'ly Sledge.'

'Which room is his?'

'Across the hall.'

'Wait here.'

Jessica went into the corridor, peering back and forth. A CCTV camera with a red LED blinking underneath was next to the lift. She couldn't remember it being there on her previous visit, so it was possible the manager had installed it given the previous 'death threat'. After strolling up and down looking for any other cameras, Jessica knocked on the door opposite Banner's. She thought she might have to try a few times but, after a few seconds, it swung inwards. The man in the doorway had long grey hair and a longer grey beard. He was wearing tight jeans and an unbuttoned checked shirt. Given the get-up, it was a sorry state of affairs that he seemed the sensible one.

'Are you, er, Sledge?' Jessica asked.

He seemed unconcerned about her being there. 'Yeah, you want an autograph, love?'

'No, I'm a police officer.'

He eyed her up and down. 'Like a stripper one?'

'No, like an *actual* one.'

He puffed his bottom lip out, not convinced. 'Right . . .'

Jessica nodded to the door behind. 'Your, er, mate called me, saying someone tried to kill him. Well, more precisely, that a ghost threatened him.'

Sledge nodded, seemingly impressed. 'A ghost? That's a new one. This one time in New Mexico, he had a bad trip and reckoned the moon was after him. He got up the next morning and wrote *The Sky's A Liar*.' He paused. 'You've heard of it, have you?'

'Sorry.'

'Never mind.' Sledge tapped his forehead. 'Anyway, he's

always been a bit paranoid. When we were in Dublin, he thought the leprechauns were after him. Mind you, that was after he'd done a giant bag of . . . well, you get the picture.'

'I think I do.' Jessica shook her head, wondering how she'd stumbled into this. 'Look, I don't have a riot crew outside and, to be honest, nobody wants to raid this place – so just tell me, did you lot take anything last night?'

'Like what?'

'I'm not going through a list. You know what I'm talking about. It's a simple question.'

Sledge put a palm on his chest. 'I can honestly say, hand on heart, that I didn't do anything last night.'

'Booze?'

'Well, obviously.'

'Girls?'

He snorted. 'It's a rock band, darlin'. What'd be the point if there weren't girls?'

'What time did everyone get to bed?'

Sledge shrugged. 'I'm still going. The girls left at two and the other lads got down about three.' He plucked a tube of Smarties from his pocket and emptied them into his hand, shoving the lot into his mouth and chomping away, before rattling the tube towards her and mumbling something that was probably, 'Want one?'

Jessica shook her head, checking her phone as Sledge eventually swallowed. 'You all right?' she asked.

'Aye, gotta keep my sugar levels up.'

'Are you one of those bands with over-the-top demands – no blue Smarties in the dressing room and all that?'

Sledge's face suddenly hardened, completely serious. 'You've got the wrong end of the stick, love. Stories like that give us all a bad name. The rider's there to keep everyone safe. It's not just what food we want in the dressing room, it's about how the lights need to be rigged, how the speakers should be unloaded, that sort of thing. If we say no blue Smarties, that's because we want to make sure the promoter's read the rider correctly. If we find blue Smarties, we know he hasn't. If he's not done that, what else hasn't he done? Our pyros could be set up dangerously and one of us have a leg blown off. Our lights might not be secure and they come crashing down on someone's head. Probably mine. That sort of thing's a test. If they've picked out the blue Smarties, then everything else should be fine.' He emptied the rest of the tube into his palm, popped a blue one into his mouth and winked. 'We're not all smackhead idiots, y'know.'

'I know, I . . .' Jessica felt embarrassed. The way he'd explained it was genius. 'Did you see anything strange last night? Not a ghost, obviously, just anything untoward.'

'No way, darlin'.'

'All right.' Jessica thought about leaving him her card but wasn't sure she wanted another member of the band contacting her at Silly a.m. She apologised for wasting his time and waited until the door had clicked closed before re-crossing the hallway.

Banner was lying face-down on his bed, naked again, his tanned arse cheeks pointing directly at her as he snored like an asthmatic pig. Jessica crossed to the dresser, pulled out a sheet of paper from the bottom of the pad and scrawled 'CHANGE ROOMS' in capital letters, before slipping it underneath the lamp. When she realised he might think the ghost had written it, she added 'MS POLICE WOMAN' to the bottom.

Benny was the hotel's night manager, a nervous, jumpy man with very little hair, John Lennon-style round glasses that didn't suit him, and flaky skin that left so much residue that it had Jessica feeling like an apple turnover was the worst dessert known to man.

As soon as she'd emerged from the lift, Benny had leapt to his feet, hurrying towards her, asking if everything was okay.

'He's not dead, if that's what you're asking,' Jessica replied.

'Oh, thank God.' He patted his chest, sending more dried skin to the floor. He was like a walking advert for leprosy. 'I should really phone the manager.'

'There's no need for that but I did notice there was a CCTV camera outside the lift on the top floor. Where's the footage from that?'

Benny motioned towards the door behind the front counter. 'Everything's fed onto the hard drives in there.'

'Can you rewind footage?'

'I suppose . . . I've never done it.'

'But you know how?'

'I guess.'

'Let's go then.'

Jessica didn't give him an opportunity to think about such petty things as data protection, warrants, permission or anything like that. Some people automatically did whatever they were told. Within minutes, Jessica was in the comfy swivel chair, avoiding Benny's flaking skin, as he searched through the digital footage. They watched as a parade of barely clad girls jinked across the hallway from Banner's room into Sledge's a little after two in the morning, before departing for the lifts forty minutes later. The camera was almost certainly breaking some sort of law, though Jessica wasn't entirely sure which. Either way, the tabloids would pay ridiculous amounts to get their hands on the footage.

They continued watching the empty corridor until Jessica emerged from the lift. She watched herself knocking on the door.

'Go back,' Jessica said.

Benny did as he'd been told, clicking the mouse and rewinding the footage, before playing it again.

'I don't get what's going on,' Jessica said.

'How'd you mean?'

'There's no way I turned up so quickly.'

Benny went more slowly the third time, with Jessica keeping a close watch on the time in the top right of the monitor. The change was so quick, the corridor so still, that she almost missed it. Jessica asked the night manager to click through the images frame by frame and then he spotted it too: the clock switched from 03:20 to 04:20 – an hour's worth of footage had gone.

Benny scratched his hand, which wasn't good as even that part of him was flaking. 'That's a bit . . . *weird.*'

'You don't say.'

'Sometimes the hard drives fill up because no one deletes the previous month's footage and then it deletes itself. It could've done that?'

'Has is done it before?'

'A few times. If there's no room to record it'll record and re-record over the final hour. I think it's a software glitch.'

Jessica wasn't convinced. 'Can anyone delete footage from here?'

'If they know how to use the software. I wouldn't know how, if that's what you're asking.'

'I'm not.'

'Has anyone else been in here in the past few hours?'

'Not that I know of.'

'Have you been on reception all night?'

'Yes.'

'You've not moved at all?'

'Well, I've been to the toilet a few times, plus I brewed up. I went to the machine upstairs to get a Twix.'

Jessica started to peer around the office. There were filing cabinets covering two of the four walls and a mass of graphs and charts pinned to the rest. 'How many people work here overnight?'

'Anywhere between three and six depending on the time. The cleaners will be in soon.'

'Why would you need six people in overnight?'

'We don't – except for special occasions. There's always a night manager and we run a twenty-four-hour kitchen, so there's a cook and server too. That's three but some of the bar staff hang around for overtime. They might help

119

out with the serving, or a bit of cleaning. With Mr Banner and his entourage, we've got a few extra on the rota because they get in late and their requests are a little . . . *extravagant* at times . . .'

'Do staff members have access to the rooms?'

'Everyone has a utility keycard but if visitors lock the doors from the inside, then there's no way in.'

That was clearly Banner's first problem – he didn't lock the door.

'Do any of the keycards double up? So if I'm in a room on one floor, could I open a room on another?'

'No, each sensor has its own individual pattern.' He clucked his tongue into the top of his mouth, rocking back and forth. 'Is there a problem? I should call the manager.'

'Probably not, I'm just checking. I know our lot asked you all of this the other day anyway.' Jessica nodded at the computer. 'Is there any way I can get a list of the guests you have staying?'

'I don't know, there's like data protection and all that. I'd have to talk to the manager.'

'All right, forget it, it's fine anyway.' Jessica took out her phone and aimed it at the wall, taking a photograph of the staff rota before Benny could say anything. From what she could see, there were six people on shift, including Benny: two women and four men. It was probably nothing, especially given Banner's instability, but Jessica thought the names might come in handy one day.

For now, she had something far more important to do.

16

Jessica sat in the hospital canteen cradling a plastic cup of hot chocolate. She'd had enough of tea and coffee for one week. There was a time when she didn't have hot drinks, then she'd been swallowed up by the job and it became second nature. If a person was going to be addicted to something, it may as well be brews. There were enough before her who'd succumbed to alcohol or other things. In Pat's case it was sugar. Thankfully, the machine-made drink was better at the hospital than it was at the station. Someone somewhere had probably created a chart of which public body had the best tea machines. There were league tables for everything nowadays.

There was a shuffling and then a woman appeared on the other side of the table. 'Hi,' she said.

Jessica peered up, mustering the best smile she could manage. 'Hey.'

Georgia was Adam's sister, a person who would have been Jessica's sister-in-law if things had worked out differently. Georgia was always immaculately turned out – glittering nails, shiny hair, big heels, the lot – but not today. Her hair was down, not in its usual tightly curled bob. A plain dark suit, much like Jessica's, had replaced her usually tight clothes. Georgia stepped around the table as Jessica stood and they hugged for a few moments. It felt unnatural and awkward, two people brought together through necessity. Jessica released her first, smiling weakly and stepping away.

'Have you been here long?' Georgia asked.

Jessica glanced up at the clock high above the counter. She'd been there for more than three hours, not seeing the point in returning home after Banner's early morning wake-up call. 'Not really.'

'You look good.'

Another weak smile: 'You too.'

It was nonsense of course. Jessica had been up crazily early two mornings in a row and if her appearance was half as bad as the way she felt, then she had the sleeping-rough-in-an-underpass look about her.

'I was up early,' Jessica added.

'I couldn't sleep, either.'

'I had to visit Blaine Banner's hotel.'

There was a pause and then: '*The* Blaine Banner? I've seen the billboards around town. I used to have posters of him on my walls.'

Jessica waved a weary hand. 'It's a long story.'

Georgia nodded, then motioned towards the door. 'Shall we?'

'Okay.'

Jessica followed her through the hospital corridors, gradually heading downwards. She'd followed the route so many times that it was automatic. She could do it with her eyes closed. They eventually ended up deep in the furthest reaches of the building, sitting outside a room on adjacent chairs, saying nothing to one another. Aside from the sound of footsteps clattering on hard floors in the distance, it was silent.

Jessica desperately tried to think of something to say, not wanting to talk about her job, but not wanting to appear rude either. What did normal people talk about? The weather? Tea? Television? 'Sooooo . . . how are you?'

Georgia had her legs crossed and was staring at a blank patch on the opposite wall. 'Good, I suppose. I got that flat I was telling you about close to the Arndale.'

'Are you still at the accountants?'

'Yes, entrenched there now. They're looking at taking on a new partner so I might be up for that at some point.'

'Good for you.'

The conversation was so painfully dull that neither of them knew how to continue. Georgia eventually gulped and then added: 'Everyone's been really great about *things*.'

Jessica gulped. 'I . . .'

'You don't have to say it. We both know why we're here. It's not as if we ever had loads in common. You were seeing my brother and that's that. We don't have to pretend.'

She didn't sound harsh, just realistic. She was right, after all. If it wasn't for Adam, they'd have never met. There were a few more minutes of uncomfortable silence, punctuated by something metallic clattering to the floor in a nearby corridor and a faint apology.

'How about you?' Georgia whispered from nowhere. 'Are you well?'

'I keep busy.'

'It's the only way.' Another pause. Georgia leant forward,

sending a gust of a grim flowery perfume in Jessica's direction. She balled both of her fists and rested them on her knees. 'Are we doing the right thing?'

Jessica opened her mouth to reply but the words didn't come. She realised there were tears in her eyes and a lump in her throat. Jessica peered to the far end of the corridor where there was an anti-smoking poster, showing the inside of a diseased lung. She closed her eyes, hoping she could hold it together. 'I have no idea. I've been trying to separate my lives – one here, the other on the outside. I don't know how to cope otherwise.'

'Did you read the leaflets they gave us about turning off the machine?'

'About fifty times. They say there are no significant brainwaves, that he could be in a coma forever.'

More silence, so chilling that Jessica shivered.

'Are you okay with the donor thing?' Georgia asked.

'That was always his idea. If the doctors say they can use his . . . *bits* . . . then . . .'

'What about scattering the ashes?'

Jessica blinked but the scene at the end of the hall was the same. She didn't want to see anyone, let alone talk to them. It was one thing to arrange all of this in advance with Adam's sister but now it was real.

'Jess?'

Jessica gulped and took another breath. She could have done without Banner's early morning wake-up call, let alone everything else that was going on. Still, if she'd not been at work, she'd only have been at home in that empty prison.

'We went to Prestatyn on one of our first dates, with his grandmother. I think he liked it there.'

'Okay.'

'I'm sorry I'm not more . . . I don't know . . . upset.'

Jessica felt Georgia's hand on her leg. They were a similar age but Adam's sister felt like the grown-up. 'I'd rather you were you, as opposed to someone faking tears and throwing yourself on the floor. You loved him and he loved you. You knew him better than I did.'

There was more silence and then the sound of approaching footsteps. Jessica opened her eyes and tried to gulp back the golf ball in her throat. There were three doctors, far more doctory than the man they'd met at the low-security hospital. For a start, they were all wearing white coats. The tallest one knew each of their names, apologising and nodding towards the room, asking if they were ready. Georgia stood but Jessica could only stare at the door.

'I don't think I can,' Jessica whispered croakily.

Georgia stood still. 'Are you—?'

'I said my goodbyes the other evening when it was just me and him. I don't think I can see him again, not with the tubes and everything else. I was with my dad in hospital when he . . . *went*. I can't do it again.'

Georgia crouched and wrapped her arms around Jessica's shoulders, kissing her on the forehead. 'It's got to be your decision, hon.'

'I've made it.'

Georgia nodded, standing as the three doctors pushed their way into Adam's room, where they were about to turn off the machines that were breathing for him. Within minutes his brain would be starved of oxygen and then the rest of him would switch off. The door was about to close when Georgia's head reappeared, her teary gaze staring straight at Jessica.

'Hey,' she said.

'What?'

'One of these days, you've got to stop blaming yourself.'

17

Jessica called DCI Topper as she was walking towards her car. He answered with a surprised 'Jess?'

'What?'

'Are you okay?'

'I'm fine.'

'You don't have to come in.'

'I'm a grown-up.'

Topper didn't reply for a moment, no doubt stung by the ferocity of Jessica's reply. She hadn't meant to sound so fierce but it was too late now.

'Fine – I'm on the way to you-know-where.'

'Why? We've not found another body, have we?'

'No, I don't really want to talk about it on the phone. If you can remember the route, I'll meet you there. Park around the corner so there's not a load of cars outside his house.'

'Okay, see you soon.'

Jessica hung up and pocketed the phone, hurrying towards the car park. Even though she knew she shouldn't she re-tuned the radio to the news station – anything that'd take her mind away from what had just happened. Unsurprisingly, they were still talking about 'Jaws Two' as the recent attack had apparently been christened.

The male presenter was in his element: '. . . police are

saying the new incident is unrelated but can that really be the case? Even if it's a copycat attack, isn't there a chance it was brought about because of the release of Damian Walker? This is Nicola from Stockport.'

Nicola sounded Irish, with a definite hint of nutter about her. 'Is that Alan?' she asked.

'It is, Nicola. What have you got to say about Jaws?'

'It's as I was just telling your researcher, they should bring back hanging. And the birch. Plus set up the stocks in Piccadilly and have people throw knives at the criminals.'

'That's a bit extreme, isn't it, Nicola?'

'No.'

There was an awkward silence and then the presenter continued. 'Right, that's Nicola from Stockport with some very forthright views. What do you think about that? Should we set up stocks in Piccadilly and throw knives at criminals? Don't forget, coming up we'll be talking to a man who'll tell us the difference between a canal, a stream and a river. Before that, this is Brother Beyond with *The Harder I Try* . . .'

Jessica turned the radio off.

Jessica parked on the wide street close to Walker's house and walked through to the cul-de-sac. Topper's 4x4 was outside the house, alongside a grubby silver Ford Focus that presumably belonged to Clayton or Millie. Jessica checked over her shoulder but there was nobody at any of the windows opposite. It was half past eleven and she already felt like she'd done a full day's work.

The front door was opened after a single knock by a

weary-looking Millie. She smiled weakly and nodded towards the living room, from where Walker's raised voice was bellowing. As soon as Jessica entered, he turned to her from an armchair, pointing an accusing finger. 'Oh, great. You've shown up to gang up on me, too.'

Walker didn't look as if he'd washed any time recently, his dwindling hair matting together, with some sort of brown food stain embedded in his shirt.

'I don't know what you're talking about,' Jessica replied.

DCI Topper and Clayton were on the sofa, with Clayton looking as if he'd done a shift in the trenches. The poor sod could barely keep his eyes open and was clearly sick of having the same argument over and over. 'As I keep saying, Eric,' he said, 'it's safer if you remain indoors. You didn't *want* to go out until I told you it was safer not to.'

Walker raised his leg, hoiking up his trousers and pointing at the tag. 'I already have this bloody thing to keep me in at night, now you're saying I can't go out during the day.'

'I'm not saying that at all. You can go for a wander in the garden, perhaps even down the road. I'm trying to tell you that it's not safe for you to be walking around populated areas, especially places like shops.'

Walker dropped his leg but wafted his hands around. 'They told me I'm free.'

'You *are* free. That's not the issue but since—'

'I didn't kill that girl. I was sleeping upstairs, like I keep telling you. Check the tags again if you don't believe me.'

'It's not a case of believing you and nobody's saying you've done anything wrong. I'm simply talking about *your* safety. You must see how being recognised could be dangerous? Those old pictures of you have been on the news for three days now.'

'And whose fault is that? Someone told them I was being let go.'

The witness protection officer was doing well to keep his voice level. 'We've been through this, Eric.'

'My name's not bloody Eric!'

Clayton was a defeated man, slumping forward and pinching his nose. Millie tried to rescue him, though she seemed jumpy too. Being around Walker was bad for a person's health. 'Nobody's telling you to stay inside,' she said. 'All we're saying is that it's safer if you do.'

He prodded a finger towards her. 'You obviously think I killed that girl.'

'I don't think anything.'

Walker pointed at Topper and Jessica, thrusting himself up from the armchair. 'Why are *they* here, then?'

Jessica answered: 'We're here to offer help and assistance.'

Walker was pacing the room, stopping by the French doors at the far end and spinning back. 'So tell them to let me outside.'

'Where do you want to go?'

'I don't know, out.' He aimed a kick at an empty space, a child throwing a paddy. It was clear he hadn't wanted to leave the house until he'd been told he shouldn't. Suddenly it was the most important thing for him to get outside, even though there was nothing specific he wanted to do. 'Maybe I should talk to the media . . .'

If he was hoping for a reaction, then he got it. Clayton and Millie tried to speak at the same time with Millie eventually getting the upper hand. 'That's a *really* bad idea. You've got a new identity and part of the terms of you leaving the hospital is that you stick to it. Everyone's spent a lot of time and put in a lot of effort in an attempt to keep you safe. Not to mention the expense.'

Walker paused by the door. 'Oh, it's always about the money, isn't it? I'm such a burden.'

'I didn't mean it like that.'

'Oh, sure you didn't. Sod this.'

Before anyone could move, Walker had sprinted into the hallway. Clayton leapt to his feet but the sound of the front door slamming boomed through the house. Jessica thrust an arm across his chest, thinking he looked like he'd had enough for one day. 'I'll go.'

She grabbed a coat from a peg in the hallway and hurried outside. Walker was already at the edge of the cul-de-sac, his legs a blur as he dashed into the distance. Jessica raced to catch him and then slotted in at his side.

'What do you want?' he hissed.

'What do you want me to call you, Eric or Damian? I personally couldn't care which.'

Her abruptness seemed to throw him as his pace slowed. 'Eric, I suppose.'

'Fine, Eric.' She thrust the coat towards him. 'Put this on.'

'Why?'

'Because it's cold and could rain at any moment – you stand out because you're not wearing a coat. It's bad enough that you're out in the open, without drawing even more attention to yourself.'

Walker stopped for a moment, slipping his arms into the jacket and then setting off again, Jessica quick-stepping to stay with him. 'You don't know what it's like,' he said. 'All those years. I didn't think I'd ever get out. I was looking forward to the small things, like going to the shops, even going out in the rain.'

'Weren't you on day release at the hospital? You must've been able to do those things for a while.'

'That's not the point. I was still supervised, still had people to report to. Now I'm supposedly free and they're telling me I've got to stay inside.'

'Where are you going?'

'Paper shop. There's one round here somewhere. I saw it when they drove me in.'

A car cruised past but didn't stop. Nobody was paying them any attention. Walker turned left at the end of the road, spotting the illuminated sign outside the newsagent. There was no way he could avoid the 'Jaws Special' *Manchester Morning Herald* sandwich board on the pavement.

More cars continued past, slowing for a T-junction next to the shop. Jessica was beginning to feel nervous at the number of people around. Not only was there more traffic, there was a smattering of pedestrians rushing back and forth. As they reached the newsagent, a man hurried out with a copy of the *Herald* tucked under his arm. He peered at Jessica and then directly at Walker before continuing without a second look. The man had been so close that even Walker stopped in his tracks, a little shaken.

'Shall we go back?' Jessica asked.

'I just want a Mars bar, or something.'

Jessica glanced over her shoulder. 'Fine – be quick.'

'You got any money?'

She delved into her pocket and pulled out a pound, wanting their jaunt to be over. 'Here – get on with it.'

'How much does a Mars bar cost nowadays? Used to be 20p in my day.'

'Yeah, well, you're in for a shock. You should see the price of Freddos.'

'What's a Freddo?'

'Never mind.'

Walker jangled his way inside and headed to the counter. The shopkeeper barely looked up as he scanned the chocolate bar, took the money, and offered back some change, which Walker pocketed. In less than thirty seconds, they were done and back outside. Walker didn't speak as he unwrapped the chocolate and started pacing back to the house, Jessica at his side.

By the time they arrived, he'd almost finished eating. Clayton, Millie and Topper were in the living room, watching the door nervously as Jessica and Walker entered.

'Everything all right?' Topper asked.

Walker ignored everyone, pushing past the inhabitants of the living room and turning on the television.

'It's fine,' Jessica replied. 'But someone owes me a quid.'

Topper started to reply when his phone began ringing. He listened, said 'okay' and then turned to Jessica, grim-faced.

'What's up?' she asked.

He lowered his voice so that Walker wouldn't hear. 'There's been an *incident.*'

18

Jessica followed DCI Topper's 4×4 towards the city centre. From the few details he'd given, it didn't sound good. He'd rustled up a portable spinning blue light from somewhere and blazed his way along Princess Road, before barrelling right and accelerating up Deansgate, Jessica in pursuit.

Topper stopped on double yellow lines outside the main bookshop, waited for Jessica to catch up, and then they dashed towards St Ann's Square. The open space was lined by shops on one side, St Ann's Church on another, and the Royal Exchange Theatre on another. In December, it was home to the Christmas market, with a collection of stalls selling crafts, plus pop-up stands with hot drinks, chocolate-dipped strawberries and other goodies. Presently, it was doused with spinning blue lights, a small militia of uniformed officers, and the type of dipshit lynch mob of which Nicola from Stockport apparently approved.

Officers were trying to maintain order, blocking the side streets that led to the square and bellowing at pedestrians to keep moving. Jessica and Topper each flashed their identification and were waved through. The afternoon was cold, the sun almost non-existent, which only bled into the nasty biting atmosphere. In the centre of the square was a statue commemorating Richard Cobden, an MP from the area who had died one hundred and fifty years previously. He was a local hero at the time, someone who'd fought to lower the price of food so the poverty-ridden people of Salford and Manchester wouldn't starve. Jessica only knew that because her magician friend Hugo had once taken it upon himself to give her a walking tour of the city's statues. She'd known Abraham Lincoln, Queen Victoria and Alan Turing; the rest were all people she'd never heard of.

Sickeningly, a thread of rope was dangling from Cobden's neck, a noose swinging loose below, thankfully unoccupied.

Topper stopped on the spot, almost wiping out a striding Jessica in the process. He stared up at the statue. 'Oh for . . . ?'

A pair of ambulances were parked on the square, four paramedics hunched over a man sitting at the base of the statue. Thirty or so uniformed police officers were surrounding a group of young men, who'd clearly been told to lie on the ground, hands behind their backs. Jessica could see four others handcuffed to lampposts around the square. Despite the police attempting to block anyone from entering the square, there was an army of people just beyond the human barricade, wielding camera phones. The local news would eat this up the moment it hit YouTube.

Topper pointed towards the statue: 'You check he's all right and I'll see if anyone needs our help.'

'Why were you and me called out?'

He shrugged. 'Anything with the name "Walker" attached apparently comes back to us.'

Jessica headed towards the statue and the four paramedics. As soon as she got close enough, she saw the blood. The man slumped at the base had his eyes open but there was a thick gash in his head that the medical professionals were trying to patch. His light top was drenched with clogged dark blood. He had grey-white hair and had to be older than fifty, perhaps even sixty. He was in shock, eyes wide, gazing through Jessica rather than at her.

Two of the paramedics were working on him, with another pair, a man and a woman, standing nearby and watching. Jessica flashed her ID at them. 'Are you all right?' she asked.

The male nodded but seemed a little shaken. 'It's a bloody good job your lot turned up when they did.'

'What happened?'

'He says he was walking through the square when that lot' – he pointed a thumb towards the group of youths on the ground – 'attacked him.'

'Why?'

Jessica already knew the answer.

'They reckoned he was that Jaws bloke that's been in the news. He said they jumped on his back and hauled him to the floor, then started kicking him in the head. One of them said, "Let's hang him", and away they went. Christ knows where the noose came from.'

Jessica gazed towards the statue and the dangling loop of rope. This was the type of thing people read about and saw in movies. A throwback to slavery in the southern United States, not the sort of barbarism witnessed in a British city centre.

'Who stopped it?' she asked.

'When we arrived there was a near-riot going on. Half the square wanted to string him up, the other half were trying to stop them.'

'I suppose that's one thing.'

Jessica stared at the victim for a while. There were similarities to the actual Walker but only in the sense they were almost the same age with grey hair. The most ridiculous thing was that, apart from a handful of people, nobody even knew Walker was living in Greater Manchester. He could have been placed anywhere, abroad even, but because of the furore that had been whipped up, people were looking for the devil everywhere.

She turned and sidled across to one of the lampposts at the edge of the square. With the sheer number of people being dealt with in the middle of the area, the ones who'd been handcuffed to lampposts were largely being ignored. The lad was white with a number two buzz cut, sticky-out Dumbo ears and an unfocused, inbred look. He probably had webbed feet.

He made a sniffing sound in her direction, voice dripping with sneering disdain. 'What you looking at?'

Jessica was close enough so that only he could hear. Today really wasn't the time for it. 'Oh, piss off, you little shit.'

'What? You should be giving me a medal.'

'How about we give you a few months inside and the biggest dickhead award?'

'What? He's that Jaws bloke. He deserves a good slap. You lot aren't doing nuffink, so we 'ave to look after our own.'

'Firstly, Einstein, you've just kicked the shite out of the wrong bloke. Secondly, we're doing plenty but by having to come down here to deal with oiks like you, there are now thirty-odd officers *not* doing what they're supposed to be.'

Big Ears lashed a foot out at thin air in the vague direction of the statue. 'That's 'im. I know it is.'

'It's not him.'

'It looks like him.'

'And you look like a deflated condom but no one's trying to kick the shit out of you.'

'Oi! What did you say?'

'You're the one with elephant's ears, you should be able to hear everything.'

Big Ears lashed out again, squirming and kicking at thin air, though he was going nowhere with his hands cuffed around the lamppost. 'Oi, I'm gonna 'ave you. I'm gonna report you. Oi! Come back. Oi!'

Jessica walked away, watching him over her shoulder, giving him a wink. With any luck, this would be his last taste of fresh air for a long time, though it was hard to tell with courts.

Topper was striding towards her, shaking his head. 'This is an absolute disaster. We're better off out of it, let someone else take the statements.'

'What have you got back at the station?'

'Paperwork. You?'

'You remember you said I could have the day off . . .'

He nodded. 'Go – if one more thing goes wrong today, I might just join you.'

19

Jessica moved her car off the double yellow lines and parked around the corner, away from the threat of traffic wardens or yobs trying to lynch pensioners. She wasn't sure which group she detested the most. Probably the yobs. *Probably.*

Izzy answered her mobile with a mouth full. 'All right?'

'What are you eating?'

'Cheese and pickle sandwich.'

'You bitch. I'd love one of those right about now.'

'Ah well, tough. What's going on? The guv said you had things on today.' Jessica hadn't told Izzy about what she'd had to do in the hospital that morning. Izzy was fantastic at not acting differently around her but this would have been pushing it too far. 'I'm in the city centre. It's carnage – some poor sod's been attacked by a bunch of morons who thought he was Walker. They were going to lynch him in St Ann's Square.'

'Bloody hell. I heard something was going on but didn't realise it was that. How did you end up there?'

'Don't ask.'

'It's bedlam here if that's any comfort. You remember our mad bride?'

'Ellie Scanlon?'

'She's in some women's magazine today talking about

her missing fiancé. They've been onto the press office a dozen times this morning and there are photographers outside taking pictures of her with the "Where's Liam?" placard.'

'That's not good.'

'You're telling me. The guv's been out all morning and Funtime's had a fit because it was originally his case. He thinks he might end up getting blamed.'

'He *should* get blamed.'

Izzy sighed. 'We both know he won't. He must have naked pictures of the assistant chiefs or something. Teflon Franks. Anyway, we're going to have to do something. This magazine's asking the press office what we're doing to find her husband and they're asking me. I'm not sure what to tell them.'

'How about, "Sod off – you do your job and we'll do ours"?'

'I don't think that'll cut it.'

'Don't they know we have a murderer to find, another murderer to protect, skinheads kicking off in the city centre, a mental rock star who sees ghosts and who knows what else?'

Izzy was munching through another bite of her sandwich, which was making Jessica feel hungry. 'I know, Jess, but I feel sorry for her. She's supposed to be getting married in three days.'

From nowhere, Jessica suddenly felt the weight of the day. She remembered what it was supposed to be like when due to get married. The feeling of enormity that life wouldn't quite be the same again, coupled with the elation that you got to hang out with someone you really liked for a very long time. Some people got married for the attention, making the day entirely about themselves and their own egos. There was nothing worse than the 'this is my big day' brigade. The monsters in white dresses who made ridiculous demands of their guests under the guise of wanting their friends to 'share' the special moment. For them, it wasn't about that at all, it was about the adulation and hero-worship. Others treated their wedding day for what it was: a union between two people who wanted everyone to know that it was them versus the world. Bring it on.

'You all right?' Izzy asked.

Jessica had forgotten where she was for a moment, gulping away the memories. 'Of course. Sorry. How's the marathon training going?'

'I did twenty miles last night in awful weather.'

'Twenty miles? Did you get a lift for part of that?'

'Nope, ran the entire way.'

'Oh, come on. This is going to cost me fifty quid. Can't you pull a hamstring or something?'

'Har-dee-har. Did I tell you Pat's after you?'

'Why? Did he want someone to go on a Greggs run?'

Izzy laughed. 'I don't know, call him.'

'I'm done for the day. The guv said I'm sorted.'

'Be done then. Why are you calling me? Go home, put your feet up and get tucked into some Ben & Jerry's.'

'That does sound good.'

'You're going to call Pat, aren't you?'

'Gotta go.'

Jessica left the side street and started to drive home in a

vague attempt to prove to herself that she actually was going to take the rest of the day off. She was outside the inner ring road, edging through the traffic lights on the East Lancs Road, when she pulled into a pub car park, switched off the engine and called the station.

Fat Pat answered with his best phone voice. Instead of his usual sarcastic northern snarl, it was Home Counties over-pronunciation.

'Is that Patrick?' she asked, squeezing her nose.

There was a suspicious pause and then: 'Who's this?'

'I'm calling to let you know that you've passed the audition to be a BBC newsreader. You start on Monday.'

His accent slipped. 'Barbara?'

'Who's Barbara?'

'Hang about, is this one of you bastards downstairs? Because if it is, I'm not joking this time, I'm going to—'

'It's Jess, Pat.'

He paused. 'Oh . . . I thought it was one of those new PCs. I swear, somebody's raided my biscuit cupboard.'

'I thought you were on a diet?'

'That's not the point. Anyway, what do you want?'

'I heard you had a message for me.'

Pat was suddenly back to his old self. '*A* message? You should see the stack I've got with your name on – paperwork that needs doing, things that need signing. What happened to that laptop you signed out?'

'It's still being used.'

'What about these messages?'

'You know where my office is, there's a filing cabinet in there.'

'Which one?'

'It's round and bin-like with loads of screwed-up paper balls on the floor.'

'Oh, you're winding me up. Like that, is it?'

'Can we do this another time? I'm off for the day.'

There was the sound of papers being shuffled, something being eaten, and a vastly overweight man huffing and puffing because he wasn't getting his own way. 'Fine. Your presence has been requested.'

'Who by?' she asked.

'"By whom". Were you raised in a barn?'

'Get on with it, Pat. I'm not in the mood.'

There was more shuffling, including what sounded like a crisp packet crunching. So much for the diet.

At first she thought he was messing with her but there was a seriousness to his voice that she'd only heard when he was giving bad news. As the person at the front of the station, he was generally the one with whom the public interacted and, when he wanted, he could be surprisingly tactful. 'I'm not sure I should tell you on the phone. Are you nearby?'

'Not really.'

'Okay, give me a minute.' The line went muffled and then Jessica heard Pat bellowing at someone to clear off and give him some space. Probably not a member of the public. When he returned to the line, he was almost whispering. 'You still there?'

'Yes.'

'You're not in trouble, are you?'

'I don't think so. No more than usual.'

'You've got a memo from Graham Pomeroy.'

'The chief constable?'

'Well, the off-on-a-sickie-after-a-heart-attack chief constable.'

'What does it say?'

'He's asked if you can visit him.'

20

Jessica continued driving on the East Lancs Road, passing underneath the motorway ring road, continuing past the golf course, and following the signs towards Walkden. It was a small town under the wider umbrella of Salford to the far north of Manchester but not quite as far as Bolton. If she was honest, Jessica never really knew where the borders started and ended when it came to Manchester, Salford, Greater Manchester and Lancashire. Broadly, it was all 'the north'. The only thing of which she was certain was that the River Irwell separated Manchester and Salford, although that was probably a dodgy piece of misinformation, too. Quite why two independent cities needed to share the same patch of land, she wasn't sure. London wasn't two cities separated by a river, neither was Liverpool, though she'd never dare suggest such a thing to Archie, not after the Anfield debacle. He probably had a list of his favourite rivers, all of which were related to Manchester in some way. It was bad enough when he started going on about football but one of his other favourites was the lecture about how Manchester was at the forefront of the modern world through building canals and kick-starting the industrial revolution. In his mind, Manchester had provided a greater contribution to the planet than the Romans and Ancient Greeks combined.

Graham Pomeroy was the former assistant chief constable of Greater Manchester Police who'd been promoted to the top job of chief constable after the damning Pratley Report. Two months previously, he'd suffered a heart attack before a press conference. Although he'd survived, from what Jessica had heard, there was little chance of him returning to work, so he was waiting for the pension to kick in and a successor to be announced.

He was also the man Jessica suspected of ultimately being responsible for the explosion that had left Adam in a coma. She'd never be able to prove it, largely because the inquest had ruled it an accident, but she knew he was part of a group responsible for controlling all sorts of wealth within the city. It was her car that had blown up, her that the fireball had been intended for. In her darkest moments, she'd plotted all sorts of things, how she could take six months off, hire a private investigator and spend her time digging up so much dirt that the media couldn't fail to pay attention. She had visions of him being led away to spend the rest of his life in prison.

Then there were the other ideas, the ones not so legal.

Ultimately, in the same way she'd separated her lives in her mind – spending evenings with Adam in the hospital in one; working and being her old self in the other – she'd found a way to pretend that Pomeroy wasn't the person for whom she ultimately worked. She figured he would one day get his comeuppance and then, miraculously, he'd keeled over in front of the media's snapping camera lenses.

Now he wanted to see her on today of all days.

Pomeroy's house was at the end of a small road and was

delicately huge. At first glance, it was no different to a normal four- or five-bedroom house in the area but the little things made it stand out. The driveway had been paved with thousands of bricks, an expanding spiral that must've cost a fortune. Even though it was October, there were hanging baskets overflowing with colour around the door, plus the bricks, windows, frame and roof were perfectly clean and clear of moss. Jessica parked outside and turned to take in the area. There were similarly large houses all around but each had something cosmetically out of place – a slightly crooked chimney, pointing that needed doing, an overgrown hedge. Not Pomeroy's. Given he'd had a heart attack, he must have a small legion of people working for him to get the place so pristine.

The salaries for the officers at the top of the tree had always been laughably high, a source of enormous discontent among those who had to work day-to-day actually doing the job, rather than giving lectures about it. This went way above that. Jessica could see the hints of a large rear garden, stretching far beyond her sightline. The front curtains were open, giving an uninhibited view through to the back of the house, where there was a sapphire glow of a swimming pool, glimmering with low lighting.

Jessica sat in her car, the engine idling, staring at the house. Did she really want to do this? On today of all days? There was no way the timing could be a coincidence given she'd been at the hospital that morning. She'd long suspected Pomeroy was watching her from a distance, looking at whose business she was sticking her nose into. He hadn't climbed as high as he had by sitting back and letting others get one over on him. Still, he'd tried to get a message to her through the station. At the very least, Pat knew her presence had been requested. Perhaps, just perhaps, he was ready to admit what he'd done.

After switching off the engine, Jessica took out her phone and found the audio recording app, pressed start, and then slipped it into her inside pocket.

'Hello? Hello? Testing. Hello?'

She stopped the recording and played it back. Her voice was a little muffled but the words were clear.

Pomeroy couldn't be so stupid, could he?

Jessica deleted the test recording, started it again and repocketed her phone before heading to the front door. She rang the bell and waited, feeling her heart thumping so quickly that it was making her feel a little sick.

The door swung open, revealing a brunette in loose chinos and a sweatshirt. 'You must be Jessica,' she said matter-of-factly.

'I hadn't told anyone I was definitely coming.'

'But you got the message?'

'Yes.'

'And you're here . . .' She stood to one side, pulling the door open further for Jessica to step inside. Once there, she closed the door and pointed along the hallway. 'It's the final door on your left.'

The woman disappeared up the stairs, leaving Jessica alone in the hallway. The walls were lined with family photographs – all featuring Pomeroy with a blonde woman, presumably his wife, but not the person who'd opened the door. If it was his wife, then she was pretty, far too good looking for him. There were seaside photos washed with a tea-stained haze; packed beaches, decrepit piers and elaborate sandcastles. Pomeroy was a young man in those pictures, thin even, which was a far cry from the pictures along the hallway, showing his bloated frog-like frame sitting outside a Mediterranean cafe, raising a glass to the camera. Jessica edged along the wall and back again, taking in the photos, feeling strange at seeing him like a normal person. It was so easy to imagine him as a hated monster, yet almost crippling to see that he'd experienced similar things to everyone else. There was even a picture of him underneath the 'Welcome To Las Vegas' sign, his arm around his wife in a near-replica of a photograph that Jessica had of her and Adam.

In a flash, unable to look at any more, she spun and focused on the final door on the left, taking a breath and then pushing her way through. The smell of disinfectant hit her straight away, catching in the back of her throat and making her gasp. The room was bright white, with long strip bulbs across the ceiling and a huge bay window. It was almost floor to ceiling, facing one end of the swimming pool and offering an uninterrupted view of the vast garden beyond. Jessica took a moment to take it in before turning to the bed facing the window. There was a steady whoosh coming from a ventilator, with tubes looping down to the bed's occupant.

Graham Pomeroy was on his back, watching her, a shadow of his former self in more ways than one. In the months since his heart attack, it looked as if he'd lost half his body weight. He was still big, but at a level where he'd probably squeeze into a Ryanair economy seat. Just. No longer Porky Pomeroy.

There was an oxygen mask across his nose and mouth that he slipped to the side as he struggled into a sitting position. Jessica stood at the end of the bed, making no effort to help. He ended up half-lying, half-sitting, his back at a crooked angle. Each time he shifted, he emitted a nasally snort. When he was finally settled, his face creased into something close to a smile. Although he'd lost weight the extra skin hadn't gone, leaving him looking doughy, like a child's plasticine creation.

He nodded towards a nearby chair. 'You can sit.'

'I'll stand.'

'How have you been?'

Jessica bit on her bottom lip, running through the ways she could tell him to sod off. In the end, she gulped it back. 'Why am I here?'

'I've heard you had a big morning.'

So he did know. Jessica had told only DCI Topper at the station about what was going on with Adam and she really wanted to believe – *needed* to – that he'd not said anything. Everything that had happened at the hospital would have a paper trail, doctors talking to doctors, somebody filling in computer records, and then Georgia could have told any number of people with whom she worked. Pomeroy could have found out from so many others. She had to believe it.

'It's none of your business. If that's all you've got to talk about, then I'm going home.'

She turned but knew she'd never make it to the door.

Pomeroy started speaking anyway: 'You're a good copper, Ms Daniel, too good. But you have to understand that some things are best left alone.'

Jessica felt the weight of the phone in her pocket, the tiny, tinny microphone poking upwards, hopefully capturing everything he was saying. She turned back, standing closer than before. 'I don't understand what you mean.'

'In my own way, I tried to tell you but there's a certain type who do this job – do our jobs – who are like dogs with bones. Nothing I could have told you, nor anyone else for that matter, would have stopped you continuing to push.'

He was speaking too cryptically.

'You'll have to spell it out,' Jessica whispered.

'I think about you every day.'

Jessica shivered at the thought, not feeling flattered, more that a slippery blood-guzzling leech was clinging onto her.

Pomeroy didn't seem to notice. 'When I woke up in hospital after the heart attack, you were one of the first people on my mind.' He stopped, sucking on his teeth. 'Sorry, you were *the* first person.'

Jessica had to look away, not wanting to see his pudgy face. She stared at the ventilator instead. 'Why?'

'I'm not sure. Perhaps I felt a bit sorry after everything that happened.'

'*What* happened?'

'You know.'

Jessica couldn't take it any longer, locking eyes with him and knowing he was going to speak in riddles. He might have guessed she'd try to record it but it was more likely he'd spent a lifetime talking in circles, not addressing the point. Even without what she suspected him of, his sort were always banging on about 'moving forward' and 'reaching out'. It was an entire sub-section of the language – flannelly management speak.

'I know what you did,' Jessica said. 'What you and your friends engineered. It was meant to be me in the car when it exploded.'

He didn't flinch. 'That's not what the inquest said.'

Jessica turned to leave, ready to go this time, but he called her back once more with a vicious guttural cough and then: 'What did you expect, Ms Daniel? Actions have equal and opposite reactions.'

Suddenly, Jessica felt a flash of burning, white-hot anger. She sprung across the room, covering Pomeroy's mouth and nose with one hand and squeezing the collection of tubes feeding into him with the other. She could feel him trying to press back against her but, in the state he was in, he was no match. She clamped down harder, *squeezing* the folds of his face together and watching his eyes widen.

One second, two seconds, three, four. Jessica stared into his bulging eyes, enjoying his fear.

Five seconds, six, seven, eight. She could feel him gasping, throat contracting, nasal passage narrowing as he started to panic.

Nine seconds, ten, eleven, twelve. Pomeroy's legs were twitching, arms flapping but there was no strength to him, as if a small child had ended up in an envelope of oversized skin.

Thirteen seconds, fourteen, fifteen, sixteen. Jessica pushed down even harder, feeling him try to bite at her. His arms were limp, one of them hanging from the bed onto her leg.

Seventeen seconds, eighteen, nineteen. Jessica let him go, stepping away but not shifting her gaze. He was gasping, reaching for his throat with one hand, the other balled and resting on his chest. Jessica moved in, standing over him and making sure he could see nothing but her. 'If you ever – *ever* – contact me again or if I ever see any of your mates anywhere around me, if I so much as sense you might be watching, then I'll be back. It won't matter how many people you've got around you, how safe you think you are, how invincible you feel – one way or another, I won't take my hand away next time.'

Jessica didn't wait for a reply, running out of the room and racing to her car. She switched on the engine and roared away, blazing along the road, taking two quick right turns and then stopping in the shadow of a tree on a side street close to a park. She sat, watching her fingers tremble on the steering wheel and then finally gave into the tears she'd been fighting since agreeing to let the doctors turn off Adam's life support.

21

DC Evesham didn't like leaning back on the sofa in the caravan. For one, it was too close to the window, which meant it was colder, but, more importantly, she was worried about the patches of damp and what might be growing within them. She perched on the edge, hunching forward and trying to balance the tray on her knees. Dave was opposite, eating off his lap but leaning backwards, seemingly not worried about the grime.

Dave's chip run the previous evening had been a spectacular success. Not only were the chips *proper* chips – none of this fries nonsense – the shop also did tubs of gravy. Legends. Then he'd gone on a dash to the minimart and come back with baked beans, spaghetti hoops, bread, milk, some Cup a Soups, teabags – Twinings! – some pasta in sauce packets, Pro Plus, cans of Red Bull, three bottles of wine and two decks of cards. In the absence of much to see from the chalet opposite, the caffeine had got them through the night in shifts and the cards had got them through the day.

The food might not be gourmet, but it reminded Ruth of her student days, which wasn't a bad thing. Not only that, Dave was a pretty good beans on toast maker. In essence, it was a simple dish that was so easy to get wrong. If the bread wasn't toasted enough, the beans would make it floppy and, well, bread-like. Overdone, and it might as well be charcoal. Dave must have had training as a head chef at some point because he'd hit that perfect sweet spot of where the bread had just started to blacken. As for the beans, they had to be steaming, not boiling. Only amateurs did them in the microwave. When it came down to it, for all the cookbooks in the world, for all the fancy dishes and the Michelin stars, there was nothing quite like a bang-on, slap-up, perfectly crafted beans on toast. And Dave Rowlands had more than delivered.

Ruth finished off the meal and patted her stomach, momentarily leaning back on the seat before remembering where she was. '*That* was spectacular,' she said.

Dave nodded along, a trail of baked bean juice along his chin and on the collar of his shirt. 'Katherine likes my cooking, too.'

Another mention of Katherine – the sixty-third that day.

'How long have you been at Longsight?' she asked.

He counted on his fingers. 'Nine years? Maybe ten?'

'You're not a bad bloke, actually, not compared to some of them.'

He looked away nervously. 'Thanks.'

'Most of the younger lads spent my first two weeks trying to cop off with me.'

'I've got a girlfriend.'

'So I've heard.' Ruth figured she might as well get it over with. 'Go on then – what's Franks's daughter actually like?'

'Not like him.'

'That's kind of a given.'

'You know why he sent us here, don't you?'

Ruth glugged down a glass of red wine and sighed. 'I probably should have said this last night but figured I wouldn't have to – that you'd snap out of it.'

'Snap out of what?'

'I know why he sent us here. I'd be a pretty awful copper if I didn't. Look, you're going out with his daughter and that's between the three of you, or the two of you – I'm not bothered. I'm also not interested in you in that way at all. Okay? Even if you have a girlfriend, it *is* all right for you to talk to other women. We're here for work, except there's not much going on. If that means we sit around playing cards, drinking wine, or whatever, then that's fine too.'

Dave was embarrassed, unable to look at her. 'Right, um . . . yeah . . .'

'So can we stop the constant mentions of Katherine? I know she exists and that's fine.'

'Yeah, er, sorry.'

Ruth picked up their plates and carried them across to the sink. There was no washing-up liquid, so she rinsed them as clean as she could and left them on the draining board, before returning to the sofa. Dave seemed to have settled slightly and was actually looking *at* her, rather than over her shoulder.

'Sorry,' he said.

'Forget it.'

Ruth pressed her hand to the window and peered towards the chalet in which the Atkinsons were staying.

The curtains were pulled – as they had been all day – with the lights switched on inside.

'You know we're wasting our time here,' she said. 'They're a couple looking to get away from the media for a few days, so they've come to the middle of nowhere.'

'They've barely left their cabin and, from what we've seen, spent large amounts of time watching the news. That's hardly escaping it.'

Ruth moved away from the window and then instantly pressed back onto the glass as the door of the cabin opened. It was dark but Mark Atkinson was backlit by the light from the within. He was tall and slender, in his forties with greying hair. From what little Ruth had seen, he seemed the athletic sort who'd hike up mountains and run back down in the rain, all while lugging a backpack around.

'What's he doing?' Dave hissed.

'I don't know.'

Atkinson looked both ways and then checked his watch before closing the cabin door and striding past the car, taking the fork on the path that would lead him deeper into Evergreen Caravan Park.

Ruth spun back to Dave. 'Are we supposed to follow him?'

'I don't know, we were never really briefed.'

She glanced back quickly but the shape was rapidly disappearing into the moonlit gloom. 'You wait and watch the cabin, I'll go.'

Ruth yanked on her fleece and hurried out of the caravan, not giving Dave a chance to argue. Mark Atkinson had a head start but she weaved between the static caravans until she was on the path fifty metres back from him. He was sticking to the tarmac and walking very quickly, seemingly knowing where he was going, although there wasn't much opportunity to veer off the track. Ruth stuck to the spaces in between the caravans, dashing forward one or two at a time and trying to keep to the shadows. Atkinson didn't look backwards anyway, reaching the end of the path and turning right. The narrow road that ran around the park formed a rectangle, allowing holidaymakers to drive up to their caravans, unload and park. He continued following it until he took another right turn, heading back in the general direction from which he'd come. He could be out for a brisk evening stroll but it didn't look like it. With his hands in his pockets and the lack of a coat, he wasn't really geared up for one.

The path was easy enough to follow but, in an effort to stay out of sight, Ruth found herself having to avoid puddles and gloopy patches of mud. She took the second right turn, dashing across the path to avoid making herself too obvious in the moonlight, when she realised Atkinson was no longer ahead of her. Ruth kept to the shadow, peering around a caravan and trying to figure out where he'd gone. She'd only lost sight of him for a few seconds. Ruth counted to five and, when there was no sign of movement, she sidestepped onto the path, standing in the open and staring towards the direction in which Atkinson had been heading.

Nothing.

Not only was there no sign of him, there was no sign of

anything. The entire park felt eerily deserted. She hurried forward a few more caravan lengths, checking from side to side and then creeping along a few more until she reached the site shop in the far corner. The white paint at the front was covered with dirt, with metal criss-cross mesh wedged behind the glass. A sign pinned to the door read: 'Closed until next season'. Ruth turned in a circle but Atkinson was nowhere to be seen. Aside from the rustle of the wind through the trees, it was silent. No cars pulling away, nothing.

Ruth crept to the nearest caravan and pressed onto tiptoes, peering through the window. All she could see was an empty carbon copy of the place they were staying. If anything, it was a little grubbier. The next two caravans were the same. Somehow, Atkinson had vanished in the few seconds she'd not had eyes on him.

With little else she could do, Ruth returned to the path and finished the loop of the park, ending up back at their caravan. She let herself in, which made Dave yelp in surprise from the far end.

'Oh, it's you,' he said.

'Who were you expecting?'

'What happened to the husband?'

'I lost him. He was following the path and I was trying not to be seen. One minute he was there, the next he was gone.'

'Where did he go?'

'If I knew that, I wouldn't have said I'd lost him.'

Dave snorted. 'Right . . . good point.'

'Has Anne left the cabin?'

'No, I've seen a shadow moving around inside but no one's come out.'

Ruth peered through the window towards the Atkinsons' car, which was still there. 'Should we call someone?' she asked.

'And say what? Mark Atkinson has gone for a walk? He's not done anything wrong.'

Ruth knelt on the sofa, cupping her hands over the top of her eyes and not shifting her gaze from the building opposite. Dave was right but she couldn't escape the feeling that she'd messed up somehow. Mark Atkinson probably had just gone for a walk but then why wait until the evening? And why go out in the cold without a coat?

Twelve minutes later, he returned, striding along the path, hands in pockets with his head down. He knocked on the cabin door and Anne appeared in the doorway, holding it open to let him in and then closing it behind him. They were definitely still both there.

Ruth moved away from the window, relaxing slightly. 'What do you think that was all about?'

Dave seemed unworried. 'Like I said, he was just out for a walk.'

'For twenty-five minutes in the cold and dark?'

'I suppose.'

'We're in the middle of nowhere.'

'Exactly – there's nothing around us. Where could he have gone?'

22

Jessica had drifted in and out of sleep through the night, expecting an early-morning call that hadn't come. When it eventually did a few minutes after seven, she was already up and about.

As she arrived, the sun was creeping above the build-ings, sending a pale orangey glow across the cemetery, eating into the single spinning blue light that had been left on unnecessarily. Jessica left her car and walked across the car park, following the hum of voices towards a collection of officers, metres of tape and more white tents in the distance. The previous night's weather hadn't been as brutal but it had rained and the ground was already sodden from the previous downpour. Jessica had no idea what time the police had arrived on the scene but it looked as if they were already winding down, with a pair of weary-looking uniformed officers heading towards a marked car, ready for bed. Laughably, a few others were standing at the edge of the cemetery telling passers-by to keep moving as there was nothing to see. Given the spinning blue lights, tape and collection of police officers, that was always going to be a hard sell.

Jessica found DCI Topper standing by himself a little off

the path, in between a pair of graves. He was talking on his phone but hung up when he spotted Jessica. 'Made it, then?' he said.

'What time did you get called out?'

'A little after five.'

'Why didn't you call me?'

'I figured you could do with the rest.'

'Are you saying I look old?' Topper opened his mouth to protest but Jessica winked at him and he smiled back, not taken in. He wasn't buying her jauntiness. 'I've never liked the name "Weaste",' she added. 'It sounds too much like "Waste". I wouldn't want to be buried in Weaste Cemetery.'

'Where would you like to be buried?' he asked flatly.

'Good question. Somewhere inconvenient, like underneath a speed hump, or something. I quite like the idea of annoying people after I'm a goner.' Jessica stared across the cemetery at the pair of white tents that were set up across the path. 'Is it the same as the last one?'

Topper nodded. 'Holly Jamieson, twenty-one, according to the wallet that was in her bag. She was found by a dog-walker with her stomach sliced open.'

'Did anything come back from forensics on the other victim?'

'Not as such – from what they can tell, there are no teeth marks, but someone cut her open.'

'So it's not an exact copycat of the Jaws attacks?'

'Perhaps not – but the rain caused so much damage that it's taking time. The initial findings might not be the final findings. From what I've heard, Superintendent Deacon's investigation isn't getting very far. They've been talking to her neighbours, her friends, some driver who saw her half an hour before she was attacked, all the people she was out with. They've not even got a suspect yet.'

'Except for Walker.'

'Exactly – who they're not allowed to speak to. Deacon must be furious but there's not much he can do. If Aylesbury tells him Walker's accounted for and off-limits, then that's that.'

'Speaking of Walker . . .'

'First call I made. Clayton spent the night there. He says Walker didn't leave the house. The electronic tag backs that up, too. He wasn't here.'

'Why is this never easy?'

'We're going to have to talk to Walker anyway, plus re-check our lists about who he was in contact with at the hospitals and so on. *He* might not have been here but it doesn't mean he has no idea about who was. Any word from Wales?'

'I'll call them again.'

Jessica moved further along the path, finding a quiet spot in front of a weathered grave for 'Mr Ferguson', who was 'beloved' by his wife and children and had died in the nineties. Jessica wondered if anyone ever had a gravestone that said how little he or she was liked. Not everyone was pleasant. *Here lies Mr Ferguson, a moaning old so-and-so.*

Rowlands answered with a sleepy-sounding groan, slurring something that was probably 'All right?'

'I thought you were supposed to be keeping watch?' Jessica said.

There was the shuffling of bedcovers and another groan. 'It's Ruth's turn. We've been doing four-hour shifts overnight.'

'Ruth? Still on first-name terms. Nice and cosy.'

'Sod off – what do you want?'

'How are things going?'

'Hang on.' The line went quiet but Jessica could hear voices in the background and then Rowlands returned. 'It's been quiet all night – no one's entered or left the chalet. There was one thing, though.'

'What?'

'Mark went for a walk at about half-seven last night. He was gone for twenty-five minutes or so. Ruth tried to follow him but he disappeared among the caravans.'

'How do you mean, "disappeared"?'

'I don't know. It wasn't her fault. There are no street lights on the site, so we only have the moon after dark. Half the time you can't see anything.'

Jessica stopped to think for a moment. 'What do you think he was doing?'

'We're not sure. Probably just going for a walk.'

'Please tell me he didn't realise he was being followed.'

'If he did, then he never said or did anything. There are a handful of people on site – three or four cars – but people aren't going outside. No one's paying anyone else the blindest bit of attention.'

That was one thing – a complaint from Anne Atkinson that she was being watched would be curtains for Topper.

'Are you sure their car was still there overnight?' Jessica asked.

'Definitely. Why?'

'There's been another death here – same as Monday.'

'Another Jaws attack?'

'Maybe. We'll have to wait and see.'

There was a pause, Rowlands wetting his tongue. 'It wasn't either of these, Jess. They've not left. We're barking up the wrong tree.'

Jessica turned in a circle, wondering what to say. She felt the same but it wasn't her decision. 'All right, just stay put and call me or the guv if something happens.'

She hung up, returning to Topper and shaking her head. 'They were there all night.'

As she was speaking, a large white van with a satellite dish on top pulled onto the edge of the pavement, ignoring the officer who was trying to wave them away. The TV news had arrived, which meant it was time for them to nick off. The helicopter would be next.

Before they could get to the car park, Jessica and Topper were intercepted by a man in a long brown coat, hands in his trouser pockets, allowing the bottom of the jacket to flare out like a cape. He had swept-back silvery hair and a crisp matching moustache, all set for the cameras.

'Chief Inspector,' he said, with a sharp nod towards Topper, ignoring Jessica completely.

'Superintendent.'

DSI Deacon nodded towards the white tents. 'What brings you out here? I know it's technically your patch but . . .'

Topper shrugged, gallantly backing down from the who-had-the-bigger-dick competition and simultaneously making it a who-*is*-the biggest-dick contest. 'I just thought I'd have a look. As you say, our patch after all.'

Deacon peered over Topper towards the road, where a second satellite van had pulled up behind the first. The race was on to yank the cameras out of the back and get them running. Deacon straightened his tie as if it was second nature the moment someone turned up with a camera. It probably was.

'That's interesting,' he purred, not looking at Topper. 'Very interesting.'

'What is?'

'Well, if HQ had any faith that your Central division were capable of finding out what's going on here, I believe this would be your operation. Instead, they pulled together a taskforce from the other districts to investigate something on your patch. What does that say about you?' He clicked his heels together and clucked his tongue to the top of his mouth, pushing himself up so that he could stare down at Topper.

In essence, Deacon was correct – officers from the North, South, East and West districts had been clubbed together to look into a central Manchester matter. He clearly didn't know anything about Topper and Jessica's unofficial activity.

'How's the investigation going?' Topper asked. 'Long list of suspects? Arrests being made? CPS champing at the bit because you're about to hand over a jam-packed file?'

They locked eyes for a moment before Deacon turned back towards the road where a third satellite van was pulling in. How many news channels were there?

'What have they got you doing anyway?' Deacon said, flicking a fleck of invisible dust from his lapels. 'Have you got a crack squad investigating inner-city graffiti? Has someone tipped over a wheelie bin on Deansgate?'

'Perhaps HQ thinks central division is far too important to be split up and babysat by senior management? How many briefings were you in yesterday?'

'You keep telling yourself that.' Deacon waved the back of his hand, shooing them away. 'Now toodle-pip and piss off before the cameras get here. They're going to want to talk to the grown-ups.'

For a moment, Jessica thought Topper was going to stand his ground and argue but he squeezed past Deacon and walked briskly towards the car park, Jessica rushing to stay at his side.

'Prick,' Topper muttered under his breath. 'You know why this is, don't you? It's because our superintendent – Jenkinson – is a right bellend too. He and Deacon are always sniping at each other over conviction figures. It's like this is all one big game. Nothing to do with serving the public, it's all about getting one over on the other.'

'At least we know for sure that Deacon has no idea what we're up to.'

Topper shook his head, sighing twice in quick succession. 'Have you seen the *Daily Mail* this morning?'

'Nope.'

'Centre pages – Ellie Scanlon with her "WHERE'S LIAM" banner.'

'Ouch.'

'No wonder the public think we're useless.'

23

When Topper and Jessica arrived at his house, Damian Walker – or Eric Seasmith as he was supposed to be known – was sitting in the armchair in checked pyjamas. He was watching television and eating a giant bowl of Coco Pops with his feet up. It was a few minutes to ten and he was flicking between the news channels, watching coverage of the scene at Weaste Cemetery.

'Have you seen this?' he said, nodding at the screen as Jessica and Topper sat on the sofa.

'We've seen it,' Topper replied.

'They're saying it's me! I was upstairs in bed.' He thrust his spoon towards the kitchen. 'Ask 'im. He was 'ere. I didn't leave the house all night.'

'We believe you, Mr Seasmith.'

'So why are you here?'

'Because we need to go back over some of the things we spoke about when we were here the first time.'

Walker threw his hands in the air, sending a splash of milk flying over his shoulder. 'I'm trying to watch the TV.'

'The quicker you talk to us, the quicker we can leave you be.'

'Fine!'

'There've been two victims this week—'

'Nothing to do with me.'

Given the provocation, Jessica was impressed the DCI was holding it together. He had far more patience than she did. She'd have lost it when DSI Deacon was having a pop at the cemetery.

'I'm not saying it is, Mr Seasmith,' Topper said, 'but there are certain familiar hallmarks compared to what happened seventeen years ago.'

Walker dropped his spoon in the bowl and turned to face Topper. 'What are you asking?'

'Is there anybody you can think of who might want to make these attacks seem similar to what's in the past? Someone who might be trying to get at you personally?'

Jessica couldn't help but marvel at the use of language. Topper had managed to apportion no blame to Walker while directly referring to the four murders committed by him. With nothing at which to take offence, Walker was left having to answer the question. He had so little wiggle room, with Topper painting *him* as the victim, that he finally seemed to engage.

Walker scratched his head with the spoon, peering at the ceiling. He slumped a little lower, no longer puffing out his chest, itching for a battle. 'There's no one obvious.'

'Did you fall out with anyone at the various hospitals?'

'There were odd spats, nothing major.'

'Spats like what?'

'Silly things over TV channels and who sat where. No big deals.'

'What about your life before all of this happened?'

He shrugged. 'I dunno, boss. I was a bit of a lone gun,

171

doing my own thing. Plus a lot of that's a blur. Speak to the doc, he'll tell you.'

'Is there anyone that you told when you found out you were being discharged?'

Walker shook his head. 'Who would I tell? Only the blokes in the hospital around me but they knew anyway. Word always gets round about a release.'

'Has anyone contacted you on the outside?'

'Only you lot.'

'Are you absolutely, one hundred per cent positive?'

'On my life, boss. I don't know nuffink about this. I just want a normal, quiet life.'

As much as she hated to think it, Jessica believed him. She'd heard almost the exact same information a few days previously but this time there were no games. In his post-hospital guise, Walker was eccentric to say the least, annoying for sure, but there was so much to say that he was innocent. The doctors' expert opinions; his electronic tag; the location of the crimes and the fact Clayton was in the house the previous night. How much more did they want before they stopped harassing him? It was no wonder he was annoyed.

Topper thanked Walker for his time and headed into the kitchen, where Clayton was resting with his elbows on the table, a cup of tea steaming in front of him. At the sound of the door clicking, he jolted backwards, waking from a momentary slumber.

'Whuh!' His feet bumped into the table leg, spilling his tea onto the surface. 'For God's sake . . .' He leapt up and grabbed a cloth from the draining board, dabbing away at the mess before sitting again, scratching at his temple. His clothes were crumpled as if he'd slept in them and he looked utterly drained, a broken man who could do with a week in bed.

'You all right?' Topper asked.

'Just tired.'

'None of us want to be here.'

He nodded. 'I just want to be home with my wife.'

Topper sat on the seat next to him, lowering his voice in case Walker was anywhere close on the other side of the door. 'What's her name?'

Clayton took a big breath through his nose. His eyelids flickered momentarily as if he'd forgotten her name. He *really* looked like he needed some sleep. 'Sonia. We've been together for almost ten years. I've hardly spent a night away from her – and now this.'

Topper offered a sympathetic smile. 'What happened last night?'

Clayton shrugged. 'Not much. He went to bed at about ten.'

'Did you stay awake all night?'

He yawned, shaking his head. 'I tried. I was on the sofa watching TV. I dozed off a few times.' Before Topper could say anything, he quickly added: 'I'd have heard the door go if he left. I'm a light sleeper. Plus the electronic tag didn't go off.'

'Could he have sneaked out the back way? Or through his window and down the drainpipe? That sort of thing?'

'No . . . well, probably not.'

'Probably?'

'I can't say for sure. I wasn't checking in on him sleeping every hour. Even when I was awake, I was only listening for noise. When you guys called earlier, I went upstairs and he was sound asleep.'

'So you can't say for absolute sure that he was here all night?'

Clayton sank lower in his chair, still yawning. 'What do you want me to say? We can share a bed next time if you prefer? His tag didn't go off and I didn't hear anything.'

Topper backed off, palms up. 'Okay, okay. Jess just needs the toilet, then we'll get off.'

Slick.

Jessica headed upstairs, poking her nose into each of the bedrooms. Two of them were empty of everything except carpets, with the third nearly as clear. Jessica crept inside, opening the wardrobe and the cupboards and then looking under the bed. Walker had remade it, tucking the covers in military-style. He was apparently still living out of a duffel bag, which was open on the floor, filled with neatly folded clothes. It was all very pristine, but offered little insight other than that Walker didn't own much. She opened the window and peered outside, noticing the drainpipe that ran next to the glass. If she had a death wish, it wouldn't take much of a stretch to reach across and slip down. Getting back up might be an issue, given the plastic pipes and brittle-looking brackets.

After putting everything back where she'd found it and nipping into the bathroom to flush the toilet, Jessica headed downstairs and went outside with Topper.

'Anything?' he asked.

'Not really. The drainpipe's a possibility, but . . .'

'But what?'

'It's a bit much to think he got his tag off, shimmied down the outside of the house, got seven or eight miles up the road to the cemetery, killed that girl and then got back again and refitted his tag. All of that without being spotted, apparently damaging the tag, or leaving a trace of blood around the house.'

'He could have picked up odds and ends from other people in the hospital.'

'What, teleportation?'

Topper sniggered but there was little humour. 'This is a mess.'

Jessica couldn't disagree. 'Do you think it's him?'

He avoided the question. 'What can we do? Arrest him? There's no proof he's done anything.' Topper took out his phone and tutted as he scrolled through the messages. 'Ugh, this is all we need.'

'What?'

'Forget all this for now, Ellie Scanlon's just about to go on ITV to appeal for her missing boyfriend. They're doing a big thing about the wedding on Saturday and HQ are doing their collective nuts about that, too. Have you looked at the file yet?'

'Not really – Franks was supposed to be handling it.'

'Why am I not surprised? Do you reckon you can—'

They were interrupted by Jessica's phone ringing. She plucked it from her pocket and held it up for him to see the identity of the caller, heart sinking. Topper closed his eyes, with the air of a man who had far too much on his plate. It was Blaine Banner.

24

Jessica knocked on Blaine Banner's hotel room door, glancing back towards the security camera and wondering what today's escapade might bring. She was expecting another flash of naked flesh, only to be met by a confused-looking Sledge. Tight jeans seemed to be the in thing, seeing as his were practically sprayed on. He was wearing a T-shirt with the band's logo on the front and peered past Jessica towards the lifts. 'Room service?'

'I spoke to you yesterday.'

'The stripper?'

'No, the police officer.'

'The police stripper?'

'Just the officer.'

He nodded knowingly, though didn't seem convinced. 'Right . . . any sign of my room service, love?'

'I wouldn't know – I'm looking for Blaine.' Sledge nodded across the corridor towards the room that had been his the previous time Jessica had been there. 'You swapped rooms?' she added.

He shrugged. 'Aye, 'twas his idea. Something about ghosts. If you could have a word about that room service, I'm busy in 'ere.'

Jessica smiled sweetly. 'I'll see what I can do.'

'Bonzer.'

The door clicked closed and there was a female-sounding giggle from the other side, leaving Jessica shaking her head in disbelief. She knocked on the door opposite, waited, then knocked again. Banner eventually swung the door open, standing with his arms wide, a bottle of Jack Daniel's in one hand, smouldering cigarette in the other. He was thankfully clothed, albeit only his bottom half. If anything, his jeans were tighter than Sledge's, as if they were in a competition to see who could be squeezed the tightest.

'Y'a'right?'

Jessica headed into the room, pointing at the cigarette. 'I don't think you're supposed to be smoking in here.'

He shrugged, taking a puff. 'Dunno.'

Jessica glanced around, noting the three smoke detectors on the ceiling that had been smashed. Small pieces of plastic littered the floor. The room was a mirror of the one across the hall but just as messy. It looked like Banner had picked up all of the clothes from the floor in one room only to carry them across the hallway and re-dump them.

'What happened to the smoke detectors?' she asked.

'Dunno, love. Think they fell off the ceiling.'

'Didn't we have this conversation about you calling me "love"?'

Banner squinted, head at an angle. 'Summat like that. I got your note about changing rooms. Good thinking, that.'

'Why did you call me this time?'

'To let you know I'd changed rooms.'

'You could've done that on the phone.'

Banner splayed his arms out. 'I thought you'd want to see.'

'Very impressive. Any more ghost stories?'

'No, I've been thinking about that. It's all a bit hazy, bit spooky, like.' He dropped the remains of the cigarette into an empty wine bottle and set about scratching his arse. Jessica wondered if this was the type of thing Izzy had been dreaming of when she said she fancied going on tour with him.

'Are you now saying you *didn't* see a ghost?'

'I'm not sure. It might've been a dream.'

Jessica was beginning to feel as tired as Clayton had looked. 'So, just to clarify, you had me come all the way down here firstly to say that you woke up and there was a ghost threatening to kill you; then a day later to tell me you didn't see one after all?'

'I thought you'd want to know.'

'Have you ever heard of wasting police time?'

Banner scratched his head with the lip of the bottle, finally getting his other hand out of his arse crack. The room reeked of cigarettes. It was a good job he had a record label to pay the bill. 'Hmm . . . "wasting police time" . . . aren't they that punk band from Portland? I think they supported us the other year?'

'I meant *actually* wasting police time. I have things to do but I've been here three mornings this week.'

He swigged from the bourbon, not even wincing as he glugged. 'Want some?'

'No.' Jessica stepped towards the door. 'I'm going to go but I don't want you to call me.'

'Not ever?'

'Fine – you can call me if you've actually been attacked, but only after you've called 999.'

'So 999 first, you second?'

'If you like – just don't call me unless something's happened. I've got things to do.'

'Oooh, it makes me all tingly when you're angry.'

'Bye.'

Jessica strode to the door but Banner got there first, planting a palm against the wood and blocking the way. With anyone else, she'd have already nicked him – there was easily enough to do him for wasting time. It wasn't even the band's management or potential negative publicity that was stopping her, it was his stupid grin. Like the naughty kid in school who somehow always got away with things because he flashed the teacher a smile.

'What?' she said.

'Are you gonna come to one of the gigs?'

'I told you, I'm busy.'

'Every evening for the next week?'

'We're trying to find a murderer, among other things.'

'Don't you get an evening off?'

'I don't understand why you want me there? There's twenty-odd thousand people a time. Isn't that enough?'

He leant away from the door, still smiling, stinking of booze and fags. 'I want to say thanks.'

'For what?'

'I dunno . . . being there.'

It sounded like a joke but he said it with such seriousness that Jessica was left holding her tongue. It was only when he took another step backwards that Jessica realised what the real issue was. Every 999 call handler was familiar with the repeat callers. They knew exactly what to say to get an emergency vehicle sent out to them – usually the magic words were 'chest pains'. It was almost always lonely individuals addicted to phoning because the paramedics or police officers offered interaction with another human being. If it wasn't for that, they'd live a pitiful existence with no friends or family, nobody with whom to spend their days. Banner wasn't abusing the emergency call system but she could see the same sense of solitude within him. A man surrounded by people but isolated from real life. He was surrounded by sycophants who'd do anything he said – even smashing the smoke alarms. Would he get in trouble for that? Of course not. Someone else would take care of it.

'I'll see what I can do,' Jessica said.

'We've got another seven nights.'

'I know.'

'Bring your friends, anyone you want. Those boxes are bloody huge.'

'I'm not promising.'

Banner winked. 'Bingo. Just don't keep me hanging, babe.'

Jessica decided to take the stairs for a bit of exercise. By the time she was a third of the way down, she realised how badly she'd judged not only the number of floors but her own level of fitness. She stopped for a rest, sitting on the top step and calling DCI Topper. He sounded as if he was about to hang himself.

'What's up with you?' Jessica asked.

'I'm at HQ expecting to see the chief constable. I've been in a waiting room for twenty minutes with no sign of anyone.'

'Sounds like fun.'

'Y'know, there was a time when I used to be an actual copper, not a message carrier. How's our rock star?'

'He's fine.'

'Are you sure? His management company were in contact again yesterday through the press office, making sure we were taking "Mr Banner's" complaints seriously.'

'What did you tell them?'

'Oh, I don't know. Someone else drafted it. Blah, blah, blah, utmost seriousness-this, highest of priorities-that. Whatever stops them running to the papers to say we're not investigating. You didn't brush him off, did you?'

'No, he's fine.'

Topper puffed a sigh of relief. 'That's one thing. What about Liam McGregor?'

'All right, at least give me a few hours, I've not even been to the station yet. Franks has had weeks to find him.'

'Ellie Scanlon's going on *The World At One*. I don't know how she managed it but it's a media blitz today. The wedding's apparently still on for Saturday and there's a story on the net calling it "The Runaway Bridegroom".'

'I'll see what I can do.'

'Jess.'

'What?'

'If you ever pull something out of the bag, make it today. I can't face another day doing briefings at HQ. I don't care if he's dead or alive, if he's still in the Lakes or somewhere in Manchester. I don't even care if she's bumped him off and has dumped the body under her bed. Take whichever officers you want. Just bloody find him, or if not that then a body that looks enough like him.'

Jessica thought about her own missing friend she'd been unable to find. It hardly boded well.

25

Jessica left her car in the hotel car park and walked through to the city centre, meeting Izzy outside the Arndale centre. It was almost lunchtime, the streets filled with people hurrying back and forth with cardboard coffee cups thrust in front of them and small paper bags filled with rip-off sandwiches. Was a slice of bread, some tomato, shreds of lettuce, processed ham and red onion *really* that expensive? Not to mention a bit of milk, hot water and some ground coffee. The world was going mad.

'Aah, this is what the outdoors looks like,' Izzy gasped.

'Your desk's going to miss you if you spend too long outside.'

'Archie's got a monk on because you didn't ask him.'

'Perhaps if he'd found a viable alternative to Walker as our slasher, then I'd give him something fun to do.'

'Bit harsh.'

Jessica set off, leading the way towards Piccadilly Gardens, Izzy at her side. 'He's a grown-up, he'll get over it. Anyway, today is technically my day off.'

'Why are we doing this, then?'

'The guv's going to have a coronary if we don't find out something about Liam McGregor. Ellie's been all over the TV and radio this morning.'

'So I saw.'

'How'd she manage that?'

'It says on her blog that she got herself an agent.'

Jessica was so surprised that she stopped on the tramlines before realising where she was and continuing towards the bus station. 'An *agent*?'

'That's what it says.'

'Isn't an agent someone who does nothing but sit around all day with their feet up, before taking your money?'

'No idea. Whoever it is got her on the telly, so they must do something.'

'Christ's sake. She'll be in the Big Brother house next. Either that or shagging someone from a boyband.'

Jessica continued past the bus station into the narrower streets at the back of Piccadilly, passing the office of the private investigator she knew and heading to the office building opposite. She had to press a button on the outer door and wait as the receptionist buzzed them in.

The woman behind the counter had blonde hair wrenched into a tight ponytail, her lengthy talons not leaving the keyboard as she peered up at Jessica and Izzy. 'Can I help you?'

The constant click-clacking of the keyboard was off-putting, as was the fact that the receptionist seemed to be some witch-like multi-tasker, though it did cross Jessica's mind that she could be striking all the wrong keys.

'We have an appointment,' Jessica replied.

'With whom?'

'Nathan Dixon from the accountants.'

'Which accountants? There are three in this building.'

'Er . . .'

Jessica turned to Izzy, who predictably knew the answer: 'Fisher Accountants.'

'One moment.'

The woman's hand flashed to the phone, scooping it under her ear and pressing a button in one fluid movement. Within half a second, she had both hands at the keyboard, continuing to type. Her telephone voice was so exceptional, she managed to sound interested in her job: 'Hello, Mr Dixon? Your middays are here. Shall I send them up?' Jessica blinked at the wrong moment, missing the phone being slipped back onto the desk. 'Floor three,' the receptionist added, smile immaculate, fingers still beavering away at the keyboard.

Jessica felt dizzy as she got into the lift and the doors dinked closed in front of them. 'Did we just see that?' she asked.

'We should definitely hire her,' Izzy replied. 'She'd have found Liam McGregor and our Jaws killer before lunch without leaving her desk. She'd have probably written a dissertation at the same time. I bet she knits with her toes, too.'

'I've heard of multi-tasking but that's ridiculous.'

When the lift doors opened again, they were met by a man in a suit a little too big for him. Nathan Dixon's black hair was short and flat, his face a bit too shiny. One of those blokes who went for waxings. The weirdo. He thrust his hand out and shook enthusiastically as they swapped names and job titles.

'How can I help you?'

Jessica took the lead, speaking a little louder than usual. 'I believe you're due to be Liam McGregor's best man on Saturday . . . ?'

Nathan peered nervously over his shoulder towards the rows of ear-wigging colleagues whose collective gazes were fixed on their computer screens, even though their ears were pricked. 'Er, hang on, give me a minute.' Nathan disappeared into a small room next to the lift doors and re-emerged clutching a large puffer jacket. 'Can we nip outside? There's a cafe down the road.'

Despite not being asked, Nathan was apparently paying. He stood at the counter at the back of the cafe looking at Jessica and Izzy over his shoulder and asking what they wanted.

'Just a Coke,' Izzy said.

He nodded at Jess: 'You?'

Well, if he was paying . . .

'Skinny latte, BLT on a bloomer and one of those shortbread things.' Jessica waggled a finger in the general direction of the biscuits, ignoring the sign at the front. Why would some fun-hating bastard spoil a good cookie by revealing how many calories it contained?

Nathan didn't seem to mind, ordering himself a cappuccino and muffin. Jessica and Izzy found a seat at a small round table and waited as he loaded up a tray.

'I wish I'd ordered more now,' Izzy whispered.

'Schoolgirl error. If someone else is paying, it's all fair game. I'd have had caviar, pink salmon and a bottle of Bolly if it was on the menu.'

Nathan soon came across with the tray, passing the various items around. Izzy was left sipping her Coke through a straw, glaring daggers in Jessica's direction. Served her right.

'How are the wedding plans?' Jessica asked.

Nathan shrugged. 'No idea. I thought it was off.'

'Ellie's going round telling everyone she's turning up to the church anyway in case Liam shows up.'

'She's not called me.' He ran a hand through his hair, grimacing and trying to spike it with his fingers. 'Sorry, no hot water again this morning.'

'Boiler problems?'

He smiled sheepishly. 'Only one.'

'Not a fan of the bride, then?'

Nathan bit into the muffin, which looked particularly good, vanilla but filled with flakes of dark chocolate. Jessica started to wish she'd opted for one, rather than the shortbread. He shrugged. 'She's a bit much sometimes. I dunno, it wasn't me marrying her.'

'Tell me about Liam.'

He sighed, shrugged, sipped his coffee and had more of the muffin. 'I already spoke to your lot a bunch of times. I don't know what else you want me to say. It's all a bit hazy now.'

'Sometimes things pop into your mind when you least expect them.'

Nathan glanced up to the clock above the door and then pulled off another chunk of muffin. Jessica snapped her shortbread in half and passed one piece to Izzy, if only to stop the evil eye she was getting.

'What do you want to know?' Nathan asked.

'Just tell us what happened as if we're complete idiots who know nothing.'

He squished his lips together, sighed, and then began: 'There were eight of us. We've all grown up together, schoolmates, that sort of thing. We went up to Keswick for the weekend. It's in the Lake District, up past Coniston and Windermere. We thought it'd be fun.'

'What did you get up to?'

'Not much, just drinking and stuff.'

'Anything else? Did you go hiking? Biking? Some sort of activity on the water?'

He shook his head. 'No, we just got a couple of hotel rooms then hit the pubs for a bit of a sesh.'

He was certainly on a 'sesh' with the muffin, having demolished it in under two minutes. Jessica had barely eaten half a sandwich. 'How was the "sesh"?'

Nathan was still fiddling with his hair. 'We'd gone up there on the Friday night and had a few – nothing messy, just a scouting session, know what I mean?'

'Yep.'

'On the Saturday, we got up late, then went out for lunch and stayed out.'

'Go back a bit – there were eight of you. How many rooms were you in?'

'Two, four in each.'

'And you were in a room with Liam?'

'Right.'

'Any problems?'

'No . . . well, he's a bit of a snorer. I mean, bloody hell, I don't know how Ellie puts up with it.'

'So you had a bad night's sleep?'

As if to emphasise the point, Nathan yawned, not covering his mouth. Lovely. 'I suppose. We slept in anyway.'

'On day two, the Saturday, you had lunch – where?'

'I've been through all this. The police went over it at the time. It must all check out.'

'If you could just go over it one final time.'

He huffed and puffed in annoyance. 'We ate at this pub – some tavern place, I can't remember the name now. After that, we had a few jars, then went on a tour of the bars.'

'Then what happened?'

'It was about eight o'clock. We were in the back room of this pub, being a bit noisy I suppose. The landlord asked if we could keep it down and we did, there was no problem. One minute Liam was there, the next he was gone. We thought he'd gone to the toilet but then it was ten minutes later, twenty minutes, and he wasn't coming back. We checked through the pub and called him, then we looked outside and started asking the other people there. It was a couple of hours later when we called you. We'd all sobered up a bit by then.'

Jessica hadn't read the full report but Izzy had summarised it well enough that she knew the details. 'I gather the police couldn't get to you right away?'

'Right, it was Saturday night and they were busy. I think there'd been a car accident, I don't really know. That's pretty much it anyway. There were people there who saw him, it's not like he could be missed – he was only wearing a mankini.'

'Why was he wearing a mankini?'

Nathan held the mug in front of his mouth, trying to hide behind it, embarrassed. 'I dunno, it was his stag do. We were messing around.'

'So there are eight of you in a back room – all lads – but one of you's in a mankini?'

He sniggered. 'What's wrong with that? We were doing dares – he had to chat up one of the barmaids, then, because she told him to get lost, he had to put on the mankini and try again.'

'Sounds hilarious.'

'Whatever.'

Jessica glanced at Izzy, whose look conveyed that Nathan had told them exactly the same as the other witnesses.

'I don't know what else you want me to say,' Nathan added.

'Was he seeing anyone else? Secret girlfriend? Boyfriend? That sort of thing?'

'No.'

'Are you sure?'

'Okay then, I don't know. Not that he ever told me.'

'What was his relationship with Ellie like?'

Nathan was withdrawing, glancing up at the clock and then checking his watch to make it extra clear he wanted to go. He downed the rest of his coffee in one. 'Dunno. Good, I s'pose.'

'You were going to be his best man, you must have spoken about it, even briefly.'

'I think it was good. She's just a bit . . . intense.'

Jessica and Izzy both nodded. Considering the blog, the placard, newspapers, magazines, TV and radio appearances, that was self-explanatory.

Nathan glanced at the clock again. 'I've got to get back. I only get half an hour for lunch.'

Jessica passed him her card and told him to contact her if he heard anything. He hurried out of the cafe and jammed his hands in his pockets, before heading in the direction of the office.

Izzy pinched a discarded corner of Jessica's sandwich. 'That's pretty much what he said last time. I've read all the statements over and over looking for discrepancies. Liam's friends all say the same. One minute he was in the pub wearing a mankini, the next he was gone. They say they couldn't find him anywhere nearby. The police took a while to get there but they couldn't find him either. At the time I think they thought he was some pisshead who'd stumbled off into the town centre and that he'd turn up in an alleyway the next morning.'

'Were there any sightings at all?'

'Nothing – not even a hoax or a fake.'

'People don't just vanish.'

Izzy didn't reply, no doubt thinking the same as Jessica – Bex had done just that, except that, as far as Jessica knew, there'd been nobody at the house during the day that she'd gone. With Liam, he'd had his friends around him. She didn't have time to drive up the motorway for a proper look at the pub or the surrounding area.

'What else is in the report?' Jessica asked.

'The usual. He's not used his bank cards, his phone's either been taken or ditched. He didn't turn up to work, obviously – there were a bunch of chocolate bars and some change in his locker but not much else. We checked his home and work emails but there's nothing there. Same for his phone records. No signs of kidnap, no ransom – not that Ellie has any money—'

'She will when she ends up doing *Celebrity Sky Diving* or whatever shite it is they come up with next.'

'That's pretty much it,' Izzy concluded. 'I know she's upset but there's only so many times you can ask the same questions.'

Jessica finished off her drink. 'How many hen dos have you been on?'

'I don't know . . . four or five?'

'How many good ones?'

'Just one – we went down to Somerset and did this adventure day.'

'Right, because the good ones are always properly organised and there are things to do. The bad ones are always "let's turn up and get pissed". Someone's always on the floor by early evening, then everyone breaks off into smaller groups and someone – hopefully not the bride – ends up copping off with someone else. It's always, without fail, rubbish.'

'What's your point?'

'Have you ever been to Keswick?'

'I don't think so.'

'It's this little town not too far away from where I grew up. Perfectly pleasant, nice and sleepy, cobbles, very English.

It's where hikers go. They get up early, set off around the lake or up to the mountains, then get back late afternoon and go to the pub. That's what it is. Why would you go there just to go drinking?'

'Maybe it's where one of them comes from?'

'Isn't Liam from Manchester? That magazine article said he was from Fallowfield.'

Izzy's eyes were screwed up as she tried to remember. 'Sounds about right. Ellie lives around the corner from the station – that's why she's picketing us, not the Lake District lot.'

'If you're going on a stag do, why Keswick? If you're into outdoor sports, then fair enough, but if all you're going to do is drink, why not the city centre? Even if you want to get away, Blackpool's up the road one way, Liverpool another. There are so many other places that are easier to get to. Nathan said they were going to "hit the pubs" but what's to hit?'

'I don't know, I didn't even think of that. What's your point?'

Jessica finished off the shortbread. For a free lunch, it had been a belter. 'I don't know. When you get back to the station, send me the details of everyone at the stag do – names, addresses, phone numbers, the lot. I'm going for a poke around.'

26

The local talk radio station was up to its usual standards. Not content with speculating about where 'Jaws' might be and warning young women not to go out by themselves, they had moved on to Ellie Scanlon's tale of police incompetence. The topic of the day seemed to be 'What's going wrong with our police?', with each caller lining up to take a kick at the Force. One woman spent five minutes explaining how 'kids' kept stealing her wheelie bin and that the police were doing nothing. She repeated 'I pay my taxes' five times before the presenter finally got bored and cut to a song.

As the music faded out, his cheesy voice dribbled through the speaker: 'That was Jet with *Are You Gonna Be My Girl?* and up next, here's Nicola from Stockport.'

Again?!

Jessica turned the radio off before the wannabe anarchist had her say. How many Nicolas could there be in Stockport? There must be a database somewhere.

As her phone buzzed, Jessica pulled over and scrolled through the information Izzy had sent. She was right that Ellie Scanlon lived close to their Longsight station – two streets over, in fact. She had the same address as Liam, with the other stag do attendees dotted around the city. Nathan's address was less than half a mile from Jessica's place in Swinton, north of the city centre. She was almost home anyway, so figured she might as well check it out. Nathan's story had been consistent throughout but there were aspects that didn't make sense. The destination would have been either his or Liam's decision, yet neither of them apparently had a connection to the Lake District. Of all the places they could go on the lash, a small Cumbrian town had to be close to the bottom of the list.

Jessica followed the map on her phone until she arrived outside Nathan's house. It was a two-bedroom new build. The type of red-brick bang-'em-up, get-'em-sold cheapo rush-job that suited nobody except the builders. People didn't really want to live in them because they were too small but were left with little choice if they wanted a foot on the housing ladder.

It was the middle of the afternoon and the estate was quiet, the majority of its residents at work, Nathan at the accountants. Jessica got out of her car and went for a walk around to the back of the property. She peered over the fence but there was little to see, other than an open bathroom window and the outline of some Lynx shower gel. After another lap, Jessica returned to her car, leaning on the back window and watching. The house really was small: two-bedroom but not enough for a family to live in unless the children were very young. Her old flat wasn't far off the same size in terms of floor space.

Eventually, she unclicked the gate and approached the front door, ringing the bell and pressing her ear to the glass. Aside from the echoing ding-dong, she heard nothing, so crouched and lifted the letterbox flap, peering through the bristles towards an open door that led into a kitchen.

'I've got a parcel,' she called, not entirely sure what she expected. 'I need a signature.'

No answer.

Jessica walked backwards along the path, watching the unmoving windows the entire way until she was at the car. She got inside and drove around the corner, parking out of sight of the house and waiting for five minutes. Trying to act as normally as she could in case there was an errant curtain-twitcher nearby, Jessica returned to the adjacent street, sticking to the fence line until she was again in front of Nathan's house. She sat on the street sign across the road, watching the house but with her phone in her hand as an excuse in case anyone wondered what she was doing.

It took ten minutes but finally there was a flash of movement. Something silvery that skipped across the upstairs hallway and vanished as quickly as it had appeared. It could have been a pet but Jessica had felt an inkling from the moment Nathan mentioned there'd been no hot water. Seeing the house only cemented her thoughts. New builds were often appalling but they generally had running water.

She crossed quickly to the front door and knocked loudly, bending to call through the letterbox. 'I can see you in there, Liam. You can either open the door, or I'll get a warrant and we'll break it down. Either way I'm not leaving.'

Jessica stepped back, waiting. Five seconds. Ten. She was about to knock again when the outline of a man appeared through the frosted glass. There was a clunk of the chain and then the door opened, revealing a man in tracksuit bottoms and a grey sleeveless running top. He had patchy short gingery hair and the hint of a beard beginning to grow.

'Hi . . .' he whispered, peering past her to the empty street.

Jessica stepped inside without being invited, making Liam edge backwards. 'You should probably take shorter showers,' she said.

'Huh?'

'Make me a brew and I'll talk you through it.'

Liam was so surprised that he shrugged and did as he was told, leading Jessica through to the cramped kitchen, drying up a pair of mugs from the draining board and then putting on the kettle. He sat on one side of a small dining table, Jessica on the other.

'I saw your best man today,' Jessica said.

'Nath?'

'Your bride-to-be's been all over the TV. We had to do something. Nathan told me there was no hot water for him to take a shower, which is strange seeing as he lives alone.'

'Oh.'

'He's not keen on your snoring, either.'

'Did he tell you?'

'Not as such – but no one can be that angry about someone else's snoring after just one night. You should really go to a doctor.'

Liam was staring at the table, arms crossed defensively. 'Are you going to tell Ellie?'

'No – you are. You're the one who's been hiding from her for a bloody month. You'll be lucky if we don't do you for wasting police time.'

His gaze shot up. 'Am I in trouble?'

Jessica stared at him for a few moments, letting him stew. 'Let's see how good your brews are first.'

He ferreted around in a back cupboard, knocking a box of PG Tips on the floor before retrieving it and asking how she liked it. A minute later and the drink was steaming in front of her.

'Is it all right?' he asked.

Jessica ignored the question. 'You were almost there, y'know? It was pretty clever, really – especially the mankini bit. People were always going to notice you in that, so there would be witnesses lining up to say they'd seen you in the pub. Keswick wasn't a bad choice. The problem with Manchester or Blackpool is the CCTV cameras – they're everywhere. Little chance of you sneaking out of a pub down here and not being noticed. Was there a car waiting around the corner from the pub in Keswick?'

Liam was staring at the table again. He had an enormous bald spot on the crown of his head, like a gingery abbot. 'Something like that.'

'You should've picked somewhere better. No one goes to the Lake District just to get pissed. Either that or come up with a better story. All you had to say was that you were all keen hikers and that you'd spent the Saturday walking. The rest of your story could have stayed the same.'

'Bit late now, innit.'

'It certainly is.'

He thumped a palm on the table, making Jessica jump. 'Ellie's always got to have her way. It was supposed to be our wedding but I've not made a single decision about it. She wouldn't even let me pick the suits. Everything's always about her. You don't know what she's like.'

'Considering she's spent a week picketing our police station and that she now has an agent and is doing the round of magazines, newspapers, TV and radio stations, I think I have a pretty good idea what she's like.'

His mouth hung open. 'She has an agent?'

'Apparently.'

'Why?'

'Because you're big news. The Runaway Bridegroom. She's going to the church on Saturday in the hope you'll turn up. I'll bet she's going to have the cameras with her just in case.'

Liam buried his head in his hands. 'Oh, bloody hell. I knew I should've faked my own death.' He got up and downed a glass of water. He was blinking rapidly, and scratching his eyes. 'Is she really going ahead with it?'

'So I'm told.'

'This is bloody typical of her – always got to be front and centre, even when there's no sodding groom.'

He slapped another hand onto the table but Jessica knew it was largely showboating for her benefit. An effort to get sympathy because she'd told him he could be done for wasting their time.

'Answer me something,' Jessica said, 'if she's so annoying, why did you agree to get married?'

Liam threw his hands up. 'It was an accident. We were watching *Corrie* and there was this couple getting married. Ellie goes, "Oh, isn't that a nice dress", and I'm like, "Yeah, whatever". Then she goes: "Perhaps we should get married?" I say – and this is a direct quote – "Maybe we should" and before I can add "one day when we have the money", she jumps in and goes "Oh, brilliant. I'll call my mum". Before I know it, she's calling her mum and all her mates, saying I've proposed and that we're engaged.'

'Why didn't you tell her you didn't want to get married?'

'Why'd you think? She's bloody mental. I'd rather marry her than tell her to her face that I'm not doing it.'

'So you'd rather be unhappy forever instead of having a simple conversation?'

'*Pfft* – you wouldn't be calling it a "simple" conversation if you knew her. If I'd said the wedding was off, she'd have burst into tears, then she'd have got her mum round, then her mates. If I'd still said it was off, she'd have threatened to kill herself, then threatened to kill me. Then she'd have cut up all my clothes.'

Liam was throwing his arms around, so Jessica waited until he'd calmed down slightly. 'What were you hoping was going to happen here?'

He shrugged. 'I dunno. I figured keep my head down until after the wedding and then come back and say I had amnesia. I'd fallen off a cliff, something like that. Nath said it was all right to stay in his spare room but I've not been able to go out. I'm stuck in here all day, every day.'

He tailed off, dabbing at his eyes, even though he hadn't been crying. 'What's going to happen to me?'

Jessica sighed, wondering if there was a delicate way to break it. 'Honestly? I'm not sure. There are hours and hours of wasted police time – interviews, searches – all that. Someone else will make a decision about that but, before anything, you're going to tell Ellie the wedding's off. Be a man about it.'

'Are you going to arrest me?'

'Not right now.'

'I don't mind if you do. I'll spend a night in the cells and tell you whatever you want to hear. What do you get for wasting police time? A few weeks in prison? A month? I reckon I could do that.'

Jessica waited for him to look up and then held his gaze. 'Go and tell Ellie.'

27

Jessica was so determined not to lose Liam that she locked him in her car and then stood outside, guarding it while she phoned Izzy. The sergeant sounded as busy as ever and was slightly out of breath when she answered. 'Is there ever a time when you're not on shift?' she asked.

'Guess who I've got locked in my car?' Jessica replied.

'Um . . . Bono?'

'Why would I have Bono locked in my car?'

'Crimes against music? Stupid sunglasses? Take your pick.'

'Better.'

'Er . . . It's not Blaine Banner, is it? Because if it is and you've not invited me, then I'm never talking to you again.'

'I've seen him topless three times now.'

'*Three times?*'

'And I've seen his arse.'

'Did you get a picture?'

'Of course I didn't. Anyway, I have neither Bono nor Blaine Banner in my car. Instead, I've kidnapped a ginger young man who's so keen to escape his deranged fiancée that he's happy to confess to any crimes we have going. I'm thinking of pinning the new Jaws murders on him. I reckon he'd cough to them.'

There was a pause as the penny dropped and then: 'You found Liam?'

'Certainly did.'

'Where was he?'

'Oh, y'know, here and there. I've not called the guv yet. I think he might recommend me for a peerage or something. I'd settle for a chippy tea, mind.'

'What are you going to do with him?'

'Can you do me a favour?'

'Only if you get me a picture of Blaine's backside.'

'I'm not going to do that. Can you do me a favour anyway?'

'What?'

'Find out where Ellie Scanlon is. She's been on a tour of the radio and TV studios so she must be somewhere around. If she's not answering her mobile, call her agent. When you've found her, let me know where she is. I'm going to drop her off a little present.'

Izzy said she would and hung up. Jessica unlocked the car and opened the passenger door, making sure that Liam was still breathing, and then locked him in again. She called DCI Topper, who sounded as excited as she'd ever heard him, indeed as thrilled as any Scotsman she'd known. It was like Scotland had beaten England at Murrayfield and then he'd found a two-pound coin on the walk home.

He muttered something about telling Aylesbury and then shoving the news 'right up' someone's arse, the name of whom she didn't catch, but there was nothing about a chippy tea. Either way, she was in his good books. If

Deacon and his Bootle Street lot could pull their fingers out and figure out who was copycatting Damian Walker's crimes, then it would go down as a productive week.

Izzy called back five minutes later to say that an 'ecstatic' Ellie Scanlon was staying in a suite at the city centre Hilton, apparently paid for by *OK!* magazine, who were now funding the wedding that wasn't going to be. They'd asked if Jessica could hold on to Liam for an hour in order to give them time to get the cameras in place. On hearing that, Jessica immediately got into the car and drove as quickly as she could to the city centre, making it in just twenty minutes.

Liam hadn't spoken for the entire journey but he did get out of the car when told, limping his way towards the hotel, his pace slowing and slowing until he had practically stopped. Jessica thought she might have to wait with him but the moment they got inside the hotel, there was a shriek from the far end of the reception. Ellie Scanlon's face was a mess of dribbling mascara, which might have been an early practice for a Halloween fancy-dress party but was more likely because of the cameraman waiting close to the lifts. Ellie was wearing a glittery red dress that did little for her or the stretched material. She bounded across the lobby before hurling herself at Liam who braced himself, slightly bent his knees, and somehow managed to prevent himself from toppling back through the doors. She was at least twice the size of him, wrapping her thick arms around his back and bear-hugging him like a wrestler trying to choke out an opponent.

'Oh my God, oh my God.' Ellie stepped away, waving a

hand in front of her face. 'Oh my God, I never thought I'd see you again.'

The dwarfed Liam looked utterly terrified, unable to get a word in as Ellie continued to shower proclamations of love upon him. Jessica was almost ready to leave when the cameraman stepped away from the lift, nervously patting Ellie on the shoulder.

'What?' she scowled, turning to face him.

'I forgot to reset the camera's hard drive?'

'What are you on about?'

'Can you do that running thing again? I missed the shot.' He turned to Jessica. 'If you could walk him in again, that'd be fabulous.'

'Are you joking?' Jessica asked.

The cameraman shook his head. 'No, it's a new camera. I've not got my head round it yet.'

Jessica stepped forward, pointing at both Liam and Ellie. 'Not that – you two. If I find out this was one big ruse to get on TV, I'm going to be mightily pissed off.'

Liam shook his head, now terrified of both of them but Ellie held her ground. 'It's *my* wedding day and *you're* not going to stop it, not now my Liam's back.'

Jessica left the hotel unsure whether she should be angry or . . . well, she wasn't sure what. She was definitely angry. She'd believed Liam at the house when he said he'd planned to keep his head down but she was also pretty sure Ellie had used the situation to her advantage. As far as she was concerned, they deserved each other.

She knew she could head home but the night was

closing in, the sky turning a navy blue as the street lights started to consider turning themselves on. The house was going to be a dreadfully quiet place if she went home now. Meanwhile, the city centre was gearing up for a Thursday night. Nights out in Manchester revolved around Fridays and Saturdays, like most places, but there was rarely a completely quiet night with the breadth of bars, comedy spots and theatres. Something was always going on.

Jessica left her car and floated through the streets, people-watching. She walked along Deansgate and then headed on to St Ann's Square, where the chaos of the day before had long dissipated. If she hadn't been there to witness the aftermath herself, she wouldn't have guessed this was where a bunch of shaven-headed morons had tried to string up some poor pensioner the previous day. Theatre-goers were beginning to mingle, with others hurrying away from their workplaces, heading for home. Jessica continued through the square, going into the Arndale centre and doing a lap of the bottom floor, then the top, not entering any of the shops before exiting onto the tramlines on the High Street. Before she knew it, as if on autopilot, she was in the Northern Quarter.

Of all the areas in Manchester city centre, it was here Jessica felt the most alive. From a rundown poverty-stricken rat-end of nowhere, it had risen to become the creative heartbeat of the city. Jaunty cafes had sprung up throughout the winding labyrinth of back streets and cobbled alleys. There was a sign that had an arrow pointing inside over the word 'cake', with 'no cake' underneath and an arrow angling towards the street. Two streets over, there was a teashop with a 1930s theme, including period signs and furniture. There were glass-fronted art galleries open until late; cramped pubs that went up over four storeys, instead of out into one big room; tattooists; a place selling wigs; two comic shops; vintage clothes shops; music bars; and Afflecks, an enormous emporium of independent goods with a sign on the wall proclaiming that '. . . On the sixth day, God created Manchester'.

The area bristled with energy and youth but Jessica continued walking past the lights, heading into the darkness of the narrower ginnels beyond, the places where shops and residents left their bins and nobody bothered to dwell. Nobody except those who had nothing else.

It was in areas such as this that Bex used to look after herself before Jessica stuck her nose in and altered the course of both of their lives. It would have been around a year since Bex last slept on these streets and even longer ago that Jessica had been around, helping another homeless man, 'Toxic' Tony.

Jessica had found Liam through a combination of luck and other people's stupidity but there had be no sign of Bex. She had thought about bringing herself to this area a few times since Bex's disappearance but never quite managed it, afraid of what she might find. The idea that living on the dirty back streets was preferable to sharing a house with her was perhaps more horrifying than not finding Bex at all. After two months of inactivity, she was out of ideas.

As she delved deeper into the far reaches of the hidden areas of the city, the glow of the street lights faded, leaving only the eerie fading blue of the sky. Jessica rounded a corner, slipping on a soaked, flattened cereal box when she spotted a heavily bearded man slumped behind a big green wheelie bin, cocooned in a large sleeping bag. He grinned a toothy smile when he saw her, pulling the cover tighter. His accent was local but masked by a deep cough. 'Got anything to eat?'

It dawned on Jessica that she should have come prepared but it was a little late now. 'I'm looking for my friend.'

'Ain't nobody back 'ere but me.'

'Can I show you her picture?'

The man eyed Jessica suspiciously, wondering if he was somehow being scammed. 'Who is she?'

'A friend. She used to live on the streets.'

'Let's see her.'

Jessica flipped through the photos on the phone and held it out for the man to see, reluctantly letting him take it when he held out a hand. He twisted the device in his hand and then made her smile by pinching the screen to zoom in. Presumably some things were universal, regardless of where a person lived.

He handed the phone back, shaking his head. 'She sort of seems familiar but I couldn't place her.'

'Do you know anyone who might know?'

He continued shaking his head. 'Girls like that don't stay on the street for long.'

'Why not?'

He started to laugh but lurched into a deep cough. When he'd composed himself, he tugged on his beard.

'Look at me – no one gives two shites. If you've got a pretty face and a pair of tits, you can get yourself out of anything.'

'Oh . . .'

'You see the big cars coming round 'ere – the Bentleys, the Jags. You think they're here for the music? Or the tea? They flash their wallets around and the girls go running. You mark my words – if she's been living on these streets, she'll be on her knees in front of some rich bloke, showing her appreciation.'

28

Jessica was dozing when her phone started to ring. It had been a week of early morning wake-up calls and there was no reason to assume Friday would be any different.

She rolled over groggily, squinted towards the clock and then picked up her phone from the floor. It was half six, which wasn't too bad, considering. Blaine Banner's name flashed across the front of her phone as it rang for a third time, which was just about typical. He'd almost certainly got in from his gig, downed a crate of lager and who knew what else, and then woken up thinking he was being attacked by a group of revolutionary pixies.

Jessica answered with a sigh. 'What is it, Blaine? I told you not to call unless it was an emergency – and even then to call 999 first.'

The caller stammered, clearly shaken. It wasn't Blaine. 'Is that the, er, police woman?'

'Who's calling?'

'It's Sledge. He told me to call this number if something happened to him.'

Jessica pushed herself out of bed, reaching for the wardrobe doors. 'What happened?'

'I'm not sure. He was found unconscious in his hotel room and they've rushed him to hospital. I think somebody tried to kill him.'

29

Perhaps predictably, the 'attempt' on Banner's life wasn't as clear-cut as Sledge had made it sound on the phone. Jessica arrived at the hotel expecting a Scene of Crime team, uniformed officers fighting off the photographers and the too-familiar satellite news vans, with reporters angling for quotes. Instead, everything was close to serene. A few guests were yawning their way out of the lifts and mooching towards the breakfast room. Most were in business attire ready for the day, though one girl was in a tiger-print onesie, seemingly oblivious to the fact she was in public. Her boyfriend was in fluorescent orange beach shorts and a vest, the pair of them ripe for sectioning.

The hotel manager was waiting next to the lifts, wearing a smart grey suit with some sort of crimson silk around his neck that wasn't quite a tie but wasn't a pashmina either. It was wrapped into something a little like a Christmas cracker and looked utterly ridiculous. He had mousy light brown hair and a smile that he probably thought was charming, even though it had more of a creepy kiddy-fiddler air about it. He intercepted Jessica before she could get anywhere near the lifts, spreading his arms and directing her towards a potted small tree in the corner of the reception area. He continued shuffling sideways, trying to hide her behind the foliage but Jessica didn't move.

'What's going on?' she asked.

'There was an . . . *incident*. Nothing to worry about.'

'Hasn't Blaine Banner been taken to hospital?'

'Shush . . . shush . . .' He peered past her, nodding and smiling towards a couple making their way to the breakfast room. 'Morning!'

Jessica glared at him. 'If you shush me one more time, something very bad is going to happen here.'

He gulped, straightening his farfalle-like neckwear. 'Mr Banner had difficulties in the early hours of the morning. He was taken to hospital by one of his bandmates.'

'No ambulance?'

'No.'

'What about the police?'

'Apparently just your good self . . . how exactly did you hear about Mr Banner's, erm, *situation*?' Jessica stared at him unmoving until he got the message and continued: 'Mr Banner's publicist and manager arrived and we came to the decision that it was best for his good reputation if news of the *incident* was kept quiet until we know exactly what occurred.'

'What *did* happen?'

'I'm not sure I'm the best person to say. It might be best if you left for now and I'll arrange for someone to give you a call later on.'

'Good idea, top thinking – I *could* do that. Or, I could nick off to the magistrates' court and see if I can get a warrant to have a peep on your top floor. What do you reckon's up there? Obviously Blaine and his friends are all clean-living, so probably tofu and oxidised water. *Definitely* not drugs or evidence of any other wrongdoing. If not that, I can pop over the road and have a word with the photographers. Ask them if anyone got a picture of the car taking Blaine to the hospital. Their news desks might be interested.'

The hotel manager was shrinking in front of her, nose twitching as if he'd had to use a toilet cubicle directly after Fat Pat. 'Ummmmm . . . perhaps I could take you upstairs, just to allay any fears you may have.'

Jessica smiled sweetly. 'Let's do that.'

If any sort of crime had occurred in Banner's hotel room then evidence was long gone. The space was packed with band members and hangers-on drinking coffee, plus two women in suits, standing close to the bathroom, simultaneously talking to each other and on separate mobile phones. Somebody had definitely cleaned up, too. The debris from the smashed smoke detectors was gone, as was the mound of discarded clothes. If there ever had been any illicit powders or pills in the room, they'd be gone as well, ingested or flushed.

Sledge was dressed almost like a normal human being. He was in loose-fit suit trousers and a T-shirt but looked shattered, a combination of a late night and genuine upset over the fate of his bandmate and friend. He was perched on the corner of a dresser, sipping coffee from a polystyrene cup. Someone had gone on a doughnut run, with two boxes of Krispy Kremes open on the bed. The one with pink sprinkles was calling Jessica's name. *You know you want me.*

'I'm not entirely sure what's going on,' Jessica said.

Sledge nodded towards the two women. 'Them lot was trying to hush it up, so I thought bollocks to that and gave you a bell.'

'What happened to Blaine?'

'I'm not sure. I was struggling to get to sleep so popped across the hallway, wondering if Blaine might want to mess around on the guitar. Some of our best stuff has come out at stupid times of the morning. You know that song *Threeway*?' He nodded, looking for a recognition Jessica couldn't provide. 'We wrote that at half four in the morning one time in Santiago. Anyway, there are two keycards per room but we've been coming and going, so I ended up with one of his. He didn't answer the door, so I let myself in. Blaine was on his back on the floor, choking. There was all this puke around him.' He motioned towards the carpet, on which, now it had been pointed out, Jessica could see a brighter patch where something had been scrubbed away. 'I thought he was a goner. I've only seen him in a worse state once – he was clinically dead in Ecuador but they used those electric paddle things to get him going and we still went out for a pint that night.'

It was a lot of information to take in.

If he hadn't already, Sledge should definitely have written an autobiography. Compared to the shelves filled with turgid shite vomited out by Z-list soap and reality stars every Christmas, his might actually have been interesting.

'What happened then?' Jessica asked.

'I sort of rolled him over, then shouted for the lads. I think someone phoned Alex—'

'Who's that?'

He pointed at the pair of women. 'Alex is our manager.' He lowered his voice. 'Absolute nutcase. I wouldn't mess with her. Blaine was still being sick everywhere but we managed to get him into a car and one of the lads zipped him across the city to this private hospital Alex sorted. When she turned up, she said we were on lockdown. No one in or out. That's when I called you.'

'Was he conscious?'

'He was drifting in and out but kept being sick. I thought he was going to bring a lung up.'

Jessica winced at the thought. Lovely. 'How were things last night?'

'Normal. We did the gig, had a few beers, came back here.'

'Was Blaine drinking?'

Sledge tilted his head to the side. 'What d'you think?'

'Isn't there a chance that he could've drunk himself into that state?'

He shook his head. 'You didn't know him, love. He could drink the contents of a horse's bladder by himself and not even slur his words.'

Jessica gazed at him for a few moments, wondering from where the comparison had come, before deciding she didn't want to know the answer. 'What time did you find him?'

'Few minutes after four.'

Before Sledge could say anything else, Alex slipped herself in between them, taking a step forward and forcing Jessica to move backwards. She had red hair permed into tight curls and was wearing the sweetest of smiles. 'Hello,

Ms Daniel, isn't it? How wonderful to see you.' She glanced down at her phone. 'I'm *so* looking forward to seeing you at one of the arena shows. Your name's been on the VIP guest list for a few days now . . .'

She took another step forward but Jessica didn't move the second time, forcing Alex to tread on the tip of her toes. 'Do you want to try moving backwards?' Jessica said.

The smile didn't leave Alex's face as she retreated slowly. 'Hopefully you've seen everything you need. I can keep you up to date during the day if you wish . . . ?'

'Where's Blaine?'

'Sorry?'

'Blaine Banner. Big guy, long hair. Doesn't like wearing clothes. Where is he?'

'Um . . . I'd have to check on that for you. What I can say is that he's perfectly well. No need for this to go any further.'

She made no effort to move, nor look at her phone, instead angling towards the door.

'I'm happy to wait,' Jessica added.

'It's just . . . um . . .' Alex glanced sideways towards the publicist, who was holding two phones, one to each ear. '. . . we were wondering if you might sign a non-disclosure form. Nothing untoward, just a simple agreement not to reveal anything you might have witnessed . . .'

Jessica nodded. 'Sounds good, absolutely fine. I'm just wondering whose arse I shove it up when I'm done.'

The smile disappeared as Alex's eyes narrowed, her tone of voice dropping an octave. 'This room is private property, Ms Daniel. The police have *not* been called here and your presence is *not* welcome. If you were to tell anyone about anything you've seen here, it would be a serious breach of Mr Banner's privacy under article eight of the European Convention on Human Rights.'

Jessica continued to nod. 'Right . . . I think I see where this is going . . .'

Alex was nodding too, her features softening slightly, point made.

'I'm going to give you two choices,' Jessica said. 'First, we do things your way. I'll leave right now because I've received an anonymous tip from an unnamed hospital source that Mr Banner has overdosed on unknown substances. Obviously that anonymous tip will have to be acted upon. Firstly, we'll have to seal off this entire area to be searched and bring everyone in this room down to the station for questioning. Obviously we'll need to know the name of the hospital where Mr Banner has been taken because he's not only a victim, he's the key witness. Of course, there's no way a story that big can be kept under wraps. Someone, somewhere's going to leak it to the media.' She paused, letting option one sink in. 'The other way, *my way*, is that you tell me where he's staying and I'll go and have a word with him myself.'

Alex kept her lips tight but didn't take long to reply. 'I, er . . . what anonymous tip?'

'I don't know – it's anonymous. I believe you're the person who's been talking to our press office non-stop for two days about an apparent threat to Mr Banner's safety? Making sure we were doing our jobs properly, that sort of thing . . . ? Perhaps the tip came from you? That'd be a story, wouldn't it? What would the record label think?'

Alex wasn't proving to be the 'nutcase' that Sledge had painted her as. She glanced quickly at the publicist and then forced a friendly smile. 'That might have been an overreaction.'

'Where is he?'

She slipped a thin Post-it pad out from her breast pocket along with a pen and wrote the name of a private hospital Jessica had never heard of. She passed it across, adding that it was in Sedgley Park, a few miles away. Jessica told her she'd find it and then headed for the lifts.

The hotel manager clapped his hands together in apparent jubilation as Jessica exited the lifts. 'All in order?' he smiled.

'I want to see the CCTV from that floor.'

'We have *procedures* . . .'

Jessica sighed, hands on hips. 'Do we have to do this again? I can nip off and get a warrant, make it all official and public, or you can just show me. I don't mind which but one really pisses me off and attracts the papers; the other should take five minutes.'

The manager didn't take much convincing, spinning on his heels and leading Jessica behind the reception desk. He typed a four-digit code into the box on the wall and then took her through the door into the back office. It took a few moments for him to isolate the correct camera and time but it was quickly clear that another hour of footage was missing, the frames jumping from three thirty to four thirty in a blink.

When he realised there might be a problem, the manager slumped into the spinning chair, finally undoing the monstrosity around his neck. 'The system does this if the hard drives haven't been tidied up.'

He wasn't even convincing himself.

'Who has access to the machine?'

'No one . . . well, the night manager.'

'Benny?'

He seemed surprised that she knew the name. 'It was Racquel last night.'

'But she'll take the odd break, yes? Nip to the toilet? Pop to the vending machine for a packet of crisps?'

'I suppose.'

'And the code to get into this room is six-six-three-nine.'

'How'd you—'

'You hardly hid it. If I know it then most of your staff probably do.'

Jessica peered past him to the rota on the wall, comparing Tuesday night's list to Thursday's. The manager blustered something about privacy but Jessica ignored him. 'Okay, I'm sure we can keep this incident nice and hushed up if that's what you want but I need some things too. First, that top floor will be quarantined until I say differently. I'll get two officers to come over and they're going to talk to everyone upstairs.'

'I'm not sure that's necessary—'

'Meanwhile, I want to talk to the three people who were working last night and on Tuesday. That's Karen Docherty, Alice Rafferty and Usman Akbal. If they've already left for the day, get them back. I want a private room in which to talk to them and some coffee.'

'Anything else?'

She stared at him, wondering if there was a hint of sarcasm in his voice. It sounded like it. Jessica turned to peer through the glass towards the reception area. 'Any chance of getting my name on that list for the breakfast buffet?'

30

When the wonders of the modern world were decided upon, the sight of the hotel's breakfast buffet surely had to be up there somewhere. Jessica wolfed down a bowl of crunchy nut cornflakes; two bacon and sausage butties – with brown sauce, naturally; and then a blueberry muffin. She also wrapped and pocketed three Danishes in case she had a craving later in the day. If she'd had a little more time, she'd have taken a bit longer to work her way through the avalanche of baked goods but work was calling.

The hotel manager set Jessica up in the smallest conference room on the first floor, which was still five or six times the size of her office and about as morbid a place as she could imagine, with dull walls, duller tables and stacks of metal chairs with blue canvas backs. She'd visited cheerier funeral homes. After calling DCI Topper to tell him she was at the hotel dealing with another Banner call out, she got to work.

Karen Docherty was in her late twenties with a brown ponytail, wearing smart dark trousers, a white blouse and a black waistcoat. She was half an hour away from finishing her shift but was literally bouncing in her seat, a ball of caffeine-enhanced energy that couldn't sit still.

'I absolutely love him,' she said. 'That's why I put my name down for all the night shifts.'

Jessica was searching through the basic list of notes the hotel manager had given her. She'd already forgotten the girl's name and the enormity of the breakfast wasn't being appreciated by her stomach. 'Is it right that you work behind the bar?'

'Yes – but we can do room service with the drinks until three. Usually there's only weekend shifts on offer but there's overtime every night at the moment.'

'What's the process when you take drinks to guests?'

'We knock on their doors and then add payment to the bill.'

'Do you have a keycard to get into the rooms?'

She held up a piece of white plastic connected to a keyring on her belt. 'We all do.'

'Have you seen Mr Banner at all over the past week?'

A grin creased across Karen's face. 'He signed my arm. I bloody love him.'

'Did you go up to his room this evening?'

She shook her head. 'Not *his* room – some of the others'.'

'What did they order?'

Karen blew out loudly. 'I can probably find you the receipts . . . there were eight bottles of wine, four of champagne, two Jack Daniel's, a Jim Beam, some vodka—'

'All right, I get the picture. What was the latest time you went up there this morning?'

'About a minute to three. They know that's the cut-off, so they call down at half two.'

'Did you see anything untoward?'

She suddenly seemed nervous, glancing towards the door and then back to Jessica. 'Am I in trouble?'

'Not as far as I know. I'm just asking what you saw.'

Karen dropped to a whisper. 'We're not supposed to talk about it. We had to sign these agreement things that we won't go to the media.'

'I'm the police – you can tell me.'

'Well, like I said, I wasn't in Blaine's room but loads more of them were across the hall. When they opened the door with the trolley, I got a peep inside and there were a couple of girls on the bed. They were . . . well, I'm not sure what it's called. What's that thing where you lick—'

'All right, I think I get that picture, too.'

Alice Rafferty was in her early twenties, blonde, pretty and one of the regular kitchen servers who did over-night shifts. She'd been out with her friends until ten the previous night and then come straight to work. She seemed a little confused by the questioning.

'Have you met Mr Banner?' Jessica asked.

She shrugged, apparently not that interested. 'A couple of times, his bandmates too. They're a bit rude, to be honest, and they're always asking for ridiculous stuff.'

'Like what?'

'One of them called down the other night to ask if we did braised armadillo. He settled for chicken.'

'Did you go up to the top floor last night?'

'Only once – at about half one, when they all got in. There was all sorts of food, so it all went up on one trolley.'

'What about Tuesday?'

She scratched her head. 'I'm not really sure. It's usually once or twice a night, so probably.'

'Has Mr Banner ever spoken to you?'

'No – I try to get in and out.' She stopped and waved a hand. 'Oh, sorry – I did speak to him on the first night. He was trying it on, asking if I wanted to see his tattoos. I said I wasn't fussed, so he asked if there was much to do in the hotel. I told him about the pool and gym and so on but he wasn't impressed, so I figured I'd tell him about the ghost.'

Jessica had been about to ask a relatively straightforward question about keycards but the final remark had thrown her off. 'The ghost?'

Alice nodded. 'It's a myth – all the staff know it. Some kid apparently died up there years ago and he haunts the top floor. I told him that on the first night and he looked at me a bit funny, then went "woooooooooo" and said I shouldn't joke about things like that.'

'Was that it?'

Alice glanced towards the door in the same way Karen had.

'You can tell me anything,' Jessica said.

'I'm not an expert but I think he'd taken something. His pupils were huge and then he told me he was scared of ghosts. I've not seen him since.'

'You definitely didn't see him last night?'

Alice shook her head. 'Sorry.'

Usman Akbal was the night security guard, whose entire job consisted of sitting *outside* the front doors – the poor sod – to ward off over-excited fans or photographers. He had little to say, other than complaining about the 'pissing rain', 'bloody wind' and 'prick of a night manager' who wouldn't let him sit *inside* the door. He'd seen nothing, spoken to hardly anyone and didn't have a keycard to access any of the rooms, let alone the ones on Banner's floor. He had heard of the hotel's ghost, however, reiterating that all the staff knew about it.

Jessica had no particular reason to disbelieve any of them, although it sounded like Banner's visions of a ghost could partially be blamed on Alice. With the idea planted in Banner's chemistry-enhanced mind, there was every chance he'd made up the rest. Before deciding what to do, Jessica needed to visit the hospital and find out what the doctors thought had happened.

Jessica sat in her car and called Izzy. 'You in yet?' Jessica asked.

Izzy sounded breezy, which was a bit much for before nine in the morning. 'No, I'm in the car – just dropped Amber off at nursery. You're on Bluetooth.'

'The line sounds lovely and clear.'

'It's a really good system.'

'Are you sure you're not in yet?'

'Nope.'

'I can hear you eating.'

There was a short pause and then: 'All right, fine. I'm hiding in your office with Archie and a pair of egg butties from the canteen.'

'Why are you hiding?'

'Funtime's not happy that we found Liam McGregor.

He says it was his case and we're glory-chasing. I think he's looking to unload a bunch of his other stuff to prove a point.'

'If it was his case, why didn't he get off his arse and find him?'

'You're asking the wrong person.'

That much was true. 'Can you do me a favour?' Jessica asked.

'I'm not saving you any. Hang on.' Two minutes ticked by until Izzy spoke again, this time in a whisper: 'We've locked ourselves in. Someone was trying the door. I think it was Franks. What's the favour?'

'I've got three names for you and need a bit of background as soon as possible.'

'Go on.'

'Karen Docherty, Alice Rafferty and Usman Akbal.' Jessica spelled the names out and then repeated them, before adding: 'It's probably nothing but make sure they're not anarchists or on any of our other lists.'

'What lists?'

'I don't know – terrorists, country music fans, whatever you can find. There could be some country versus rock war going on.'

'Have you been visiting Blaine again?'

'Not yet.'

Izzy's pen finished scratching and there was the sound of typing. 'Have you seen the news?'

'What?'

'Ellie and Liam – the wedding's on after all. Everything's set for tomorrow.'

'Are you joking?'

'I guess she bullied him into it. They're going to broadcast it live on UK Weddings or whatever the channel's called.'

'This is unbelievable. What about doing them for wasting police time? Him at the very least.'

'Now *you're* joking. What do you think the papers will do to us if we arrest them for that? Even the CPS won't want to be that unpopular. Besides, he was hiding under our noses – if we make too much of a fuss, it'll look bad for us too. I think everyone wants to forget it ever happened. Want to know the good news?'

'I hope this is chocolate-related.'

'In a way – we've all been invited to the reception.'

31

'Hey, babe! You came.'

Blaine Banner grinned at Jessica as she plopped herself in the chair next to his bed and plonked a bunch of grapes on the side table. He had a room to himself at the private hospital and was wearing a gown, sitting on top of the covers with a drip attached to his arm. Aside from a little tiredness, he seemed perfectly fine.

'I'm pretty sure "babe" was on the list of things you weren't supposed to be calling me,' Jessica replied.

He started twisting the tube that was stuck to his arm. 'I think all this hospital stuff is playing havoc with my memory.'

'I'm sure that's it.'

Banner started to reach for the grapes but Jessica slapped his hand away. 'What?' he protested.

'I bought those thinking you could eat them but I'm reliably informed you've not long had your stomach pumped.'

He grinned, flashing his bright white teeth. 'You've gotta get it done a couple of times a year just to keep the ol' digestive system running.'

Jessica ate a grape herself. 'I really don't think that's how it works.'

'Don't knock it till you've tried it. There's nothing like a good stomach pumping to set the pulse racing.'

'I'll take your word for it.' Jessica swallowed another grape, watching Banner as the grin slipped, exposing the act. 'What happened?' she asked.

'It was back.'

'What was back?'

'The ghost. I woke up and it was right over me. I tried to reach out but couldn't move. I think it had tied me up. Then it started tipping booze down my throat.'

'The ghost made you drink?'

'I know it sounds mental.'

'What was the drink?'

He shrugged. 'Whisky, vodka, whatever.'

'Are you sure you didn't just drink it?'

'Course not, I know my limits. There are far too many pretty girls in the world to want to end it all.'

He sounded sincere but it was hard to know, not because he was necessarily a liar, more because his powers of recall were unreliable to say the least.

'If you were on the bed when you were being forced to drink, how did you end up on the floor?'

'No idea. Next thing I knew, I was here.'

'Are there any marks from where you were tied up?'

He held up his wrists, rolling back his sleeves but there were red marks up and down from where his bandmates had hauled him into the vehicle. It was madness they hadn't called an ambulance. The band manager, Alex, had put Banner's life at risk because she was so obsessed with negative publicity. She could definitely make it in Greater Manchester Police's press office.

'Do you remember anything else?' Jessica asked.

'No.'

'Did the ghost say anything?'

It was a question Jessica thought she'd never ask.

'Um . . . sort of. It was like, "wooooooooooo", and then kept saying, "why haven't you told them what you did?"'

'What did the voice sound like?'

'Sort of ghosty.'

'Male? Female?'

'I don't know.'

Jessica had another grape as Banner tried sitting up higher and then delved into the gown, scratching his backside.

'What *did* you do?'

'I don't know! If I start confessing to every commandment I've broken, we're going to be here a long time. How many girls does the Bible say you can be with at the same time? Two? Three? It's got to be at least three.'

'I don't think that's covered.' Jessica stood, taking her grapes with her. 'Stay here and get better. We're talking to people at the hotel to see what we can find out.'

'I've got a gig tonight!'

'Well, I'm not a doctor, but you should probably stay in bed.'

'Are you coming?'

She turned back. 'We'll see.' She was about to open the door to leave when one final thought struck her. 'Blaine.'

'What?'

'*Lock* your hotel door. Actually pull the catch. Don't just close it.'

'Anything you say, babe.'

Jessica had a pair of missed calls as she left the hospital and called Izzy back before she reached the car. 'Still hiding?' she asked.

'We got found out – Archie found a video on YouTube of some bloke falling down the stairs and was laughing so hard he gave us away.'

There was a muffled cackle in the background, followed by a: 'It was bloody funny though.'

'What have you got?' Jessica asked.

'We've been looking at those three names from the hotel but there's not much to report. No criminal records, no cautions, nothing really. We can go deeper with phone records and the like – up to you.'

'Forget it.'

Jessica didn't think any of the three had anything to do with Banner's 'incident' and still wasn't convinced it was anything other than a drinking session that had gone too far. The missing security camera footage was a curious one, perhaps a coincidence because of the system recording over itself but unlikely. Other than knowing for certain it wasn't a ghost, Jessica had little idea what was going on – and Banner wasn't helping, nor were the band manager or the hotel manager, who both wanted everything hushed up. If only Banner locked his hotel room, it would solve the problem. There were only a few nights left of the tour and he'd be done.

Izzy was making a low humming noise.

'What?' Jessica asked.

'I'm not sure. Something about those names seems familiar but I'm not sure what. I've tried Googling them but nothing comes up.'

'Do you mean they're familiar to you personally, or in general?'

'I'm not sure. It's probably nothing.'

'I just saw Blaine in a hospital gown, by the way.'

'What did he look like?'

'Like a man who'd had his stomach pumped.'

'I bet he's still hot.'

'What's the name of your husband again?'

Izzy laughed and hung up.

32

The rest of the day had an end-of-the-week feel to it, which was rare, even though it was the actual end of the week. According to Clayton, Damian Walker hadn't left his house, with Jessica and Topper's sub-investigation into the pair of copycat murders petering out because there was nowhere else to go. They'd discovered no secret grudges from Walker's time in secure hospitals, nor any family or friends he might have to assist him. From what they could tell, he'd made no attempt to contact anybody since being released, either in person or by phone. He said he didn't even have a mobile and Clayton and Millie both said they'd seen nothing to dispute that. With his electronic tag apparently secure and Clayton sleeping on Walker's sofa overnight, everything else was tied up. He was a free man, after all. If he wanted to send the witness protection officers packing, he could, yet he'd not even objected to Clayton sleeping at his house.

If their investigation had hit a wall, then DSI Deacon's was in an even worse place. He and his team had been interviewing friends, family members, neighbours and seemingly anyone with a pulse but had found no link between the two murdered girls, nor any evidence of who might have killed them. He'd been lobbying to speak directly to Walker but the chief constable had denied the request, assuring Deacon that Walker was not the killer. Without that, Deacon was left clinging to the hope that the forensic results would appear at some point soon. Those poor sods always got it in the neck anyway but the tsunami of Manchester rain had really screwed them on this occasion. They'd apparently promised that there'd be a definitive report within twenty-four hours – although, as DCI Topper pointed out, there was every chance the report wouldn't have much to say. They already knew both girls had been killed by having their stomachs sliced open.

While that was going on, officers had interviewed the entirety of Blaine Banner's entourage on the top floor of the hotel. There was no scene to preserve seeing as it had already been cleared by his management, plus everyone was claiming they saw nothing. The rest of the CCTV had been thoroughly examined but everything between half past three and half past four had been wiped – or 'recorded over' as the hotel manager claimed. He told the interviewing officers that it happened a lot, blaming the glitch on everything from the programmers to his staff's ineptitude in clearing the hard drives. It was fishy to say the least but Banner was hardly a reliable witness. Not only that, both the hotel and band managers were so keen on keeping everything quiet that their cooperation was questionable. Nobody was even sure there'd been a crime and the longer they spent chasing after the band, the more man-hours were being wasted. The only glimmer of light was that the story of Banner's overdose – or attack – hadn't leaked. Even Jessica wasn't sure what she believed.

After a day of frustration, Jessica parked outside her house, dreading heading inside. An unproductive day at work was still preferable to a silent evening by herself. She'd still not had time to deal with what had happened in the basement room of the hospital, locking the memory away and focusing on the job. It was all she had. Once the work ended, everything else would have a chance to take over.

Her key scratched the lock when she realised there was someone behind her. Jessica turned to see the bedraggled shape of Bex's mother, Helena. They'd only met a handful of times before and Jessica had never been quite sure what to make of her. Helena's addiction to drink, drugs and men had driven her fourteen-year-old daughter onto the streets, a fate that was almost too awful to contemplate. In the past year, she'd cleaned up her act, living in a controlled block of flats for recovering addicts. She'd made an effort to track down her daughter and attempted to make amends. Then Bex had disappeared and both she and Jessica had been left looking to each other for answers that neither had. This was the first time Jessica had seen Helena in more than a month.

She looked a lot like her daughter, with long straight black hair, a narrow face and a rounded dome of a nose. Despite the physical similarity, she lacked the spark and sharpness that Bex possessed; not to mention the tattoos and piercings. She also looked as if she could do with a wash. Her hair was greasy and beginning to clump together, and her nails were filthy.

'Oh, hi . . .' Jessica said.

Helena looked as if she'd been recently crying, red rings cupping her eyes. 'Have you heard anything?' she asked.

Jessica opened the door, nodding inside. 'Do you want to come in?'

The woman shook her head. 'What are you doing to find her? Aren't you supposed to be the police? If you can't find her, who can?'

Jessica took a breath. 'We had this conversation a month ago. It's not as easy as you make out.'

Helena scrunched her lips together, glaring back, but Jessica found it difficult to judge whether the anger was genuine. Bex disappeared a short time after her mother made contact for the first time in years. Jessica had seen plenty of coincidences through her work – and they were far more common than people might think – but it was almost too much to believe that the two events weren't connected. It was hard to see past the woman who drove her fourteen-year-old daughter onto the streets.

Helena's voice was a growl: 'What have you actually been doing?'

Jessica peered past her towards the houses on the other side of the road, not wanting a scene in front of the neighbours. 'Come in for a bit.'

'I'd rather stay here.'

'I've been doing what I can.'

'And what's that?'

'I've logged her information with the missing persons bureau, plus we've got tags on things like her bank account. If there's any sign of her anywhere, I'll know straight away.

I've spoken to her friends and tutors, not to mention my neighbours. Nobody knows anything.'

'So my daughter just vanished into thin air? Poof! One minute there, the next she's gone.'

Jessica stepped backwards into the house hoping Helena would follow. If they were going to do this, it could at least be out of the cold. Until now, their irregular interactions had been civil but Helena was a spiky character and this had always been going to happen at some point.

'I'm trying my best, Helena.'

'So where is she? Where's my daughter? She was in your care and you scared her away.'

Jessica wanted to deny it but there was a part of her that agreed. She didn't know why Bex had left but there was at least a chance it was because of her.

Helena wasn't done. 'It's you, isn't it? I've been reading up about you. What was that thing with your boyfriend? Didn't he run off, too? I saw that report about the car he was in. He'd rather blow himself up than live another day with you.'

Her eyes bored into Jessica, wanting the words to hurt. They did.

Jessica felt her nails digging into her palms as she balled her fists. For the most part, getting older had taught her to keep a lid on the temper that she'd so struggled with in the earlier parts of her career, but this . . .

Helena continued to glare. 'What? Nothing to say . . . ?'

Jessica stepped off the porch, two quick steps bringing her eye-to-eye with the other woman. She kept her voice low, just loud enough for Helena to hear. 'How's the drinking going, Helena? I bet you miss the taste of that alcohol slipping down your throat? What was your drink of choice? I bet it was vodka – is that what you used to drink when all those men used to come round your house? I've heard some sick things in my time, dealt with some real disgusting people, but there's something particularly vile about a woman who invites round a group of men and then encourages them to watch her teenage daughter sleep.'

As she spoke, Jessica continued advancing, giving Helena no choice other than to back along the path towards the pavement.

'She was fourteen. *Fourteen!* What sort of mother are you? Not even that, what sort of *person* are you? You're disgusting – a horrible, disgraceful excuse for a human being. Now get lost and don't let me see you anywhere near my house again.'

Jessica was at the edge of her path, with Helena on the edge of the kerb. They glared at each other and, for a moment, Jessica felt sure the other woman was going to launch herself forward and start an actual fight. Helena seemed shocked by the spite but that was good, exactly as Jessica wanted.

Eventually, she took a half step away from the road, still staring at Jessica. 'If I did everything you say and pushed my daughter away, then at least I can hold my hands up and admit I've made mistakes. I know why she left me and I don't blame her. But what did you do? I was a terrible mother – but what does that make you?'

33

Jessica's house felt as empty as ever. Helena had stormed off having had the last word because there was nothing with which Jessica could respond. As much as she didn't want to admit it, everything Helena said was true. Jessica had no idea why Bex had left. The teenager's phone and the laptop she always used had been looked at by experts, who'd found nothing. Bex's friends insisted that she had been happy, having recently enjoyed her eighteenth birthday, and that she was looking forward to going to college. All of that tallied with Jessica's own experiences.

She thought about the support group and wondered if she should return the following week. Telling her story had been cathartic in some ways but listening to other peoples' tales had made her feel selfish because there were so many others going through what she was. She wasn't special. It also left her with a strange sense of guilt at all the missing persons cases she'd dismissed over the years, assuming deep down that husbands, wives, boyfriends, girlfriends and young people had walked out for a reason. That those left behind were somehow at fault for driving their loved ones away.

The statistics felt as mind-boggling now as when Jessica had first seen them – how could a quarter of a million people disappear every year and there not be some sort of national outcry? Fewer people died of cancer, fewer still through road traffic accidents, yet they received a much greater level of coverage and scrutiny.

Jessica stood in the doorway of Bex's room, gazing at the young woman's meagre possessions and hoping something she'd previously missed would suddenly appear. She'd looked under the mattress, in the wardrobe, even under the carpets. She'd leafed through books page by page in case there was a hidden note, yet there was nothing anywhere.

'Where are you?' she asked the empty room.

Jessica jumped as the phone in her pocket started to vibrate. Bex was at the front of her mind and, for a moment, she expected to look down at her screen and see the teenager's name. Instead, it was DCI Topper.

'I'm off shift!' Jessica said.

Topper sounded rushed. 'Me too. Have you got the telly on?'

'Why? What are you watching, *Celebrity Piles*?'

'Put the news on.'

Jessica went downstairs, hunting through the drawers underneath the television until she found the correct remote, and then turning it on. It only took her a moment to recognise the house on the screen: Walker's.

'Are you seeing this?' Topper asked.

'Why are the cameras outside his house? I thought he had lifelong anonymity?'

'Me too.'

*

The scene on the streets surrounding Damian Walker's house was a mass of people, police officers, journalists, cars and satellite vans. The bright white lights from the top of the video cameras burned bright in the evening sky as reporters did their pieces for the local and national news. Hundreds of people were massed behind a taped barricade that looked flimsy to say the least. They were bundled up in coats, scarves and gloves, unworried about the dark and cold.

Jessica parked close to the nearby shop and edged through the crowds, sensing their simmering anger that a known murderer had been placed in their community. As well as adults, there were children clinging onto their parents, scared stupid by the unfolding scene. There wasn't the same ferocity as in St Ann's Square but it felt like the bubbling, clinking lid on a pressure cooker, building and ready to pop.

The blue and white police tape stretched from tree to tree across the width of the road, manned by a dozen uniformed police officers who were glancing at each other nervously. If things were to kick off, they'd have no chance, but deploying a riot squad could make the situation worse, inciting a battle rather than preventing it.

Jessica flashed her ID card and they lifted the tape, allowing her through as a howl of protest went up behind. She heard the word 'Shame!' being shouted at her but didn't turn. Hopefully the ill-feeling would ebb away when the temperature dropped a few more degrees, though she couldn't help but wonder where the Manchester rain was when it was really needed. A well-timed deluge would send the protestors scattering.

Far from anonymous, Walker's house was under siege. Three marked police cars were directly outside, with officers hurrying in and out. At the very least they were *looking* busy, which was half the battle when the news crews were around.

Topper was leaning against the garage, wearing a long trenchcoat like a flasher. 'How's your Friday going?' he asked.

'Spiffingly,' Jessica replied, before nodding to the house. 'What happened?'

'Someone put his name and address on the Internet and it went viral.'

'Do we know who?'

He shrugged. 'I'm not sure it matters – as long as it wasn't one of us. It went on the message boards of the *Herald*'s website at about half four and we didn't even realise. The paper says they don't have staff to monitor comments unless they're reported. Within half an hour, it had been copied and pasted all over the web. By the time we saw it, things were already too late.'

Jessica peered towards the open front door, her heart thundering, remembering the poor bloke some mob had tried to lynch. If they'd done that to someone innocent, what would they do to Walker himself? 'Did they get here before us?'

Topper stepped towards the house. 'Come on.'

He led her through the front door into the kitchen. Sitting in the centre of the table, in the same place Walker's bowl of Coco Pops had been a few days previously, was his electronic tag. There was a neat slice through the side of the plastic from where it had been sawn off.

Jessica wasn't sure if she was relieved. 'He made a run for it?'

Topper pointed towards the fridge, where there was a smear of blood across the floor. 'We're not sure.'

As they were looking around the scene, a uniformed officer bundled in behind them, out of breath. 'Sir . . .' He waited until Topper had turned. 'You're going to want to talk to one of the neighbours. She says she saw the whole thing.'

Jessica and Topper followed the officer out of Walker's house, across the road to a mirror-image house. The inside was eerily similar to Walker's but with more clutter on the walls. It felt lived-in.

The owner was a retired woman in a flowery dress and pinny. The kitchen smelled intoxicatingly of baked goods, the oven humming away in the corner. She fussed back and forth, leaning over to peer inside and then resting against the sink, offering them both cups of tea and then explaining that her grandchildren were coming over in the morning. Neither Jessica nor Topper had the heart to break it to her that it was unlikely anyone would be allowed into the area any time soon.

Topper was doing well to be diplomatic given the speed with which they needed the information. 'I gather you might have seen something happening across the road earlier today,' he said, talking as if they were having a cosy chat about a cat that had fallen off a bin.

The woman nodded. 'I had to pop to the shops for some margarine. I'd just got in when I heard them shouting.'

'Who was shouting?'

'I don't really know. They were next to a silver car across the road. I was at the back of the living room and didn't see much.'

'What did you see?'

'They were getting into the car.'

'*Who* was getting into a car?'

'Two fellas. It was hard to see, all a bit of a rush really. I was trying to get things into the oven. There was a white man and a black man.'

Jessica and Topper exchanged a glance: Walker and Clayton – and Clayton's silver Ford Focus.

'How do you mean, getting into the car?' Topper asked. 'Was there anything strange?'

'I'm not sure what you mean.'

'Say you and I were to go to a car, you might head for the passenger's side and I might go for the driver's. We'd both get in and close the doors. Was it like that?'

Her brow rippled before she started nodding. 'Now you mention it, I suppose it was a bit strange. They were both on one side and then the white man went round to the other. I think he was driving.'

'Was there anything else unusual?'

'Are you saying something bad's happened? I did wonder what all the commotion was over there. That house has been empty for ages. I assumed it was squatters or something.'

She clearly hadn't seen the news.

'Can you re-run everything through your mind and think about exactly what you saw?'

Her forehead scrunched into a series of wrinkles. 'Umm . . . the black one was holding his head. I thought he might have bumped it on the car roof but . . .' She scratched at her head. '. . . I suppose he could have been bleeding.'

'Why do you think that?'

'He was wearing a white shirt that had a red pattern – but maybe it wasn't a pattern.' She slapped her thigh. 'Oh, I *knew* I should have told someone. I didn't want to waste anyone's time. What do you think's happening?'

'Did you see anything else to make you think one man might have hurt the other?'

She screwed her lips together and then puffed out a short breath. 'There was something silver – only a flash. I thought it was car keys but perhaps . . . I suppose it could have been a knife. Is that what you think?'

Jessica looked through the kitchen door towards the front. It was quite a distance from the back of the woman's living room to where Clayton's car would have been parked and she didn't know how good the witness's eyesight was. It was as likely to be a knife as it was keys. Either way, it seemed possible Walker had kidnapped Clayton and driven off in his car.

'Anything else?' Topper asked.

She shook her head slowly before the oven started to ding, capturing her attention. Topper thanked her for her time and they headed back onto the street.

'Not exactly a concrete statement, is it?' Jessica said as they walked back towards Walker's house.

'Where's a proper neighbourhood busybody when you need one?'

There was a cry of annoyance from the back of the houses, where the protesting neighbours were massing and the cameras were filming. Jessica half-expected a gang of angry locals to pour around the corner, pitchforks in the air, but there was nothing.

'We'll have to get Clayton's number plate and then see if any of the cameras have seen it leaving the city,' Topper added.

'Was there anything else in the house?'

He shrugged. 'The house was empty by the time our lot got here and then we've had the mob outside to deal with. There aren't enough officers free because it's Friday night and most of them are on pisshead patrol in the centre. The front door was wide open and we don't know if anyone went into the house before we did. If there were any clues about where Walker was going, then they're not there any longer.'

'We're going to have to hope that number plate shows up some place soon.'

Topper fought back a yawn. 'Do you reckon we're that lucky?'

34

DC Ruth Evesham peered through the caravan windows towards the cabin opposite. She and Dave kept the main lights off, not wanting to make it too obvious they were in. She checked the time on her phone – exactly half past seven.

'He's off again,' Ruth said, turning over her shoulder towards Rowlands.

'Mark Atkinson?'

'Who else?'

'Perhaps he just likes an evening walk?'

Atkinson was dressed in the way he had been the previous evening, in a slim-fit fleece, with athletic trousers and walking boots. He closed the cabin door behind him and then stood by the boot of the car, talking to someone on his mobile phone. It was cloudier than it had been on previous nights, with only the merest hint of moonlight peeping through. The light from his phone screen lit up the side of his face, showing a peppering of stubble, though he was otherwise in shadow.

'What's he doing now?' Dave asked. He was sitting across from Ruth, with not enough room for them to peer through the same window together, not unless they were uncomfortably close and there was little chance of him letting that happen. Rubbing elbows was as good as cheating on his girlfriend.

'Talking on his phone.'

'Perhaps he's come out for a bit of peace?'

'He's been for a walk at the exact same time two evenings in a row. This would be the third.'

Dave was sipping from a cup of tea, looping his fingers through the handle for warmth. It did get bloody cold in the caravan and they hadn't risked fiddling with the gas in case it poisoned them during the night. Ruth had no idea why people came to a place like this for a break. A break from what? Presumably they had perfectly good houses with four walls and a roof, so why give that up to sit in a cramped tin box?

'You should follow him tonight,' Ruth said.

'Me?'

'I've lost him two nights in a row. I can't get close enough without him spotting me, so I've been hanging back but then he disappears.'

'Where can he be going?'

'I told you, I don't know.'

Ruth had been for a walk in the daylight, following the path in the direction Atkinson had headed for in the dark, yet she couldn't see where he might have gone. There were a handful of unremarkable caravans two or three deep between the path and the hedge marking the edge of the site but they all appeared to be the same. Ruth had skirted between them but there was no chance of examining each one without drawing attention to herself. There was a small wooded area beyond the boundary and a few thinner patches in the hedge through which Atkinson could have gone but Ruth didn't like leaving the caravan for too long. She and Dave had been dumped together to keep an eye on the Aktinsons, with a remit that was loose to say the least. The fact that Mark was disappearing for twenty or so minutes each evening might mean something but the priority was to avoid being seen watching the couple. Not only that, she and Dave were both struggling from the lack of rest. They were doing four-hour shifts overnight and through the morning, before eating together in the evening, but the broken sleep pattern was getting to them. The boredom was stinging, too. Aside from playing games on their phone and cards with each other, there was little to do. Phone reception was patchy, working perfectly at times and then not at all at others. They couldn't even risk reading anything substantial in case they lost focus on what they were supposed to be doing.

By a long way, these had been the most trying days of Ruth's career.

Mark Atkinson continued talking on his phone as Ruth glanced backwards at Dave. 'You're quiet.'

'You're not going to believe what's happened.' He looked up, eyes glinting. 'This is on the BBC News website – Walker's gone AWOL. Someone leaked his identity and he's taken off. They're saying he's kidnapped some protection officer. There's a full-on manhunt going on.'

He handed Ruth his phone and she scanned the article, before turning her attention back to Atkinson, who was still on the phone at the back of his car.

'Why didn't anyone let us know?'

'Dunno – perhaps they've forgotten we're here?'

Ruth turned around, eyebrows raised. 'Don't even joke. What did the guv say earlier?'

'Blah, blah, blah, he appreciates our efforts, it won't be forgotten. That sort of thing.'

'Any word on when we can get back to Manchester?'

'He didn't say. Presumably either when these pair go home, or when they find out who's been killing those women.'

'This is ridiculous. What are they doing up there?'

Dave didn't answer, continuing to read the article on his phone. Meanwhile, Atkinson hung up, turning in a semi-circle and then setting off along the path.

'He's walking again,' Ruth said.

'What can we do?'

'I want to know what he's up to.'

'He's probably just stretching his legs. I bet he has a routine at home where he goes out for a jog at half seven every night.'

'Why wouldn't he go out when it's light? Why not the morning? He and his wife haven't left the chalet all day. They're on holiday – why aren't they going out? There are cafes in the centre. Or, if he likes walking, they could be out hiking. All they've done is sit inside.'

Dave was distracted by his phone. 'Perhaps they're doing . . . y'know . . . ?'

'All day? They're not seventeen.'

'I don't know – it's good for us they're not going out, else we'd have to find a way to follow them. Either that or call in to say we've lost them. Their car's not left the spot they parked it in.'

The shape of Mark Atkinson was beginning to be swallowed up by the shadows, so Ruth tugged on her shoes and tied them tightly. 'I'm going out again.'

Dave suddenly seemed animated. 'Don't.'

'Why?'

'Because our number one thing is to not be seen.'

'Sod that. He's up to something.'

Before he could protest any more, Ruth was out of the caravan, dashing around to the front. The path formed a rectangle around the site, so, instead of following Atkinson, Ruth headed in the opposite direction. She'd lost him in a similar place on both previous nights and if she ran, she could go the other way around and get there before him.

She stayed on the path, trying to keep her footsteps light and not make too much noise. With the lack of light, it was difficult to see where she was going but there was enough of a difference between the path and the mushy uncut lawns for her to trace the route. Within a few minutes she was at the spot at which she'd lost Atkinson. There were a dozen caravans on each side, with wide spaces between them for cars to park alongside.

Ruth turned, looking for a spot to hide, and then edged onto the grass, feeling her feet sink as she stretched her hands out in front of her, trying not to bump into anything. Footsteps were echoing from tarmac somewhere nearby – surely Mark Atkinson – so she dashed ahead, squishing and sliding her way towards the hedge. She could feel the mud *in* her shoe, squelching between her sock and the sole. Ick. With little other choice unless she wanted to risk being seen, Ruth squeezed herself through the hedge. The spiky tendrils scratched at her hands, snagging on her clothes as she forced herself against them, pushing as hard as she could until she popped out on the other side, landing on her knees in a puddle.

'Hello?'

A man's voice was calling from the other side of the hedge, somewhere around the area from which she'd left. Ruth held her breath, not wanting a thin plume of air to drift above her, giving away her location. She slowly crawled away from the mud, edging up a grassy bank in absolute silence until she was behind a tree.

'Hello?'

The voice sounded again. It was surely Mark's, definitely not Dave's. Ruth was in a position where she could peer over the hedge back towards the park but it was so dark that it was difficult to make out anything but the block-like caravans. She thought she could see a person – Mark – before realising that it was a water butt wedged against the side of a caravan.

When she could hold her breath no longer, Ruth blew out as slowly as she could, using her muddied hand to shield her mouth from view. She counted to twenty, then fifty, but there were no other noises beyond the hedge and she didn't dare move. Being caught trailing Walker's surviving victim and her husband was the worst thing that could happen. DCI Topper would be disciplined at the very least and her and Dave's careers would be in the balance, not because they hadn't followed orders but because they were incompetent enough to be spotted. Policing was a complicated matter, especially for a CID officer. There were long lists of guidelines and rules, which were all very well and, for the most part, adhered to. But there were grey areas, too, and it was when working within those that there was one rule and one rule only: don't get caught. The best officers weren't necessarily squeaky clean – they just knew how to make it look that way.

Ruth continued counting. Eighty. Ninety. One hundred. Two hundred. When she was convinced there was no one on the other side of the hedge, she crept back down the bank, finding a spot in the hedge through which she squeezed, this time taking more care. She edged towards the path, squinting into the darkness in case Mark Atkinson was nearby. He wasn't, so she headed back to the caravan, feeling the weight of the mud and water clinging to her clothes.

As soon as she arrived back, Dave was on his feet. 'Where have you—?' He stepped away when he saw how dirty she was. 'What happened?' he asked.

'I fell in a puddle.'

He jabbed a thumb towards the cabin. 'He's been back for a while. Went straight inside and hasn't come out. Were you spotted?'

'I don't think so. Now, if it's all right with you, I'm going to take a shower.'

'Okay.'

'And Dave . . .'

'What?'

'You're following him tomorrow.'

35

Jessica had headed home to bed a few minutes after eleven on Friday night when it was clear there'd be no immediate news of where Walker had disappeared. She woke up early, half-expecting her phone to ring, and then sat in bed watching the morning news. The stations were full of up-to-date pictures of Walker, all pretences of his new identity gone as they reported that he'd kidnapped a protection officer and taken off. As far as Jessica knew, the press office wasn't briefing that he was responsible for the killings of the two young women that week, but it made little difference because people were drawing their own conclusions anyway. Jessica was supposed to be on a day off but there was little chance of that happening.

Her phone started to ring at a few minutes to seven. She was expecting Topper or Blaine Banner but the name flashing on the screen was far more surprising than that. Jessica thought about ignoring it before changing her mind.

'What do you want, Helena?' she said.

Bex's mum was whispering, her voice slightly slurred. 'Jessica?'

'You know it's me.'

'Sorry, um . . . last night. I'm sorry about that.'

'Fine. Apology accepted. I'm sorry too. Whatever you want. Do you know what time it is?'

Helena didn't seem to hear her. 'Look, I've been asking around my old crowd for weeks. Don't worry, I'm not using again but I know people who know people, if you get what I mean.'

Jessica sat up straighter, suddenly interested. 'Are you all right?'

'It's not that – one of my old mates came round last night. He reckons he saw her.'

'Bex?'

'Who else?'

'Where?'

'He couldn't remember. I showed him a picture but he was pissed off his face. He was certain it was her, though. I would've called but . . .'

'Where is he now?'

'He's on my sofa. Can you get here?'

It was a few minutes after seven and Jessica wanted to be at the station for half eight at the latest in order to make the morning briefing.

'I'll come right now,' Jessica said.

'Hey – there's one more thing.'

'What?'

'He's a bit, well . . . dodgy. You can't nick him or anything, he'll never speak to me again.'

Jessica was scrambling on the floor for a pair of socks. 'Fine.'

*

Helena lived on the top floor of a two-storey block of flats not far from Hyde Road, close to the greyhound and speedway stadium. There was a row of eight white-fronted flats on the ground floor, with eight more above and then a parallel row opposite. The two buildings were separated by a patch of lawn strewn with washing lines.

All thirty-two apartments were maintained by a collective of charities and the council, who were sponsoring the drug- and alcohol-free project. The residents were all former addicts, given somewhere to live for a period of time in which to get their lives together. Helena should have already moved out but had been given a grace period because of what had happened with Bex. Alcohol was banned, with any breaches resulting in eviction. The rules were harsh but the rate of rehabilitation was high.

Jessica made her way to the upper floor, heading along the balcony and knocking on the double-glazed door of a flat in the middle. Helena opened it instantly, nodding Jessica inside without a word. She looked a mess, her hair dirtier than the night before. She didn't look as if she'd slept, eyes wired open through a cocktail of substances that were hopefully legal.

'He's in there,' she hissed, pointing at the living room.

'Are you—?'

'I'm fine. Talk to him. He needs to be gone before inspection.'

'What's his name?'

'Leon.'

The living room was a stinking mess. There were two curry tubs on the floor, sticky brown goo welded to the sides, with a sprinkling of yellowy rice scattered nearby. More worryingly given the terms of Helena's residency, there was a pair of empty vodka bottles lying close to the window. Jessica peered from the bottles to Helena, who offered a knowing shrug. Helena picked up the takeaway tubs and fished a pair of forks from underneath the armchair before disappearing towards the kitchen.

Apart from the mess, the other thing of note in the living room was the man lying face-down on the sofa, crocheted blanket stretched across his back. He was mixed-race, the movement of the breath in his chest making it look like he was doing press-ups without trying. A pile of clothes was on the floor next to him.

'Leon.'

He didn't move, so Jessica crouched next to him, hand on his back, speaking a little louder.

'Leon!'

He groaned, head rocking from side to side. 'Ugh.'

'Wake up, Leon.'

He moved in a flash, rolling onto his back and grabbing Jessica's wrist, *squeezing*. 'Who are you?'

Jessica wrenched herself away, using her free hand to shove him in the chest. He was strong, his arms and torso toned. The blanket lay across his lap but he was otherwise naked.

He stared at Jessica. 'H? Where are you?'

'Helena's busy.'

'Who are you?'

'I'm someone looking for her daughter – Rebecca, or Bex. I'm told you've seen her.'

Leon scratched his chin, where there was a thin rash of stubble. He was in his twenties, far younger than Helena. Almost creepily so. 'You're five-o, aren't you?'

'I'm what?'

'Five-o. Old Bill.' His gaze shot guiltily down to his pile of clothes. 'Bollocks to this.'

He reached for his clothes but Jessica kicked them away, scattering them across the floor and exposing a polythene bag of greeny-grey flakes. They both looked at the bag and then Leon snatched for it, throwing Jessica staggering backwards. She used the headrest of the sofa to steady herself and, as Leon lunged forward, Jessica booted his legs out from under him, sending him cannoning chin-first into the hard floor. Before he could do anything else, she was on him, straddled across his back, snapping her handcuffs around his wrists. He tried thrashing his legs, but without his arms he was like an upside-town tortoise.

'Are you going to sit still?' Jessica said.

'Piss off.'

'I don't have time for this, Leon. I only wanted to ask you about my friend but you had to be a dick about it.'

'Where's H?'

'Never you mind. Now, do you think you can behave?'

'I want my lawyer. I know my rights.'

She dug one of her knuckles into the base of his spine, pushing enough to make it hurt. 'You're not under arrest and you don't need a solicitor. All you need to do is answer a few questions.'

'What about the weed?'

The bag had squirted along the floor and was resting

against a chair leg. It was bundled into roughly the size of a tennis ball, a good few quid's worth. She knew she should call it in but, by doing so, it'd not only get Helena evicted, it would stop the man from telling what he knew. Jessica shifted onto the sofa as Leon rolled onto his back, grimacing as he slid into a sitting position, fighting against the cuffs. He was wearing a pair of boxer shorts and socks but nothing else.

'You're not going to get out of the cuffs,' Jessica said.

'Whatcha want?'

'I told you – I want to know where you saw my friend.'

'I'm hungry.' He glared at her, eyes narrow. 'I ain't talking till I've ate.'

Jessica moved to the back of the room, opening the door into the kitchen. Helena was sitting at the dining table, cupping a mug of tea.

'Can you put some toast on?' Jessica whispered.

'I need him gone.'

'I'll sort it.'

Two minutes later, Jessica was sitting on the floor next to Leon, feeding him the toast as he shuffled uncomfortably, complaining about the cuffs. When he'd finished eating, Jessica took out her phone and scrolled through the photos until she found the one taken of Bex on her eighteenth birthday. She was grinning, offering a peace sign to the camera, nose piercings glinting in the light. Jessica tilted her phone so that Leon could see the screen and then flicked through a couple more.

'Where did you see her?' she asked.

Leon's brow was furrowed, at least giving the impression he was thinking. 'I told H last night – I can't remember.'

Jessica nudged the bag of cannabis with her foot. *'Think.'*

'She got a spider's web?'

A tingle slithered along Jessica's back. She searched through her photos, finding one of Bex in a short-sleeved top and holding it up. There was a spider's web tattoo on the teenager's forearm.

'Aye . . . something like that. I don't really recognise *her*, but that tatt . . .'

'Where've you seen it?'

His nose twitched as he screwed up his face, trying to scratch it while unable to use his cuffed hands. 'Can you itch my nose, like?'

'You mean "scratch".'

'Whatever.'

Jessica leant in and scraped the side of his nostril, before he pulled away.

'I can't remember,' he added whinily.

'How long ago did you see it?'

'I dunno, maybe a month back?'

'And where were you a month back?'

He shook his head. 'I can't remember! I get around.'

Jessica nudged him with her knee, making him rock back and forth, unable to support himself. *'Name some places.'*

'I'm in Manchester a lot.'

'Where else?'

'I dunno . . . Birmingham, Newcastle. I was in London

last month. I had a weekend in Blackpool, then I was down in Bristol. I told you – I work all over.'

Jessica stared at him, not wanting to ask what the nature of his 'work' entailed. She could guess. 'I'm going to ask you one final time and I want you to give me a proper answer – *where* did you see her? Listing half the cities in the country doesn't help.'

He shifted backwards, breathing heavily through his nose and eyeing the bag of drugs. 'I'm pretty sure it was up here somewhere but I can't tell you what I don't know.'

'Which places are we talking?'

'Manchester, Liverpool or Newcastle. Maybe Blackpool – but that was a really hazy weekend.'

'And this was a month ago?'

'I suppose. I was down south for the summer, going round the festivals.' He wriggled on the floor. 'You gonna let me out now, or what?'

Jessica eyed him, wondering if he was lying. He could have made up anything and it would have been in his better interests to name a single place. He'd not done that, he'd been vague because it was genuinely all he could remember. Jessica couldn't believe Bex was in Manchester, certainly not the centre, so that meant Liverpool, Newcastle or Blackpool.

'Turn around.'

Leon did as he was told and Jessica leant down, unlocking the cuffs. He snatched his clothes from the floor, stuffing the bag of drugs into a large pocket of his hoody. Without another word, he ran for the door, moving so quickly that he almost tripped over the doorstep. He righted himself at the last moment and then slammed the door behind him.

After a few moments of silence, Helena crept in from the kitchen, hands behind her back. 'I didn't do anything with him. I'm still clean.'

'I don't care.'

'What did he say?'

'Does Bex have any links to Liverpool, Blackpool or Newcastle?'

Helena shook her head slowly. 'You'd know better than me.'

Jessica sighed, fearing that was the case. She didn't have a clue. 'I've got to go,' she said.

Bex's mum nodded at the empty bottles. 'Can you take those with you? Please don't be seen.'

36

Jessica made it to the station just in time for the morning briefing, which wasn't what she thought it might be. Instead of a team-wide update, Acting Chief Constable Aylesbury had commandeered DCI Topper's office, sitting behind the desk and taking a phone call as Jessica and Topper sat on the other side of the desk like a pair of naughty schoolchildren.

Aylesbury was dressed down in chinos and a jumper, probably ready for the golf course. She could hear only his side of the conversation, which consisted of 'yes', 'I understand', 'absolutely', 'who said that?', 'well, you know what I think of her – if her brain was as big as her chest', 'I couldn't agree more', before he finished with, 'well, I don't bloody know where he is'. He slammed the phone down with an echoing thunk of plastic and metal.

'I'm supposed to be flying to Malaga tomorrow,' he said. If he was expecting sympathy, there was none forthcoming. 'This is a monumental balls-up. I don't blame you two, nor the officers at this station, but . . .'

He didn't finish the sentence, leaving it unclear who he did actually blame. It definitely wouldn't be anyone in senior management, and certainly not himself, considering he'd set up two investigations to essentially do the same thing.

Aylesbury nodded at Topper. 'What did the night reports bring in?'

The chief inspector fidgeted, uncomfortable at being displaced from his own desk. 'Officers went to Clayton Gordon's house but it was empty . . .'

Now it was time for the *really* bad news.

'From what we can tell, his wife is missing, too.'

Aylesbury gulped and Jessica didn't blame him. This was the first she'd heard of it. They didn't just have a missing witness protection officer, his wife had gone too.

'The rumours are true?' Aylesbury whispered.

'I don't know how the story got out, Sir. I didn't find out until I got in this morning. Her name's Sonia and we've had officers trying both their phones. There's no answer from either and no trace. We've spoken to her friends but no one's seen or heard from her.'

Aylesbury nodded quickly, scratching the back of his hand and clutching at invisible straws. 'Were they definitely together? No separation, divorce or anything?'

'Clayton told us about his wife the other day. He was looking forward to all of this being over so he could get back to her.'

'So, after Walker kidnapped Mr Gordon, he drove to his house and took his wife, as well?'

Topper's gaze flickered sideways to Jessica. 'We don't know – that's what seems likely. Sonia Gordon was six months pregnant, she—'

'Well, isn't that just brilliant?' Aylesbury slumped back into the seat in a huff.

Topper cleared his throat and then continued: 'We've

been going door-to-door on their street last night and this morning but reports are inconsistent. Some say they saw a silver car but they couldn't identify any distinguishing features. It's not as if silver cars are rare – plus that's Clayton Gordon's vehicle anyway. They'd have seen it regularly. We've not found anyone who can say with absolute certainty that they saw it yesterday.'

'What about traffic cameras?'

'A couple of sightings. We isolated the car about half a mile away from Walker's house but that was from last night, before any of our lot had got to the scene. There's two more near to Clayton Gordon's place, so there was every chance they were there. We're still trying.' He paused but Aylesbury didn't reply, so Topper continued: 'I spoke to the night team this morning for the handover. The working theory is that Walker flipped when he saw that his name had been leaked. He whacked Clayton Gordon, stole the car, and then drove to get Sonia Gordon for leverage.'

Aylesbury sighed, his morning of golf and holiday to Spain both in the balance. 'I've got to liaise with the press department, then get back to HQ. I need something to tell people – they're still fuming that Walker was placed back in Manchester, let alone that he's on the run. That's before we even talk about those two dead girls. Now we've got two kidnap victims. Three if you count the unborn child.'

Jessica could see the fear in his face – not that he was worried about the fate of Clayton or Sonia Gordon, more that he could see the permanent chief constable's job slipping away because this had happened on his watch. Typical.

'Why would he want hostages?' Jessica asked.

Aylesbury's gaze flickered to her, annoyed, before he focused back on Topper. 'Yes, why would he want hostages?'

'It's hard to say. He's not contacted anyone but we figure there might be a point when he'll make demands. Perhaps another new identity, perhaps safety. Perhaps . . .'

'Perhaps what?'

'Well, the latest attacks could have been him after all.'

Aylesbury's eyebrows shot up. As the go-between, he'd been assuring DSI Deacon that Damian Walker was *not* responsible for the attacks, trying to play a game of investigating Walker without making it look as if they were looking into him.

The tension was broken by the ringing phone. Although it was Topper's, Aylesbury snatched it up, gruffly answering with: 'Yes?'

This time, the single half of the conversation left Jessica cold, knowing something incredibly bad had happened. She watched Aylesbury's face sink, like a melting waxwork as he shrank lower into the seat. 'Are you sure that's what they're saying?'; 'Are they absolutely sure?'; 'Where did they get that from?'; 'Why didn't we know this earlier in the week?'; 'You tell them from me that this is on their heads.'; 'What? No – of course we're not telling the press.'

He slammed the phone down a second time, leaning back in the seat and breathing in noisily.

'When did this job become all about smart-arses in

white coats?' he said, not expecting, or getting, a reply. Eventually he added: 'They found a hair on Casey Graves's body from Monday night. It was a stray one that they missed on the first sweep because the rain had made it stick to her own. That's their story anyway.'

'Who does it belong to?' Topper asked.

Aylesbury blinked and looked up, hands clamped together. 'Who do you think?'

'Walker?'

'Correct – he must have got that tag off and killed her after all. One day, that's all it took. He spent all those years banged up, conning those idiot doctors, and the moment he got out, he was back to his old ways. You wait until I get that security tag lot on the line. I'll make sure everyone knows it was their mistake, not ours.' He paused, breathing heavily as neither Jessica nor Topper risked speaking. His career was disintegrating in front of them. 'At least we know why he took off with the Gordons,' Aylesbury added, though it was little consolation. He nodded at Topper. 'We've got to find Walker.'

He said it as if it was a brand-new idea no one had yet come up with. There was a killer on the loose and the chief constable thought it might be an idea if he was found. Genius. That was presumably the sort of insight which merited a six-figure salary.

'Every force in the country is looking for him,' Topper pointed out. 'The photos of him, Clayton Gordon and the car have been circulated as widely as we can manage. We're doing what we can but the expanded coverage makes it worse in some ways because everyone's phoning in and we're having to wade through everything to see what's plausible and what isn't. It's still very early on a Saturday. A lot of people won't be out of bed yet.'

'So we're relying on lazy people to get themselves up and put on the news? Perfect.'

Jessica thought it was a bit harsh to call people still in bed at half-eight on a Saturday 'lazy' but Topper had just about summed it up.

'What have your lot been doing all week?' Aylesbury added, eyeing Topper. 'You were supposed to be looking into Walker.'

Topper was doing magnificently in keeping his temper. 'We have been, Sir, but the records from seventeen years ago aren't as complete as we would've hoped. We've been checking properties he might have, places he lived, even areas he knew growing up. He was quite a loner back then and things aren't that different now. He has no family so there's not a lot of people we can run things by.'

'What about hospital feuds?'

'We've looked into that and couldn't find anything. As far as we can tell, he was a model patient. That's why they released him.'

Aylesbury was tapping on the table, looking for a way that the situation could be blamed on anyone who wasn't him. The security tag company were already going to be hung out to dry and now he had a second target. He wagged a finger unnecessarily. 'Those doctors, those bloody doctors. I hope they don't think they'll get off lightly in all of this. Someone made the decision to let him go and this is what he's done.' He snapped his arm forward, checking a chunky silver watch and then thrusting the chair back and standing. 'I've got to go. I have a conference call at nine, then the Home Secretary will want an update.' He reached the office door and turned as he opened it, offering a firm-sounding 'find him' before striding off along the hallway.

Jessica and Topper were alone, saying nothing as a second door banged from the far end of the corridor and then there was silence.

'I'm not even supposed to be here today,' Topper said.

'Me neither.'

'It's a good job he told us to find Walker, else we wouldn't have known.'

Jessica didn't laugh. 'Is there something you want me to do?'

'You don't have to be here.'

'If you are then so am I.'

Topper rounded the desk and took his usual chair, reaching down and fiddling with the height. 'I've not been in long. I had the morning handover then came straight here. I don't know who's downstairs, so just check everyone knows what they're doing. I'm sure they do.'

'Anything else?'

He winked. 'Find Walker. Deacon and his lot will be after him too, so there are more officers than we know what to do with.'

This time, Jessica did laugh. 'Good thinking – I'd not thought about finding him.'

She was on her feet, about to head downstairs when Archie walked past the glass. He knocked on the door and was waved in, turning to Jessica. 'I've been looking for you.'

'I'm on a day off, sitting at home watching cookery shows. Can't you tell?'

'I managed to get hold of someone at Ashworth this morning – a friend of a friend – and they did me a favour. We've been asking about people Walker might have fallen out with in hospital, people with a grudge, but I figured I could ask who he was on a ward with.' He glanced at Topper. 'Don't ask where it came from – but this is a list of names.'

He handed Jessica and Topper a sheet of paper each and she scanned the list of names. There were around twenty-five, all men.

After a few moments, Topper looked up. 'Have you found out anything in particular about these people? The names mean nothing to me.'

Archie turned to Jessica, saying nothing. She wondered how he knew because it had happened before either he or Topper had started working at the station. 'I recognise one of the names,' she whispered.

Topper stared at her but Archie was looking at the floor. He knew.

'Who?' Topper asked.

'Randall Anderson,' Jessica replied. 'He tried to kill me.'

37

Visiting the secure hospital was uncannily similar to nip-ping into a prison for a non-cosy chat. Usually there would be a long list of hoops through which to jump but, with time at a premium in finding Damian Walker, Acting Chief Constable Aylesbury had spoken to whoever he needed and the paperwork for Jessica's visit had been rushed through.

There was a high wall around the hospital perimeter and, once inside, Jessica had to show her ID card and then pass through a metal detector. She left her jacket, bag and phone in a locker and followed the escort through to the visiting area.

The wide room was empty, with two dozen tables and chairs bolted to the floor and vending machines lining the walls. Jessica picked a table in the middle, sitting and waiting with her eyes closed. It had been seven years since she'd last seen Randall Anderson. That was the name by which she knew him but he'd been originally Nigel Collins. He'd killed at least four people and then cornered Jessica in her own flat and almost murdered her too. It was one of her first major investigations but so much had happened since that there were large parts that felt like a dream. There was so much she would have done differently if she had the chance to go back.

There was a clunk of the door and then Jessica peered up to see two men in dark blue uniforms marching into the room, shoulder to shoulder. They were big and burly arse-kicking types but without the obvious handcuffs of a prison guard. As they neared her, they parted, revealing the man behind. His eyes locked instantly onto Jessica's, as if he'd been waiting all this time for her. He wasn't secured: no handcuffs, nothing around his legs, no imminent threat of a tasering if he did something out of line.

Randall still had the good looks that had attracted Jessica's friend Caroline. He was a little under six feet tall, his head shaven, with glimmering cobalt eyes the colour of the ocean in Photoshopped holiday brochures. He was wearing jeans and a T-shirt, with a spiky tattoo peeping out from his top on his right arm. He'd lost some weight – mainly muscle – with the ripped shoulders and upper arms replaced by a slightly skinnier appearance.

He sat opposite Jessica, planting both hands onto the table palms down. She found herself staring at them, remembering his fingers around her throat before she realised what she was doing. She looked towards the back of the room. The porters, nurses, guards, or whatever they were had retreated to the doors with a nod of acknowledgement in Jessica's direction and were busy sharing a Toffee Crisp. Usually it would make Jessica feel hungry, but her throat was dry, her thoughts cluttered. For a moment, she couldn't remember why she was there.

'This is cosy.' Jessica zoned back into the room as Randall spoke. 'You're looking good,' he added.

Eye contact could be an incredible weapon when used

in the right way. When Jessica was in an interview room with another officer, they'd work together, collective gazes barely leaving a suspect, making him or her feel they had nowhere to escape. Here, the roles were reversed. Jessica could feel Randall watching her, wanting her to return the stare. He made it feel like the room was smaller than it was, the walls edging closer, no longer a huge visiting room, instead a small cell containing just the pair of them.

'Do you know how many visitors I've had in the past seven years?' Randall asked.

Jessica didn't reply.

'None – having no family does that to you. When they came to me this morning and said I had a visiting request, I thought it was a wind-up. They're not big on jokes in here but I figured one of my new friends around here had arranged something. Then they told me the name. They said it was up to me, that the request was urgent but that the decision was mine. How long do you think it took for me to say "yes"?'

Jessica could still feel the tug of his stare, willing her to look away from the vending machines and at him instead.

'I don't care,' she replied.

He clicked his fingers. 'That long. I've been hoping for so long that you'd come. I even asked my doctor a year or so ago to see if he might reach out to you. He said I wasn't ready but then here we are. Funny how things work out.'

'I'm not here for a conversation.'

'What if that's why I'm here, Jessica?'

She had to stop herself shivering at the sound of her name. It slithered from his lips, finishing with a flourish.

'Then you'll be disappointed. I only need to ask you one thing.'

'I don't think I'll be disappointed. I'm recovered – ask my doctors. The only reason I'm here is because they don't think the public would be ready for my release. I'm hoping to move to a lower-security prison. Weekends out, evenings off, away-days. I can't wait.'

Jessica didn't know if there was any chance of that happening but the thought of running into him in the city centre was horrifying. She could still remember the weight of him on top of her, his fingers around her throat, the prickle of his stubble as his skin brushed against hers. She thought it was out of her system but it was only by sitting across from him that Jessica realised it wasn't.

Randall tapped his temple. 'They give me medicine that stops me thinking. I feel it in my mind, slowing me down. Sometimes I don't even remember her name . . .' He paused, waiting to see if Jessica would respond, before adding: 'How is Caroline?'

'That's none of your business.'

'I heard she got married . . .'

'I'm not talking about this. It's not why I'm here.'

'So why *are* you here?'

'You already know.'

'The Devil.'

Jessica could resist no longer, shifting her attention to the man across from her. He was smiling slightly, pleasantly even. If she didn't know who he was or what he'd done, she'd think he was a perfectly nice guy who wanted to say hello.

'We called him "The Devil",' Randall added. 'Because of the whole Damian thing. You must have seen *The Omen* with the devil child?'

'How well did you know Walker?'

'As well as you know anyone in here. You have to be careful about who you latch on to. You never know who might turn.' He rotated a finger around his ear and then leant in, whispering: 'They don't like you doing that around here.'

Jessica knew he was toying with her, playing up to the image of a man in a secure hospital. There was no way he'd be behaving in such a way if his doctors were nearby. At the realisation that he was acting, Jessica sat up a little straighter, feeling more in control. She'd been a different person seven years ago – she'd gone up against bigger and better people than Randall Anderson since. He was no one to be afraid of.

'You had things in common with Walker?'

'I suppose. Neither of us remembers the crimes of which we were accused.'

He was looking for a reaction. Neither of them was simply *accused* of crimes, both of them were guilty.

'You don't remember what you did?'

'I was overwhelmed by grief at the time. It's all a blur. Like when you wake up and can't quite remember the last dream you had. Damian succumbed to the drugs but his situation was similar. We had a lot in common.'

On entry to the hospital, Jessica had been told not to engage with Randall about his crimes but she was struggling not to be pulled in. She tried to be sympathetic when it came to issues of mental health, to believe that doctors knew what they were talking about, but it was hard to reconcile that with the carnage left in their wake.

'How long were you here with him?' Jessica asked.

'A year, perhaps longer. I was the first person he told when he found out he was moving to a different hospital. I was pleased for him.'

'Did he ever talk about places he visited? Somewhere he used to live? Holidays he used to take? That sort of thing.'

'Aah, so we're onto business already. What would it be worth if I told you?'

'What do you think I can offer you?'

'Answering a question with a question – classic diversionary tactics.'

Randall picked up his hands from the table for the first time, shifting in his seat and causing a squeak that made the two men by the door turn and look.

'Well?' Jessica asked. 'You can't think I can do anything about you being here – not that I would anyway.'

'So why are we talking?'

'You're here for rehabilitation, right? If you're better, if you've dealt with all the issues you had before, if you're a reformed character, why wouldn't you want to help another person in need?'

'Heh.' Randall was nodding. 'That's good – turn it around onto me. I thought you'd just threaten me, get angry and whack the table.'

'Maybe in the old days.'

'Who would I be helping?'

'Two people are missing, a husband and wife. They've been kidnapped by Damian Walker.'

'Hmm . . . that's a bit of a pickle, isn't it? I honestly thought he was being sincere. I thought he'd enjoy his freedom and make the most of being on the outside. Something must have happened.'

He started drumming his fingers, *tap-tap-tap-tap*, fishing for details.

'I don't have time for this,' Jessica hissed. 'They've been missing since last night.'

'So you're saying I have the fate of two people in my hands? I could be the difference between life and death? Wouldn't it be lovely and ironic if *I* was the one who saved them? With everything you must think of me? That would leave you with quite the sense of cognitive dissonance. You know what that is, don't you?'

Jessica pushed her own chair backwards. 'I've got to go.'

'It's when someone holds two contradictory opinions at the same time. You'd still hate me, but you'd have to be grateful, too. Wouldn't that be fascinating?'

'I'm going.'

He slapped the table lightly. 'You're not. It's why *you* came instead of someone else. How many people work with you? Tens? Hundreds? Anyone could have visited me – but it was you. If you didn't want to see me, to talk to me, someone else would be here.'

'Clayton Gordon and his wife Sonia – they're the couple who are missing. She's six months pregnant.'

'So I'd be saving three lives? It gets better.'

'Do you know anything about where Walker might be, or don't you?'

'It's not a yes or no question. I'd have to say . . . *maybe.*'

'So tell me.'

This time the eye contact was mutual – and Jessica knew she had him, playing up to his ego. She didn't care if his giving the information was self-serving and if Randall thought it would provide redemption, she just wanted it.

'There was a farm that Damian used to talk about.'

Randall swirled his hand, making it look as if he was searching for the details, even though Jessica could see that he was still acting.

She waited.

'I think about you a lot, Jessica. You and Caroline in that little flat. I don't suppose you're still there now but it's nice to think of the pair of you. I often wonder how close you were as friends. Were you friends, or *friends*?'

'Are you done?'

'It's kept me company on many a night thinking of you both and what good friends you were.'

'The name.'

'Why so hasty? I've been waiting such a long time for this little tête-à-tête.'

'Do you know the name of the farm?'

'Are you going to return? I'd love to talk again. We could make it a regular thing. I wonder if my doctor might think it cathartic?'

She could see that he knew something else about the farm, the name or the location, but this would be the last time they saw one another. It was no wonder he was trying to draw it out. Just a few more seconds, a bit more patience. Hold on to the anger . . .

'Jessica . . . ?'

'What?'

'Will you be back?'

'For what reason?'

'To allow you to see how much I've changed and how sorry I am.'

'You can show that by telling me what you know.'

He nodded. 'If I'm able to help you, I'd like to see you afterwards so that you can talk me through it.'

'Your doctor would have to make that decision.'

'He was fine with it this morning – let's assume he will be again.'

Randall looked at her expectantly, leaving Jessica to wonder if it was a game after all. Was he trying to manipulate her, or did he genuinely want her to see that he'd changed. Did it matter?

'We'd have to see – there are a lot of hypotheticals.'

For a moment, neither of them said anything, then the silence was broken by the sound of the bin lid clunking close to the door. One of the porters had discarded the chocolate wrapper.

'It's as good as you're going to get,' Jessica added.

Randall was nodding slowly again. 'It's named Patchworth. I believe it belonged to one of his stepfathers. Did you know he had four dads growing up? His actual one left when he was a baby. His mother never remarried but she had a succession of boyfriends. All off the books for benefits purposes, of course. As soon as Damian became comfortable with one, she moved on to the next. What do you think that would do to a young person? The upheaval, the lack of a father figure. It's all about outcomes for you, isn't it? No thought about why a person may do what they do.'

'Where is it?' Jessica asked.

'No idea – perhaps you can tell me when you return?'

38

As it was, Patchworth Farm was ridiculously easy to find. After retrieving her things, Jessica called DCI Topper from the hospital's car park to give him the information. By the time she'd reached the main road, her phone was ringing with details of where they were off to next. With the time it had taken to set up the visit with Randall, it was now late afternoon, the sun beginning to dip on what had been a surprisingly pleasant day. The clocks were due to go back that evening, which would only make the daytimes feel shorter. She'd never really understood why the clocks couldn't stay forward, giving everyone a little more daylight in the afternoons. The only explanation she'd heard was something to do with Scottish farmers. Well, bollocks to them – it wasn't even half five yet it was nearly dark. Twenty-four hours later and it'd be as bleak at half four. Ridiculous.

Jessica drove south, following the motorway ring road until it turned into winding country roads, overgrown hedges blocking the remains of the daylight. Jessica continued following Topper's directions, out of Manchester and into the borders of the Peak District around twenty-five miles south east of the city centre. It didn't take long until she knew she was in the right place. Two large police vans were parked on the verge, blocking one side of the road, with an unmoving convoy of marked cars behind, including an ambulance in the centre.

Jessica parked at the back, showing the officers her identification and slipping between the cars until she found herself at a stile. A large group of officers were on the other side, hidden in a field under the shadow of an ancient tree. Topper was by himself, the bottoms of his trousers caked with filth from the muddy field. He looked as tired as she felt, with the fact he was there at all testament to the pressure he was clearly under. He should've been at home, on the sofa with his other half, watching some delusional nobody sing a bad cover version. Instead, he was literally mucking in, hoping it would soon all be over. Go in, rescue Clayton and Sonia Gordon, arrest Damian Walker, charge him for the two murders and the kidnap and then go home. Easy peasy.

Yeah, right.

'I was wondering if you'd be here in time,' Topper said.

'Where's the farm?'

He pointed past the tree towards the outline of a tall building.

'Why are we waiting?' she added.

'We don't know if there's anyone there. One of our lot crept along the hedgerow but there were no cars at the front and no sign of movement. It's not been a working farm in a long time. There's a for sale sign at the front.'

'Did you find out who it belonged to?'

He shook his head. 'We got a name but there's no connection to Walker.'

'Randall told me it was a glorified stepdad. A boyfriend of Randall's mother.'

'That might be the case. He could have been feeding you a story.'

Jessica took a breath, nodding slowly. She'd been thinking that too.

'What's the plan?' she asked.

'For us? Sit back and wait. There's a tactical firearms team who are going in.'

'In where?'

Topper pointed towards the tree again. 'There's a farmhouse on the other side. It's dark and we don't think there's any electricity.'

'Do we know the floorplan?'

'We don't know anything. We're not even sure if it's two floors and an attic, or three. Our scout got a few photos but he had to keep himself out of sight.'

Jessica pushed herself onto tiptoes but could see little over the hedge other than the vague outline of the angled beams that signalled the very top of the house.

Underneath the tree, the firearms team were receiving their briefing. They were all dressed in padded dark clothes, ninjas in the night, ready for the word go. The sun had almost disappeared, with perhaps five or ten minutes until everyone was ready. If they had known for sure that Walker was inside, they'd have already gone. It was always a nervy moment when tactical firearms teams were involved, with so much that could go wrong. Ideally, there would be no shots fired on any side.

With the signal given, the figures in black ghosted

towards the road, with Jessica having to squint to see what was going on. They massed at the back of the vans, handing out the weapons and night-vision equipment. When they were done, the commander turned to Topper, offering a pair of the goggles. 'Want one?'

'Do I have to sign anything?'

'In triplicate if you can. We only accept blood.'

He tossed them across to Topper and then found another set for Jessica, before giving them a headset each. When they were ready, everyone moved along the lane towards the entrance to the farm, the firearms officers each clutching a machine gun across their chests. Considering the size of the boots being worn, there was a surprising grace to the team's movement, like a group of trained ballet dancers working to a routine. With the goggles on, everything appeared in shades of green, real life brought down to the level of a computer game. One of the men opened the gate and the firearms officers moved through one by one in quick succession. Jessica and Topper were at the back, walking past the crusted 'Patchwork Farm' sign that was being engulfed by the overgrowing hedge.

The farmhouse was as ramshackle as Topper had suggested. At one time, it would have been a glorious creation, with long lines of steepling windows across two floors and pointed turrets at the top. Since then, the chimney had collapsed, leaving a small stack of bricks protruding from the top, with at least as many slates missing as remained. There was a large courtyard at the front, covered with mud, straw, grass and dust. Next to the house was the rusting frame of a tractor, its tyres deflated and useless. Off to the side was a large barn, its wooden roof riddled with holes as winding vines stretched across the surface.

The firearms team moved in such unison that Jessica was left feeling like a spare part, standing towards the edge of the courtyard. A handful of officers darted around the line of the hedge towards the back of the house, more swarming towards the front. A few others headed for the barn before the message hissed through over the headsets that there was a silver Ford Focus on the inside.

It was really happening – Walker was here. Not only that, they never would have found him without Randall Anderson's help.

He could still shove his cognitive dissonance up his arse, though. Jessica knew what he was and had no mixed feelings about him.

She focused on the house, to where the officers had taken up positions. There was a series of confirmations over the headsets that everyone was ready and a few moments of silence.

Then the shouting started.

39

A battering ram thundered through the front door, sending splinters of wood spinning in all directions as the officers poured inside, shouting at the inhabitants to get on the floor. There was a series of bright white sparks – disorientating flashbang grenades thrown by the officers – and then smoke began to pour from the smashed windows.

DCI Topper started to walk slowly towards the scene, hands in his pockets, though Jessica could tell he was nervous from the way his shoulders were tensed. He probably had his fists clenched. She was anxious, too, counting the seconds as the officers' boots boomed across the hard floor. It had been three seconds . . . four . . . since the flashbangs had gone off and no further shots had been fired.

Thump-thump-thump.

Jessica could hear nothing through the headset but the sound of the officers pouring through the house. Still the smoke seeped through the shattered windows.

Topper was whispering under his breath, nervous enough for the pair of them. 'Come on, come on . . .'

'Down! Down!'

A man's voice echoed through the radio before a few seconds of silence and then, finally, 'Target secure.'

'Is it Walker?' the commander asked.

'Confirmed, Sir. Suspect is in custody.'

'Any sign of the Gordons?'

There were more thudding boots and then another silence, definitely longer than the first, agonisingly so, before a second voice replied: 'Confirmed, Sir. Gordon is secure.'

Whew. Get in.

Topper advanced towards the door, Jessica just behind. Beyond, there were bare floorboards and the remains of a kitchen. An oven and fridge stood at one end, the once white fronts crusted with dust and dirt. A solid wood dining table was pushed up against a wall that had paper peeling from the top. A handprint was clear in the centre of the table, framed by the coating of dust. There was a long row of cupboards around the walls, most of them without doors, stringy cobwebs clinging to the corners. A bottle of dust-coated washing-up liquid was sitting on the counter top but the kitchen was otherwise empty. Somewhere, there was a reality TV production company dying to do the place up.

Smoke was pooling at the top of the room but the air felt clear to breathe as they stood together, peering around the space. Topper removed his night-vision goggles and Jessica did the same, blinking as she tried to acclimatise to the low-level light. A dim bulb was glowing from beyond a door through which Topper headed.

They emerged into a hallway with a set of creaking wooden steps on one side. Jessica and Topper waited as a pair of officers led Clayton Gordon down the stairs. He was leaning on one of their shoulders for support and there was a gash on his head, the dried blood creating a crescent-shaped scab that arched across his eyebrow. His hair was encrusted with either dust or plaster, his expression dazed.

'Clayton?' Topper said.

The man looked to the chief inspector but there was little recognition.

'Are you okay?' Topper added.

Clayton stared through him.

'What happened?'

He responded with a croak but there were no words.

'Where's Sonia?' Topper asked.

At the mention of his wife's name, Clayton's eyes widened as he finally focused on them, attention switching from Jessica to Topper.

'Sonia?'

'Didn't Walker take her too?'

'I . . . yeah, he did . . . I . . .'

'Where is she?'

Clayton started to blink rapidly and then rub his eyes. He coughed something that Jessica didn't catch before stumbling into the officer who was supporting him. Topper nodded to the man, who hoisted Clayton slightly higher and then eased him slowly towards the kitchen.

Topper took the arm of the second officer, nodding upwards. 'Was there anyone else up there?'

The man readjusted his gun to aim towards the floor. No accidents here. 'It's clear.'

'What about the third floor?'

'It's an attic – we've been up but there's no one around. It's full of old junk.'

'Where was he?'

'Gagged and tied to an old radiator with some rope. Apart from the whack on the head, he seems all right. Probably just shock.'

'Okay, make sure the paramedics see him.'

The officer nodded and then moved into the kitchen, leaving Jessica and Topper alone in the hallway. They exchanged a glance with no words needed to convey their nerves. If Clayton Gordon was here, then where was his wife? The only point of relief – if it could be called that – was that they now knew for sure that Walker had kidnapped Sonia too. They'd been guessing before.

Topper turned to Jessica: 'Any word from that Evergreen caravan place?'

Jessica checked her phone but Rowlands hadn't called or messaged. 'Nothing. We can probably get them back.'

'Soon.'

Topper continued along the hallway, into what would have once been a living room. There was a fireplace with a pile of bricks at the bottom, plus a dust-coated flowery sofa. More to the point, there were half a dozen armed officers in a circle, their weapons aimed at Damian Walker, who was lying face-down on the floor, hands cuffed behind his back.

'Was he armed?' Topper asked.

'No, Sir.'

'Stick him on the sofa.'

Two of the armed officers yanked Walker to his feet,

lifting him across the room and plopping him on the settee. He didn't resist, going limp and allowing himself to be moved and then slumping forward into a sitting position and staring at the floor. Aside from a crusty rug in the centre and the bricks of the collapsed chimney, there were creaky exposed floorboards stretching across the rest of the room, with a tall lamp in the corner that had an old-fashioned dim yellow light bulb glowing at the top. It was the type that'd never pop but would leave a sizeable dent in an electricity bill. Walker was half in shadow, the wrinkles in his face seeming deeper and ageing him even further.

'You can leave us,' Topper said, offering the nearest firearms officer a 'thank-the-lord-no-one's-been-shot' look. The best firearm operations were always the ones in which not a single shot was fired, if only to save everyone from an awful lot of paperwork.

The officers moved out slowly through the kitchen and back towards the courtyard. If they were really lucky, someone would have magicked up a few flasks of tea as a reward.

There was an eerie silence gripping them as Jessica, Topper and Walker were left alone. From nowhere, her phone fizzed, cutting through the mood. It was a few minutes after six and Jessica peered down at Izzy's text message, before holding it up for Topper to see.

'Ellie & Liam wedding went off without hitch. On evening news!!!'

Topper echoed Jessica's thoughts with a single raised eyebrow that said it all. After the week Jessica had endured,

Ellie and Liam were off earning tens of thousands from trashy magazines, while she and Topper were stuck in a creaky farmhouse with a murderer. Jessica would never be able to escape the sneaking suspicion that Ellie had played them all, despite the apparently heartfelt anguish of her blog. She didn't know whether to feel sorry for Liam, or figure he'd brought it all on himself.

The floorboards screeched as Topper stepped across until he was in front of Walker, towering over him. 'Where's Sonia Gordon?'

Walker was rocking back and forth, his hands cuffed behind him. He didn't look up as he answered: 'Who?'

'If you've done anything to her—'

'I don't know who you're talking about.'

'Look at me.'

It took a while but Walker did as he was told, shuffling backwards and grimacing from the awkwardness before peering up. He was taking his time in answering the question, wasting everyone's time.

'I'll ask you again,' Topper said. 'Where's Sonia Gordon?'

'I don't know who that is.'

'Clayton Gordon's wife – the clue's in the name.'

He shook his head. 'I have no idea what you're on about.'

Topper glared at him but the answer wasn't forthcoming. 'Right – you can wait there then.' Topper picked up his radio, telling everyone listening that finding Sonia Gordon was a priority and that they could tear the place apart.

Over the next hour and a bit, they sat listening as

officers ripped through the house, pulling apart boards and doors to find their way into the deepest reaches. Others were checking the barn, the fields and bushes beyond. All the while, Walker sat and stared, probably making the most of his final few hours on the outside. He said nothing except continuing to deny he knew who Sonia Gordon was.

Eventually, the sounds began to die down and the eventual message came through that she was nowhere to be seen.

Topper took a deep breath and turned to Walker. 'Where is she?'

'I don't know who she is. If I did, I'd tell you.'

'You kidnapped Clayton Gordon and drove him here . . .'

Walker huffed out a sigh. 'I wouldn't say "kidnap".'

'What would you say?'

'I sort of . . . borrowed him.' He glanced from Topper to Jessica, looking for sympathy. 'Someone knocked on the door and asked if I was Damian Walker. I said no but there was no sign of you lot and I panicked. Clayton wouldn't let me leave and one thing led to another and . . .'

'. . . you hit him on the head.'

Walker shrugged. 'I s'pose. I wanted to get to somewhere I knew would be safe. By the time I started thinking straight, it was a bit late.'

He could say that again.

'If you were thinking straight, why did you tie him to a radiator?' Topper asked.

Walker was fidgeting, squirming around on the sofa like

a rodent with an itch. 'He was trying to talk me into letting him go, saying it would all be okay, but I knew it was all over. He was talking gibberish, saying I'd made an angry mark and condemned him as well as me. He wasn't making much sense and I couldn't think straight.'

Jessica glanced at Topper, then back to Walker. 'An angry mark?'

'That gash on his head, I suppose. I didn't mean to hit him that hard but he kept going on, saying I couldn't leave. It was instinct. He didn't stop talking to himself up there – that's why I gagged him. He was mumbling for hours and then shouting. I was telling him that I didn't want to hurt anyone but he's a bigger nutjob than they say I was.'

That seemed unlikely.

Topper replied: 'So you didn't go to the Gordon house?'

Walker shrugged. 'Why would I? I don't know where he lives. Look, I know I've messed up but this is just a blip. I need to see my doctor. We can get this straightened out. If you think about it, it's not such a big deal. I was under stress, people were coming to my house and you weren't there to help. It's all a misunderstanding . . .'

'A misunderstanding?'

'I didn't know what I was doing.'

'With Clayton or the two women?'

Walker's eyes narrowed as he looked from Topper to Jessica and back again. '*Two women?*'

'Casey Graves and Holly Jamieson. We know you killed them. That's why you kidnapped Clayton, isn't it? To make sure you had a hostage when you went on the run.

You realised you made a mistake.'

Walker's head was rolling, his wide eyes flashing between the two of them. He tried to stand but Topper shoved him backwards. Without his hands to support himself, Walker flopped onto the sofa.

'I told you, I didn't kill those girls.'

'It's over, Damian. You should never have been released. One of your hairs was found on Casey Graves's body. We know. There's no need to mess us around any longer.'

He shook his head ferociously. 'It wasn't me – I didn't kill her. I was in bed.' He nodded with his head, unable to use his hands. 'You planted it, or someone did. You want to fix me up.'

Topper shook his head. 'If that were true – which it isn't – we wouldn't have taken a week to find it. A small strand of your hair was matted by the rainwater within hers. If they hadn't gone through her scalp hair by hair, it would never have been found. There's no point in denying it. The evidence is rock solid with Casey and they're still looking at Holly's body. You killed them in the exact same way as you murdered your other four victims.'

Walker arched sideways, banging his head into the armrest. 'No – the voices have gone. I've not touched that stuff in years. Ask Doctor Marwick, he'll tell you.'

Topper hoisted him up straight. 'I'm not going to ask you again, where's Sonia Gordon?'

Walker was still shaking his head, fighting to escape until Topper placed a forearm across his chest, pinning him to the sofa.

'I don't know who that is!' Walker protested.

Topper gave Jessica the nod, so she headed into the courtyard, signalling for some of the officers to come and remove Walker from the house. He wriggled the entire way as he was dragged and then lifted up by four men before being dispatched into the back of a van. Jessica and Topper stood in the farmhouse's doorway, watching the scene in front of them as the firearms team started to pack up, ready to go home for the night. If they were really lucky, it'd be the whole weekend.

'We're going to have to tear this place apart to try to find her,' Topper said. 'We were *this* close to having it all sorted.'

'Why would he deny taking Sonia Gordon? He admitted kidnapping Clayton. Well, more or less.'

'Who knows? Clayton confirmed she'd been taken. We'll have to ask him again if he has any idea where his wife is. Then we'll need search teams . . . it's going to be a long night.' He arched back, cricking his neck. 'Nothing's ever simple, is it?'

The courtyard was now illuminated by headlights and spinning blue lights as the various emergency vehicles manoeuvred their way around. Jessica and Topper walked towards the ambulance, where a pair of paramedics was sitting on the back step, chatting quietly to each other. They looked up as the two officers neared, smiling thinly.

'No shots fired,' one of them said.

'Thankfully,' Jessica replied.

'Do you still need us?'

'Where's Clayton?'

They both looked back blankly. 'Who?'

'The hostage – black guy.'

The paramedic pointed a thumb over his shoulder. 'Oh – he said he was fine. Last I saw he was walking that way.'

Jessica peered around the ambulance in the direction the paramedic had indicated – the barn. At first she walked slowly but then her pace quickened, with a desperate sense that they'd missed something. The door was on the far side but there were so many gaps in the walls that Jessica shoved aside a crooked plank and slipped inside. The space was enormous but dank, the air clammy and thick, clinging to her throat. A second rusting tractor was abandoned in the corner with piles of scrap metal up against the far wall. Jessica moved into the centre, turning in a circle and peering into the darkened corners before she clicked the button on her radio.

'Has anyone seen a silver Ford Focus?'

There was a pause and then: 'The one in the barn?'

'Right – except it's not here any longer.'

40

It was half-past-seven on the dot when Mark Atkinson went out for his usual evening stroll. Across the way as they sat in the darkness of the caravan, Ruth exchanged a glance with Dave letting him know it was his turn after her disastrous muddy escapade the evening before. They'd been at the caravan park for five days and it was a pathetic testament to their time there that a man going for a walk was the most exciting thing they'd spotted. Everyone's time was being wasted but Ruth couldn't lose the feeling that something was going on that they'd missed. It was probably innocent but there was still a mystery and, like any half-decent officer, she wanted to discover what it was.

Atkinson was walking slowly along the path, hands in his pockets.

'Shall I follow him?' Dave asked, sounding nervous.

'Up to you – you could head around in the opposite direction but it didn't do me much good.'

'I'm just a bit . . . heavy-footed. I make too much noise when I'm walking. Jessica says I go up and down stairs like an overweight hippo.'

'So walk on the tips of your toes.'

'I'm not very good at that either. I have balance issues – always have done, ever since school. We were doing this play of *Jack and the Giant Beanstalk* and I was supposed to be—'

'He's almost out of sight.'

Dave peeped through the window at the disappearing figure. 'You'll definitely be better at this sort of thing.'

'Yeah, that's why I fell in a puddle and came back covered in mud.'

There was little time to argue, so Dave hurried to the other end of the caravan and eased the door open before clicking it closed behind him. Ruth watched him scamper across the car park, dashing from shadow to shadow as he followed the route Atkinson had taken. It was fair to say that he wasn't an athlete. He moved with the grace of a drunken orang-utan with one leg shorter than the other before being swallowed up by the darkness. She wondered if she should have gone, after all. This ridiculous operation was bound to be wrapped up by the end of the weekend.

Ruth cupped her hands over her eyes and gazed across the tarmac, past the Atkinsons' car towards the chalets. There was a narrow gap in the curtains of their flat, a flickering light beyond. If the rest of the week was anything to go by, Mark would be gone for at least fifteen minutes, leaving Ruth with a small window for a bit of a nose. She made her way out of the caravan as quietly as she could, keeping to the edges of the shadows as she looped a long way around the car park until she reached the side of the single-storey building.

From a distance it looked outdated and it was little better close up. The walls were speckled with raised dimples of pebble-dashing, with a black grimy smear of filth clinging to the base. The gutter was filled with leaves, creating a soiled pool of water that was bubbling with foam. Even in the middle of summer, this would be depressing, but in the cold and dark of October, it was even worse.

Ruth edged around the side of the building, feeling the prickles of the wall jabbing into her back. The Atkinsons' sporty-looking green hatchback was a few metres away, its rear window glinting from the sliver of light seeping through the crack in the curtains. She crouched, picking up a small stone and pinging it towards the vehicle. It ricocheted with a satisfying *thwick* but no alarm sounded, leaving her free to approach. Ruth had the cover of darkness but the angle of the moon made the spot directly outside of the Atkinsons' flat lighter than anywhere else in the car park.

Typical.

She crept closer to the window, staying low and trying to avoid the grittier areas of the car park. The slit between the curtains was narrow but Ruth managed to manoeuvre herself into a spot that allowed her to peep from side to side, gazing into the living room of the flat. Anne Atkinson was sitting on the sofa, legs curled underneath her, talking on a mobile phone. The device was wedged between her shoulder and ear, allowing her to move both hands around animatedly.

Across the room, the television was showing the news – some story about a political visit, nothing particularly interesting. The rest of the living room seemed bare and cold: basic furniture and unimaginative prints to decorate the walls. On the table in front of Anne was a pile of board games, Mouse Trap, Guess Who? and Operation among others. It wasn't Ruth's idea of a relaxing getaway – but it was still better than the pack of cards with which she and Dave had whiled away their time.

Anne slipped her legs out from underneath her and took the phone into her hand, leaning forward and nodding. She was smiling, delighted at whatever she was being told. Ruth tiptoed closer to the window, ducking underneath the glass and straining her ears, trying to catch anything that was being said. Whoever owned the park couldn't clear the gutters, clean the walls, or generally tidy up – but the bastards had installed windows so bloody thick that they kept all the sound in.

Ruth glanced down at her watch – seven minutes had passed since Mark Atkinson had left the apartment and if he was genuinely out for a brisk walk and wasn't stopping, it wouldn't be long before he returned. Ruth backed away a few steps and risked another peep through the gap in the curtains to see Anne standing with her back to the window. Acting on instinct, she stepped forward until her nose was practically touching the glass of the window, giving her a complete view of the inside. Tucked against the far wall were a pair of packed bags and a small suitcase, with coats draped across the top.

Sticking to the shadows, Ruth looped back around the car park, heading for the caravan opposite. If Anne and Mark Atkinson were leaving that evening, should she call someone? Or wait until they actually left?

Ruth scrambled up the steps to the door of the caravan,

easing herself inside and finding her spot on the sofa next to the window. Her earlier attempts at avoiding the mouldy damp patches had been long forgotten. If she was going to get some sort of respiratory infection, then she'd already have it. She could sue the park owners, her employers and, if possible, Wales, at a later date.

For a few minutes, nothing happened. Ruth kept an eye on the car park, while glancing away to her watch at regular intervals. Fifteen minutes passed, then twenty. This was as long as Mark had been away for on previous days. Assuming he was sticking to his routine, he should be back any moment.

Except that he wasn't.

The clock ticked around to five to eight, then eight o'clock, but there was still no sign of either him or Dave. Ruth thought about calling Dave's phone but the dozy sod had probably left the volume up and the sound would give away his position. If they were lucky, he was currently hiding somewhere in full view of whatever was going on.

At three minutes past eight, Mark strode past the caravan into the car park. Ruth shrank away from the window as he turned to peer over his shoulder, anxiously looking from side to side. The lights were off inside the caravan and she was fairly sure he couldn't see her, but there was something about the confusion in his eyes that left her panicking too. He stopped next to the car, one hand on the bonnet, as he scanned the darkness. After a few moments, he checked his watch and then headed into the flat.

Ruth waited. Four minutes past eight. Five past. No sign

of Dave. Ten past, quarter past: still no sign. She took out her phone and found his name in her contacts book, pressing to call. For a moment nothing happened and then there was a vibrating sound from underneath the coffee table. Ruth crouched and picked up his phone, seeing her own name on the screen. She ended the call, pocketing both phones and then exiting the caravan. Worried that either of the Atkinsons could leave the flat and spot her, she retreated around the back of the caravan, moving quickly until she was at the far corner, eclipsed by the shadows but with a full view of the block opposite. Ruth started backing along the path, knowing she couldn't go on a loop of the park by herself because someone had to keep watch. With short glances over her shoulder, she continued moving until she reached the junction where the path turned at a right angle and stretched deeper into the park. She could just about still see the block, where the cabin door remained closed, the car untouched. Ruth turned, squinting into the distance towards the long rows of caravans. Dave should have been on his way back but he was nowhere in sight. It was half past eight and he'd been gone for an hour.

'Dave!'

Ruth's voice hissed into the distance, echoing slightly among the empty metal boxes.

'Rowlands!'

Nothing. Where on earth could he be? She'd pushed through the hedge, fallen in the mud and hidden behind a tree without taking this long to get back to the caravan.

'Dave!'

She edged back and forth, trying to keep an eye on the flats while at the same time giving herself a better view of the caravans further in the distance. The moon was freckled by clouds, not as bright as it had been on previous evenings, but she could still see a fair way along the path yet there was no sign of any movement at all, let alone DC Rowlands.

'Crap.'

Ruth mumbled under her breath and then scampered back towards the caravan. She couldn't watch the Atkinsons and look for Dave at the same time, but keeping an eye out was the one thing for which she was there. If Dave was stuck in a gully somewhere, he'd have to get himself out.

Just as she reached the corner of the caravan, Ruth froze, pressing herself against the metal and feeling the cold through her clothing. Mark Atkinson was in the doorway of the flat with a bag under his arm. He plipped open the car and then dropped it in the boot before heading back inside. In a flash, Ruth dashed into the caravan, throwing herself onto the sofa and peeping through the window to the car park beyond.

Anne and Mark Atkinson were ready to head home.

41

Jessica walked around the perimeter of the barn in case she'd missed an alcove somewhere. The place had already been searched when the team was looking for Sonia and there were few hiding places. Topper was at her side, saying nothing, which only made her feel more nervous.

As they reached the gap in the wall through which they'd entered, he finally spoke in a whisper. 'Why would Clayton have left?'

'What if Walker didn't kidnap his wife after all?'

'If he didn't, then where is she?'

Jessica took out her phone and checked the time – it was just after half past eight and they'd been hanging around the site for three hours. She scrolled through the home screen and dialled DC Rowlands, muttering 'come on' under her breath. After five rings, the phone was eventually answered – except not by him.

'Dave's phone,' a woman whispered.

'Ruth?'

'Is that DI Daniel?'

'Well, yes – Jessica – what's going on?'

There was a sigh and then Ruth replied: 'It's all a bit of a mess. I don't know how much Dave's told you but Mark Atkinson has been going for a walk every evening. He does a loop of the caravan park. We've been trying to follow him – well, *I* have – but he disappears two-thirds of the way round.'

'What do you mean, disappears?'

'I don't know. There's not really anywhere for him to go. There are a lot of caravans and then a hedgerow with woods beyond. Dave went out this evening to follow him but he's not come back.'

'How long ago?'

'About an hour. Mark's only usually out for about twenty minutes, not even that. He was gone for over half an hour tonight.'

'Where's Atkinson now?'

'He's back – I think he and Anne are getting ready to go, they're putting bags in the boot. I don't know what to do.'

Jessica glanced sideways at Topper and then across towards the police van. 'Are they leaving right now?'

'No, he put a bag in the boot and then went back inside. I'm not sure what they're up to.'

'I'll call you right back.'

Jessica hung up, quickly told Topper what was going on and then dashed across to the police van. Walker was sitting inside one of the cages, hands now cuffed in front of him with his elbows resting on his knees. He glanced up, peering towards Jessica and Topper as they climbed inside.

'What do you want now?' he asked.

'You said Clayton was mumbling incoherently – that's why you gagged him.'

'Believe me, don't believe me. I don't care. You've already fixed me up.'

'What was he saying?'

Walker stared back at her, shaking his head. 'What docs it matter?'

'I need to know.'

'It was nonsense.'

'You told us something about him saying you'd made an angry mark.'

'I told you. It was an accident – I didn't mean to hit him. We were in the kitchen and he was saying I couldn't leave. It just sort of happened and then he was bleeding.'

'Was he definitely talking about the mark on his head?'

Walker's face creased in confusion. 'What?'

'Could he have said something like, "You'll make Mark angry?", or something similar?'

He shrugged, forehead wrinkles rippling. 'I dunno. Call me what you want but I told you, he's a nutjob. He spent the whole time talking to himself. He's the one who needs help.'

'Think really carefully – what did he actually say?'

Walker didn't even pretend to make an effort, leaning back and raising his manacled wrists. 'Yeah, right – you want my help after all this.'

Jessica didn't have time to argue or barter. She backed out of the van, slamming the doors behind her and turning to Topper. His mouth was open as he ran through the same scenario she was imagining.

'What was it Clayton told us in Walker's kitchen that time?' Jessica asked.

Topper knew exactly what she was talking about. 'He said he wanted to be at home with his wife. I thought it was because he was working long days and having to sleep over at Walker's.'

'Me too. How long do you reckon it'd take to drive from here to that holiday park place in Wales? Three hours?'

'If you stuck to the speed limit. Less if you had your foot down.'

Jessica turned to look at the empty barn and then took out her phone again. It was answered before Jessica had even heard it ring. 'They're still in the flat. I'm not sure what's going on,' Ruth said.

'Any sign of Dave?'

'No.'

'Ruth, this is absolutely imperative. Whatever you do, you can't let that car leave.'

'What about finding Dave?'

Jessica glanced at Topper, who was saying nothing. Somehow she'd wound up making the decisions and she guessed he was feeling the pressure of having sent Rowlands and Evesham to Wales in the first place. Not only that, he'd wasted more than an hour by having the team pull apart the farm and its grounds looking for someone who most likely hadn't been there in the first place. It wasn't his fault, not really; a bad decision was easy to identify in retrospect.

'You're only one person,' Jessica said. 'Stop that car leaving and keep yourself safe. Dave will have to look after himself.'

'What if he's in trouble?'

Jessica took a breath. Rowlands was her oldest friend at

the station. He'd been there long before Topper, even before Izzy. Unbeknown to her – the detective who'd somehow missed what was directly in front of her – he'd spent years pining for her before giving away his real feelings. That had been when she was in love with Adam, when times were different and she wished he'd shut his mouth. They'd got past that, rekindling a friendship built upon piss-taking and not really growing up.

'He'll have to look after himself,' Jessica whispered, before hanging up.

42

Stop the car? What on earth did that mean? Ruth had no clue about anything to do with vehicles. Her car was something that got her from one place to the next. As long as she kept feeding it petrol and visited the garage once or twice a year, it kept going. She'd never really understand that band of men – *always* men – who banged on about horsepower-this and torque-that, not to mention cylinders, compressors, linkage, transmissions, beds, pumps and all the other bollocks.

Grow up, for God's sake. Her younger brother had stopped zooming toy cars around when he was ten.

She'd long figured that the more a man talked about engines, the smaller he would be in crucial areas. It was a classic case of trying to compensate. This was the one time she wished she had some petrol-headed bellend around. He'd come up with something simple about detaching the 'gravity belt', or something else that sounded made up. A simple flick of a switch that would disable the car without making it obvious it had been interfered with.

Ruth stared across the car park to where the cabin door was still open a fraction, as was the car boot. Being told to look after herself was one thing but how would it seem if she stayed put while the Atkinsons pulled away *and* her colleague was dying in a ditch somewhere? Words were cheap but it was actions that defined a career.

She crossed to the kitchen, hunting through the drawers until she found something close to a vegetable knife. The tip was pointed but barely left a mark on the sideboard as she stabbed it. The blade itself was blunter than a DC Archie Davey chat-up line.

Ruth crept out of the caravan, heading in the same loop as when approaching the block earlier. She was about to cross the car park closest to the main entrance gate when she froze, pressing back into the hedge as Mark Atkinson emerged. He slung a second bag into the back of the car and then turned, calling something into the chalet. Moments later, Anne emerged with the suitcase. She handed it over and Mark wedged it into the back, slamming the boot with such force that it sounded like a gunshot. Ruth held her breath as the pair stood at the back of the car. For a moment, she thought they were going to get inside, meaning she was too late, but instead they headed back into the cabin and closed the door.

With no time to waste, Ruth tore across to the car, not bothering to stay low. She slid to a halt next to the back wheel closest to the petrol tank and dropped to the ground, keeping one eye on the flat as she removed the knife and slammed it into the tyre. The rubber was hard, fighting back against her, but Ruth was on her knees, pressing down with as much force as she could manage. Her arms were straining, burning from the effort before she stopped.

The cabin's door remained closed.

This time Ruth ran her fingers around the tyre, finding a space where the tread was at its widest. She squeezed the tip of the knife into the groove, levered herself up and then jammed down, putting her entire body weight on the weapon. For a moment, it felt as if the knife itself might give but then, mercifully, the blade slipped through the rubber. As soon as the tyre started to deflate, Ruth whipped the knife out, stabbing three more times in quick succession, the tip slipping in more easily with each jab as the pressure sank. She was about to scuttle back towards the hedgerow when her heart jumped as the cabin door flung open. She was shielded from view but only until either Anne or Mark moved around to the driver's side.

'Is that the lot?' Mark asked. Bizarrely, considering how long she'd spent watching him, it was the first time Ruth had heard him speak, knowing for sure it was him. His voice was deeper than she'd expected.

'I think so,' Anne replied. 'The cases are in the back.'

Ruth edged around towards the front of the car, trying not to skid on the grit.

'Have you got your purse?'

'Yes, but . . . my phone's inside somewhere.'

Ruth risked a glance over her shoulder. Mark was standing in the doorway of the building, staring into it with his arms crossed. There was no time to form a better plan, so Ruth stayed low, half sneaking, half running towards the shadow of the nearest caravan. At any moment, she expected Mark to yell after her but there was nothing. By the time she reached the corner, enveloping herself in the darkness, Mark still hadn't moved, his back to her as he peered into the building.

'Shall I call it?' he asked.

Ruth didn't hear the reply but Mark had his phone out anyway. Moments later, there was a tinkling sound from within and then Anne emerged with the device in her hand. Ruth didn't dare move, even though the dampness of the grass was seeping through the seat of her trousers. She was cold and knackered, mentally if nothing else. She felt out of her depth. This wasn't what she'd signed up for. As Anne slipped her phone into her bag, Ruth remembered that her own still had the volume turned up. Trying to move as little as possible, she stretched out her legs, slipping her fingers into her pocket and fingering around the edge of the device until she managed to turn it off. She'd left Dave's in the caravan.

Whew.

Mark was in the driver's seat as the car flared to life. The headlights burned across the car park, shining brightly into the caravan in which Ruth and Dave were staying. If she'd been watching from the window, she would have definitely been spotted. The car surged forward, stalling, before he started the engine again. Ruth had a perfect view through the passenger window, where Anne had her eyes closed and was resting her head against the glass. At the second attempt, Mark drove forward, turning towards the exit gate and then starting to reverse. The *flap-flap-flap* of the back wheel was dragging even louder than Ruth had thought it would, the rear end slumped to one side. For a moment, she thought that Mark was going to continue driving anyway but then the brake lights burned red and the driver's door opened. With the engine still idling, Mark walked around to the back of the car, hands on hips as he peered at the flat tyre. He placed a hand on the rubber and then withdrew it, staring at his palm and then turning in a circle, gazing into the shadows that surrounded him. Ruth remained still, holding her breath and trying to ignore how wet she was. Surely he couldn't see her? He'd have had to have eaten nothing but carrots to be able to spot her and yet his eyes lingered upon the spot in which she was sitting. Or did they? He was turning slowly, straining to see into each dark shadow, spending a second or two on each before moving on.

'Hello?'

His voice slinked through the darkness, more of a demand than a question. Ruth didn't move, didn't breathe.

Eventually, Mark leant back into the car and switched the engine off. He muttered something Ruth couldn't make out and then Anne climbed out of the passenger seat. Mark opened the boot and they removed the three bags, placing them on the ground before he lugged out a heavy-looking jack. With his attention focused the other way, Ruth slid backwards, getting herself even wetter but somehow making no noise as she glided the entire length of the caravan. She had no idea how long it took to change a tyre but that was the length of time she had to find Dave.

Who said she couldn't do two things at once? Three if she counted looking after herself.

Ruth scrambled to her feet and dashed across the

pathway. Instead of following the loop around the park, she was going to head straight through the middle . . . which was all well and good, aside from the unexpected waist-high chainlink fence in the centre. Ruth was running so quickly that she almost impaled herself on the barrier, sliding to a halt just in time and grazing her hands as she snatched at the metal to stop herself from barrelling into it. Bleeding palms, wet arse: it was turning into quite the night.

Delicately, she lifted herself over the fence, landing with a splat in a patch of mud on the other side but reckoning it was too late to care now. She skipped around an upturned bin, hurdled an errant set of steps that had blown over, and then dashed for the path. She emerged in a breathless huff, turning from side to side in an effort to figure out the area in which she'd lost Atkinson on the previous occasions. The caravans looked largely the same, aside from a few different shades of scratched, fading paint. Ruth found the correct place and crossed the path, finding a spot in between the caravans and the hedge through which she'd fallen the day before.

'Dave?'

Her old drama teacher used to carp on about stage whispers and would have been proud of Ruth's effort, even if there was no reply. In the immediate area, there were nine or ten caravans on each side of the path, plus the woods beyond. Where could he be?

'Dave?'

Ruth jumped as a bird of some sort launched itself into the air beyond the hedge, squawking in what was no doubt a deliberate attempt to scare the living crap out of her. There was a flutter of leaves and branches, and then the bloody thing disappeared into the night. Ruth checked her watch – it was seven minutes since she'd left Mark Atkinson to change the tyre and she was pretty sure he wouldn't have been able to do it in that time. She certainly hadn't heard the sound of a car engine.

Unsure of what else to do, Ruth approached the nearest caravan, heading up the small set of steps and leaning to peer through the adjacent window. She cupped her hands to shield her eyes from the glare of the moon, gazing across the built-in sink and draining board into the darkness at the back of the caravan. It had the exact same layout as the one in which they'd been staying: stale, dull and depressing. There was nothing out of place, however, and definitely no sign of a police constable.

Ruth checked over her shoulder and then moved to the next caravan, repeating her actions but noticing nothing out of place. She tried two more but there was nothing to see except for limescale-topped draining boards. Eleven minutes had passed since she'd left the front of the park and it would take her at least five to get back. She was running out of time.

'Dave?'

She waited, listening. Perhaps he'd got himself trapped underneath something and couldn't shout back.

Nothing.

Ruth was about to move to the next caravan when she spotted the smear on the door handle of the one across the path. It was on the opposite side from where she'd been searching, not on the rows near to the hedge but on the section that led towards the central divide. She crossed the path, checking both ways, until she was in front of the door. There was a definite mark on the cream surface underneath the handle, a graze from someone's fingers or knuckles. She'd first assumed it was mud but the closer she looked, even in the dim light from above, the more it seemed a coppery red as opposed to brown.

Just in case it was important, Ruth didn't touch the scuff itself, using the tips of her fingers to try to pull down the handle. It didn't give, so she strained sideways to peep through the kitchen window. The interior looked identical to the other caravans she'd been hunting around.

'Dave?'

Nothing.

Ruth jumped down the steps and did a quick lap of the caravan, though she wasn't tall enough to peer through the windows on any of the other sides. There were no other marks on the metal, nothing to see . . . except that she had a feeling. When she arrived back at the front, Ruth tried the handle again before checking the time – she had to be getting back to the front of the park, so it was now or never. Heck, it was only her career . . .

The spaces underneath the caravans were peppered with all sorts of junk – scrap metal, sodden planks of wood, bricks, rats . . . no, definitely not rats. *Stop thinking about rats.* Ruth crouched, feeling her thighs and knees creak from the damp, the running, the climbing. She stretched underneath, patting the ground until her fingers closed around a rough-edged half-brick. It felt heavy in her hands, the idea weighing as much as the object. She'd always been dreadful at throwing at school, not only when it came to distance but direction too. In a track and field PE lesson, she'd narrowly missed impaling Mrs Grant when she'd slipped and launched the javelin sideways. It had whistled through the air, sizzling past her teacher's chest and then spiked itself into the run-up for the long jump. If she'd tried to do it, she'd never have managed it.

Ruth stood at the bottom of the caravan steps remembering the javelin incident. She had to be better at throwing now, didn't she?

Only one way to find out.

Ruth pulled back and hurled the brick, watching as it sailed in a perfectly straight line and rattled through the window next to the door, sending a cascade of splintering glass with it and creating a fist-shaped hole. Take that, Mrs Grant. It was only ten years too late. And it had echoed around the park. Ruth didn't have time to care if either of the Atkinsons had heard it, heading up the stairs and using her elbow to knock a few loose shards of glass away from the window. She reached through carefully, straining and stretching until her fingers were brushing the door latch. She'd done the breaking, so entering was the next natural step. The two went hand in hand. Beans and toast, Manchester and rain, breaking and entering.

As soon as she got inside, Ruth could taste that there was something wrong. At first she wasn't sure what but then her first breath of air left her chest feeling heavy. Her vision swirled for a moment before righting itself and allowing her to focus. She stared towards the sofas and the coffee table but the area was empty, as was the kitchen, aside from the brick and broken glass. Beyond the first door was the bathroom but the manky shower and cheap-looking toilet was clear. The further Ruth went, the cloggier her lungs felt, as if somebody was scratching at her chest. The next door opened into a bedroom, but the bed was stripped and there was no sign of anything. One to go.

The air tasted foul, as if she'd just eaten something with too much pepper. Her tongue clung to the top of her mouth, her throat itched. Slowly, Ruth pushed open the final door, stepping backwards in alarm at the sight which met her. DC Rowlands was on the bed, head slumped forward, eyelids lolling up and down. The only reason he was still sitting was that he'd been tied back to back to a black woman. They were each gagged, feet bound together and wrists tied, but she looked in a far worse state. Her eyes were closed and weren't even flickering.

'Dave?'

He twisted his neck slowly to look at Ruth but could barely keep his eyes open, his chin flopping forward onto his chest.

43

Ruth stepped backwards into the kitchen area and took a breath before returning to the bedroom. She untied Dave's gag and then set to work on the woman's. She assumed it was Mark Atkinson who'd trapped the pair of them. He'd used long football socks as gags, tying them into a double knot. As soon as she'd released the woman's mouth, Ruth turned her attention back to Dave. His head was nodding forward and back, his eyes opening and closing. It was only when she followed the direction in which he was bobbing that Ruth realised he was trying to tell her something. Beyond the bed, directly underneath the window, was a heater that was burning hot. She knew nothing about that sort of contraption but it seemed obvious it was from there that the toxic fumes were pouring. Ruth twisted the dial at the top and then stretched up and opened the window.

Suddenly, Wales was the greatest place on earth, full of wondrous clean air that poured into Ruth's lungs. She took three mouthfuls and then turned to face the pair on the bed. Dave's eyes were half-open as he struggled against his bonds but he didn't seem to be getting anywhere.

'You all right?' Ruth asked, immediately cursing herself. On a list of stupid questions that had ever been asked, it was right up there.

He nodded.

'Was it Atkinson?'

Another nod.

Ruth was about to head into the kitchen when she remembered she still had the knife from slashing the car tyres. She delved into her pocket and set to work on the rope that was tying Dave and the woman together. It felt like a stiff washing line, some mix of metal and cord that scratched at her fingers. The knife was making little impact either.

'Dave?'

His eyes had closed, his head flopping forward like the woman's. Ruth's palms still felt raw after the impact from the fence but she gritted her teeth, clasped the knife as hard as she could, and then yanked up on the rope with one hand, down with the knife with the other. In an instant, the twine went loose, dropping into the prisoners' laps. Ruth grabbed one end and started pulling, tossing it to the side until they were separated. Their arms and legs were still tied but she didn't have time. Without the rope to support them, Dave and the woman each drooped sideways, heads colliding as they landed on the bed.

Neither of them moved.

Ruth returned to the window, pushing her cheeks into the gap and taking a deep breath. Dave was her colleague, probably even her friend, but the woman had been unconscious from the moment Ruth broke in and had to be the priority. She rounded the bed and hooked her hands underneath her armpits, trying desperately not to let her head drop as she dragged her backwards off the bed.

Bloody hell, she was heavy.

If everyone got out of this safely, Ruth was going to pay for the woman to go on some sort of Slimming World course. Everyone always thought their weight was under control until their unconscious body needed to be dragged out of a poisonous caravan bedroom and then the truth set in.

Ruth dug in her heels and *pulled* as hard as she could, her back cricking, neck straining as the woman plopped off the bed and started to slide along the floor. Ruth kicked the broken glass to the side and continued to pull the woman through the kitchen, still cursing her weight before she realised the obvious.

Oh no.

She wasn't fat, the woman was pregnant . . . and Ruth had just dragged her off a bed.

This was so bad in so many, many ways. Ruth managed to pull her into the main doorway but there was a drop of a metre or so to the ground, and no way she could let the pregnant woman drop. She was limp, arms slumped by her sides, head drooping at an angle. Ruth was out of choices and out of time. She jumped down from the caravan, moving the steps out of the way and then reaching up underneath the woman's armpits and lifting as hard as she could.

Everything hurt.

She felt like one of those weightlifters at the Olympics, the ones whose arms and legs looked as if they might rip in half before they heaved up an impossible weight and then screamed their heads off. Ruth felt like screaming but was in too much pain to get the sounds out.

Moments later and it was all over. Ruth crumpled to her knees, placing the woman on the grass as carefully as she could.

Now for Dave.

From nowhere, she felt rejuvenated, hopping up into the caravan and heading into the bedroom, where Dave was in a sitting position, rubbing his head. He'd somehow got his legs free.

'We've got to get outside,' Ruth whispered.

He nodded, acknowledging her presence but seemed unable to hold himself up. Ruth looped a hand across his back, resting underneath his armpit and hauling him to his feet.

Bloody hell! He didn't even have the excuse of being pregnant. The constable spent half his time eating salads, too, so he must have been a real porker in months gone by.

Ruth dragged him into the kitchen and towards the front door. His efforts to move were paltry to say the least.

'Come on, Dave, there's a drop to the ground.'

He mumbled something that sounded a bit like 'Mummy', eyelids still heavy as Ruth left him leaning on the sink while she hopped outside and found the stairs again. Back inside, she supported his weight once more.

'Two steps, Dave. Well, three. You're going to have to help yourself. Follow me.'

She went first, backing down the steps and reaching up to try to stop him falling. Dave managed the first step perfectly adequately . . . well, in a staggering zombie end-of-days way.

'Come on, Dave, nearly there.'

He tried the next step but tripped, lurching forward and crashing down face-first onto the grass with a splat.

'Oops, sorry, mate.'

Ruth reached down to help him up but there was a crunch from behind. She spun, ducking instinctively as something whistled through the air, narrowly missing her head.

Lucky girl.

Mark Atkinson was standing over her clutching a tyre iron but the swing had taken him off-balance, leaving him stumbling into the side of the caravan as Ruth faltered sideways. He straightened himself, side-stepping across the pair of bodies and forcing Ruth to take a step backwards. She felt in her pocket for the knife but it wasn't there, lost somewhere in the caravan.

'My, my,' Atkinson said, 'aren't you the little hero?'

Ruth pressed herself up, ignoring her aching back, pulsating thighs, and scraped palms. She felt like shite. 'I'm Detective Constable Ruth Evesham and you're under arrest.'

He nodded, lifting the tyre iron slightly in his grip, feeling its weight. 'Is that right?'

'You do not have to say anything but it may harm your defence if you do not mention, when questioned, something which you later rely on in court. Anything you do say may be given in evidence.' She paused for a breath. 'Do you understand?'

Atkinson's eyes had narrowed, as he stared at her. 'You're serious?'

Ruth took another step backwards, gaze flickering past him to the path beyond.

Atkinson broke into a smile. 'You think I'm going to fall for the old someone behind me trick? Is that what they teach you nowadays?'

He stepped towards the prone, groaning DC Rowlands, the tyre iron raised above his head, ready to cave the defenceless constable's head in.

44

Three hours to the caravan park? Yeah, right. DCI Topper had driven like a maniac, aided by the blues and twos blazing a path in front of him. Misguided judgemental people claimed *she* was a bad driver but Jessica was hanging on for dear life as the chief inspector barrelled around corners, took the racing line at every possible opportunity and generally drove like a man possessed. Wait until she told Fat Pat about this . . . assuming they survived, of course.

It would have been simpler to contact the local police, except that Jessica had spent the best part of forty-five minutes attempting to do just that. She was passed from one person to another, trying to find out which force had jurisdiction over the tiny corner of Wales to which they were heading. It was Saturday evening and, by the time she managed to speak to the right person, she was told that it would take another forty-five minutes to get a team into place – 'everyone's off-duty, you see'.

In the end, she told him to forget it.

They didn't forget it. The line of police cars roared into the caravan park, closely followed by Topper's 4×4. They screeched to a halt at the wall of vehicles ahead. There was an ambulance, five police cars with 'Heddlu' written on the side, a green hatchback, and, crucially, a silver Ford Focus.

Jessica was out of the car before Topper had switched off the engine, racing across the car park towards a group of uniformed officers. 'What's going on?' she asked.

One of the officers pointed towards a single-storey Cold War throwback masquerading as a block of cabins. Dim orange light was seeping from two of the units and Jessica opted for the nearest, opening the front door and heading inside.

DC Evesham was sitting on a sofa, sipping from a cup of tea and looking a little worse for wear. Her damp hair was matted across her head and she was wrapped in a rough-looking blanket.

'You all right?' Jessica asked, out of breath.

The constable held up her hands, revealing a criss-cross of scratches. 'Well, I cut up my hands, I've hurt my back, my thighs are killing me, my ankles are on fire, I got a bump on the head and I'm sodding freezing. If you put all of that to one side then, yes, I'm bloody fantastic.' She broke into a grin, adding: 'I'm fine.'

Jessica returned the smile. She knew that feeling. 'Everyone else?'

'No shots fired.'

For the first time since leaving the farm, Jessica started to relax. She'd tried calling both Rowlands' and Evesham's phones throughout the journey but there had been no answer. Nothing had come in over the radios either.

'Sonia Gordon?'

'She was taken away in one of the ambulances. She's okay but a bit shaken. I guess we'll find out about her baby.'

'Dave?'

'He went off in another ambulance.'

'Is he—?'

'He's all right – but he's probably broken his nose. If anyone says anything then it was his own fault. If he wasn't so heavy, I could have supported him.'

'What happened?'

Evesham rolled her eyes, sipped her tea and then told Jessica how she'd found Rowlands and Sonia Gordon in a caravan on the far side of the park, slowly suffocating to death in a small bedroom with a dodgy heater. She didn't know why Mark Atkinson hadn't just killed the pair of them – Dave especially – other than the fact that he was a little squeamish until he was really pushed. One of the officers had told Ruth that a safety panel had been removed from the heater, meaning it was pouring gas into the room.

Jessica interrupted Ruth as she reached the point where she'd turned to see Atkinson with the tyre iron. 'Where is he?' Jessica asked.

The constable pointed through the window towards the remaining ambulance that had a ring of police officers around it. 'He's okay, he just got his arse kicked.'

'Clayton?'

Evesham indicated towards the police van next to the ambulance. 'He saved me. Mark thought I was trying to do the old look over your shoulder thing, not realising that Clayton actually *was* behind him. I have no idea how he got here or where he came from. I didn't even know who he was when he first showed up.'

'What did he do?'

'He was looking at his wife on the floor and I could see the veins popping around his temples. Next thing, he'd launched himself at Atkinson, rugby tackling him to the ground. He was swinging and swinging, punch after punch.' She tilted her head to show a small gash next to her ear. 'He caught me as I was trying to pull him off. Atkinson was already unconscious and if he'd hit him any more, he'd have killed him.'

Jessica sighed, wondering if Ruth knew the full extent of what Clayton had probably done. She doubted it, or else the constable might not be calling him her saviour.

'Are you sure you're fine?' Jessica asked.

'I could do with a few days off.'

'The guv might be able to help with that. The chief constable will probably have a thing or two to say as well. That's if he's not gone on holiday before then. The higher up they get, the harder it is to get them off the golf course.'

Ruth finished her tea and put the mug down. 'Are you joking?'

'Maybe. What happened to Anne Atkinson?'

'Next door.'

Jessica offered another sympathetic smile and then returned to the car park. The police van and the ambulance were both moving slowly around in a circle, flanked at the front and back by the 'Heddlu' cars. Someone, somewhere, was going to have one hell of a lot of paperwork to do and it definitely wasn't going to be her.

After watching them leave, Jessica knocked on the door of the chalet next door and heard Topper's voice telling her to come in. The living room was exactly the same as the cabin in which Evesham was in, but this time Anne Atkinson was sitting in an armchair with a uniformed officer on either side and Topper on the sofa opposite. Her arms were crossed, lips pressed firmly together. She was close to Jessica's age but looked so much older. Her brown hair had a grey streak through the centre, with flecks of white peppering her eyebrows too. She was pale and looked severely underfed, the blemishes of Walker's attack on her seventeen years previously crystal clear, even though there were no visible marks.

Jessica exchanged a look with Topper, who told her with something akin to telepathy that Anne wasn't speaking. She raised her eyebrows and sat on the sofa, with Topper taking the hint. He stood, telling the other officers to follow him and leaving Jessica alone with Anne.

'Clocks go back tonight,' Jessica said. 'Or forward. One or the other. I bloody hate this time of year.'

Anne looked up, saying nothing at first before asking where her husband was.

'You must know where he's off to,' Jessica replied.

'He was trying to keep me safe.'

'I'm sure he was. So, tell me, is this what you wanted?'

The other woman stared across the room towards Jessica before unfolding her arms and slowly, deliberately, rolling up her top and exposing her stomach. Splayed across the area around her belly button was a mish-mash of intersecting cuts and scars, the physical marks to match the mental ones.

'Do you think I wanted this?' she whispered, her voice

disconcertingly calm. Jessica couldn't pull her eyes away from the horrific mutilations until Anne dropped her top. 'Well?' she added.

'Of course you didn't.'

'Right – but *he* did it anyway. And then you let him go.'

Anne spat the words towards her but this was a conflict Jessica was never going to win. Anne Atkinson had had her life stolen as a teenager and whichever way people wanted to dress up rehabilitation and society's duty to give people a second chance, no one could deny her the anger that she felt at being let down.

'Whose idea was it?' Jessica asked.

'Does it matter?'

'What about Clayton Gordon? How did you find out who he was?'

Anne bit her bottom lip, shaking her head. 'You don't know?'

'Someone will tell us – probably Clayton himself. If you want to help your husband and yourself, it may as well be you.'

Anne didn't reply for a short while and, when she did, she clutched her stomach and stared at the floor. 'He came to us saying that Walker was going to be released with a new name – Eric Seasmith. He was disgusted that that animal was going to be on the streets. He told us all about the cosy little house in Didsbury. *We* can't afford to live somewhere like that, but look at him – Walker, Seasmith or whatever you want to call him. He kills four women and cuts me open, then gets to come out to that. He never even went to prison.'

'So you repaid Clayton Gordon by kidnapping his wife and bringing her to a caravan park in the middle of nowhere?'

Anne didn't flinch. 'It wasn't like that. We wanted Walker to pay. *I* wanted him to pay.'

'So why not just kill him? Find out from Clayton where he lived and do the job yourself?'

'Because it would have been too obvious. We'd be some of the first people you'd look at because he doesn't have connections to anyone else. Plus what punishment is that? We wanted . . . *I* wanted to see him suffer. To actually go to prison. To die there.'

Jessica waited, knowing the next question was *the* question. She already knew the answer, or at least thought she did. Anne was right that they'd have been under suspicion, which was why they'd escaped to the middle of nowhere, giving themselves perfect alibis for the two murders.

'So, because of that, you held Clayton's wife hostage and forced him to kill those girls just to prove a point?'

Anne's reply took a while and, when it came, it was more of a breath than a whisper. 'I wanted him to pay.'

It was the only explanation that made sense. Walker's electronic tag hadn't gone off because he hadn't left the house. Clayton had stolen one or two of his hairs from a pillow or a comb and then planted them on the bodies. He was the one who'd left the house at night.

'Why two girls?'

'Because you're so useless. We'd – *I'd* – read up about things like this and he couldn't just leave the hairs somewhere obvious, else it would look wrong. I figured a hair within the hair would be best but you couldn't figure it out. I thought you'd bodged it.'

'It was the rain.'

Anne shrugged. 'As soon as you found out it was Walker and arrested him, Sonia would've been allowed to go. No one was trying to hurt her. But you couldn't do your jobs, so we had to make sure.'

The disconnect with which she spoke was terrifying – nothing mattered to her except revenge. Meanwhile, Holly Jamieson had died because of sheer bad luck. If it had been a dry night on the evening Casey Graves was attacked, there was every likelihood the forensics team would have found Walker's planted hair quicker. There was also a very good chance he would have been convicted for something he didn't do.

Jessica had more or less all she needed. Whether either of the Atkinsons or Clayton repeated it on tape with a solicitor at their side was another matter. For now, it'd do.

'How did Clayton know where you were?'

'Sorry?'

'If he knew you were here all along, why wouldn't he have raced here to free his wife?'

'I have no idea how he found us. He roared through the gate and then said he'd kill me if I didn't tell him where his wife was. I didn't actually know but, well . . . I guess he found her.'

Jessica was confused before the truth hit her. Topper had given him the information by accident when they'd been in the hallway at the bottom of the stairs in Walker's farmhouse. He'd asked Jessica if she'd heard from Evergreen. Clayton had been in the doorway of the kitchen resting on the officers for support and could have easily overheard. It was no wonder he'd roared off.

For a moment, she almost blabbed the answer but, when the doodoo hit the fan, Jessica figured someone else could work it out. Either that, or Clayton would tell the truth. It definitely wasn't going to be her.

'I hope you and your husband have your stories straight,' Jessica said, standing.

'Does it matter? We're supposed to live in a decent society and you've all let me down.'

Jessica paused by the door, one hand on the catch. 'When you were plotting your revenge on Walker, did you think about the innocent people you'd be affecting? Not just those two girls but Clayton Gordon, his wife and their unborn kid?'

Anne turned, staring straight into Jessica's eyes and rolling up her top. 'Who was there to look after me? Only Mark – and look at what you've done to him. Walker did this. All of it.'

Jessica opened the door. 'No, he didn't.'

45

SUNDAY

Jessica didn't want anyone to know but she actually enjoyed the warm-up act ahead of Blaine Banner's gig. It was some bloke with an acoustic guitar singing songs about how people shouldn't trust the police, the government or anyone else in authority because they were all corrupt. The crowd went wild, cheering each of the incendiary lyrics as the inhabitants of the box from which Jessica was watching looked awkwardly at one other.

As the scraggy, bearded revolutionist strolled off the stage, the roadies piled on and started to get it ready for Banner and co. The box given to them by Banner offered the best view in the house, sitting in between two levels of seating, high but not too high and level with the edge of the stage.

Jessica took two glasses of champagne from the server and crossed the box, offering one to Izzy, who was wearing tight jeans and a black Blaine Banner T-shirt. She was also far too excited, hovering around the edge of the balcony and bellowing at the roadies to get a move on.

'Drink?' Jessica asked.

Izzy pushed away from the edge, flopping into a seat. 'I'm training, remember.'

'Just one?'

'No, one will mean two, then two will become three. I'm going to do this marathon one way or the other – and then I'll drink.'

'How about you drink now and then you *don't* do the marathon and I don't have to pay you fifty quid.'

'How about you stop being so stingy and sponsor me more than fifty quid?'

Jessica put down the champagne flute on the ledge in front of her friend. 'Every group of friends always has a show-off. Someone does a 10K, so someone else has to do a half-marathon. Not to be outdone, that first person has to come back and do a full marathon. This competitive nature is a really bad character trait. You should speak to someone.'

Izzy picked up the champagne glass and handed it back. 'Thanks for the invite.'

'Thank Blaine, not me.'

Izzy peeped over the railing towards the stage. 'Oh, believe me, I will do. Is it definitely nailed on that we get to meet him after the show?'

Jessica turned to where Izzy's husband was in conversation with DC Rowlands and Katherine Franks. 'Yep – everyone gets to meet him, you *and* you husband.'

'Spoilsport.'

Jessica laughed, downing one glass of champagne and then starting on the other. It had been that sort of week.

Izzy was fiddling with her phone: 'Did you see the wedding photos?'

'Thankfully not.'

She turned it around, zooming in to show a grinning Ellie and gurning Liam McGregor.

'He looks constipated,' Jessica said.

'She probably had a fork up his arse, directing him to the altar. They're doing a twelve-page special in *OK!* this week, plus a Channel Five special next Saturday.'

'Unbelievable.'

'The magazine are paying for them to go on honeymoon to Antigua with the proviso that they get to send a photographer too.'

'I should've bloody left him hiding at his friend's house.'

'No you shouldn't.'

Jessica stood, picking Izzy up and giving her a hug. 'Thanks,' she whispered.

'For what?'

'Being you.'

She stepped away, offering a weak smile as Izzy's husband cut in. He was tall and dressed in a suit, utterly out of place next to his rocker wife. Jessica doubted he'd ever been to a gig before.

'Everything all right?' he asked, pecking Izzy on the head.

She winked at Jessica, smoothing her T-shirt and pointing at Banner out of her husband's view. 'Everything's fine, hon.'

Jessica turned and almost overbalanced as Archie made his way down the steps, clutching four beers in one go.

'They're free all night,' Jessica told him as he fumbled backwards, putting the drinks on the floor. He was wearing a Manchester United shirt with 'LEGEND' on the back.

'Aye, I didn't know if they'd be hoiking the price up later, so piled in while I could.'

'Free's free, Arch.'

He grinned at her and then his smile shrank as he nodded sideways to a young woman with long blonde hair and a matching United shirt. 'This is Arwen,' he said. 'We're, er, sort of seeing each other.'

Arwen had her hand outstretched, nails each painted with the Red Devils' logo. Aside from the shirt, she was stunning, with a wide pixie-like smile and cute nose. She was closer to Archie's age and, probably crucially, shorter than he was.

'Hey,' Arwen said.

Jessica shook her hand. 'All right?'

'Arch has told me all about you.'

'Has he indeed?'

Jessica's gaze flickered to Archie, whose panicked expression told her that he hadn't told his girlfriend *everything* about them.

'He says you're a cool person to work for?'

'Shhhhhhhhh . . .' Archie cooed but Jessica slipped in between him and Arwen, her back to him.

'Were those his exact words?'

'Yes.'

'What else did he say?'

Archie pushed his way around Jessica, taking his girlfriend's hand. 'Not much . . . just the usual. Come on – we should see if they've still got food on the go.'

Before Jessica could ask anything else, he was dragging

his girlfriend up the steps in the general direction of the hot buffet.

Jessica glanced around the box but it was almost entirely couples. Dave was in the corner, making the most of his broken nose as Katherine fussed over him, fetching him drinks and food. As soon as her back was turned, the cheeky sod winked in Jessica's direction. If he could get away with it, he'd milk this for months.

At the back of the box, Jessica's magician friend Hugo was playing with a pair of hoops, interlocking and unlocking them as Caroline watched, trying to figure out how he was doing it. Jessica hadn't seen them in a while but it felt like a night for friends – even if she was a singleton in a world of couples. She'd still not had the heart to tell Izzy what had happened to Adam.

'Hey.' Jessica turned to see DC Evesham offering her another glass of champagne. 'You looked like you were running low,' she said.

'I'm not sure it's possible for a drink to get low in this box.'

There was a piece of tape across one of the constable's temples and sore-looking scratches on her palms, though she was otherwise unmarked. 'Thanks for the invite,' she said.

'I think it's the least I could do. Besides, this is *definitely* not a gift to the police force. There's no way I'm declaring it anyway. Did you get your time off?'

Evesham plonked both hands on her hips. 'Two sodding days – and they owed me that in overtime anyway. The ungrateful bastards.'

Jessica didn't want to laugh but it slipped out anyway. 'Welcome to Longsight.'

'Did you hear about Sonia Gordon's baby?'

Jessica nodded. 'I don't know what kind of life the poor kid's going to have with its dad in prison but the only reason it survived at all is because of you.'

Evesham shrugged. 'I'm just surprised they're not sending me on a health and safety course to teach me how to lift properly.'

Jessica laughed again. 'Now I *know* you're one of us.'

Before she could say anything else, the lights dropped and a large cheer went up. There were a few moments of silence and then somebody started playing a bass line. Izzy was screaming as loudly as anyone – louder – bellowing 'Blaiiiiiiiiiiiiine' at the top of her voice. In an instant, the lights blinked on and Blaine was front and centre belting out the opening lyrics of *Threeway* into the microphone. Not bad for a man who'd had his stomach pumped recently.

Izzy was dancing perilously close to the edge of the balcony, her husband looking on nervously. Archie and Arwen were next to one another in their matching shirts, while Rowlands was leaning on Katherine's shoulders as if he was a bloody war veteran instead of an overweight sod who'd fallen off some stairs. Even Caroline and Hugo were holding hands, gazing down towards the action. Only Evesham was alone but she didn't seem to mind, waving her arms in the air and singing along.

Jessica watched her colleagues . . . her friends . . . from the back of the box wishing the people she really loved were with her. One day, she'd have to come to terms with what had happened to Adam. There was only so long she could pretend it wasn't happening. That was, hadn't *happened*. But Bex . . .

As the first song blurred into the second, Jessica crept out of the back of the box, heading into the concrete-clad corridor. She headed to the other side and sat on a ledge with her eyes closed, enjoying the degree of silence. The music was muffled, blaring in the background and that meant she didn't have to be with others.

'Hiya.' Jessica opened her eyes to see Arwen with her Red Devil nails and Manchester United shirt. She was perfect for Archie. 'I'm looking for the toilets,' Arwen said.

Jessica pointed towards the end of the corridor.

'Are you all right?' Arwen asked.

'Bit of a headache.'

'Not really your thing?'

Jessica shrugged. 'Not today.'

'Have you been to many gigs before?'

'A few . . . I never get the encore thing. I work for the police, so what if I did what they do? I get everyone in a room Miss Marple-style and tell them I know the identity of the murderer. I talk them through the crimes and the build-up and then, before naming names, I walk out, turn the lights off and stand in the hallway. Everyone in the room has to clap their hands and stamp their feet until I go back and put them out of their misery.'

Arwen sniggered, although Jessica wasn't sure she got it. 'At least the music's good,' she said.

'I suppose.'

'My dad's a big fan but I always preferred the early Banner-Rafferty stuff before Blaine got famous.'

'Right . . . I've never heard of it.'

'It's really good – you should track it down. I'll give Arch some details to pass on.'

'Thanks.' Arwen smiled sweetly and set off along the corridor towards the toilets when Jessica called her back. 'What stuff were you talking about?' she asked.

'The Banner-Rafferty collaborations. You can get them as a bootleg but they're not well known. Bob Rafferty is the guy who started off with Blaine way, way back when they were gigging in pubs – that's when my dad started watching the band. I think they were at college together. For whatever reason, they went their separate ways. Blaine became a big star and Bob's got his own band that do pub gigs around here. There were rumours he was going to be the opening act but I guess not.'

Jessica slipped her phone out of her pocket and returned the smile. 'What's the name of that bootleg website?'

46

It was a few minutes before eleven when Jessica got out of the taxi and headed into the hotel where Blaine Banner and his band had been staying. Benny was on the front desk and immediately recognised her, panicking at the thought that something else had happened.

'How's business?' Jessica asked.

His eyes darted past her, looking for trouble. 'All right . . . should I call the manager?'

'Is Alice working tonight?'

'She's in the kitchen.'

'Can you tell her I'd like a little chat? I'll be in the bar.'

Jessica headed to the far end of the reception area and slipped through to the bar. She ordered a glass of rosé and found a snuggly booth that was lined with soft crimson velvet. Lovely. If she was honest, she was feeling a little tipsy after the champagne and now the wine but what the hell, she was off-duty and it had been one hell of a week.

Alice emerged from a door at the far end a couple of minutes later, wearing her uniform of a dark skirt with a white blouse and a tie. She walked confidently across the floor before slotting in on the other side of the booth.

'Did you want me?' she asked, tucking a strand of blonde hair behind her ear.

'How old are you, Alice?'

'Twenty-two.'

'Good – the bar closes in two minutes so what would you like?'

'I'm on duty, we're not allowed to drink.'

'You sure?'

Alice examined her and then turned. 'Oh, sod it. I'll have one of those apple VK things – the sugar will keep me awake all night.'

Jessica did the honours, approaching the bar and ordering the drink before returning to the booth. Aside from the barman, it was just the two of them.

'I've just been at the Arena,' Jessica said. 'Blaine Banner's putting on one hell of a show.'

'Okay . . .'

'What's your dad's band like?'

Alice froze with the bottle halfway to her lips. 'Oh . . .'

'Oh, indeed.'

'Am I in trouble?'

'Tell me about your dad.'

Alice paused. 'Am I—?'

'Just do it, Alice. We're two women having a drink.'

She took a large drink of the vile apple concoction and then coughed. 'My dad started a band when he was a teenager, eighteen or nineteen, younger than me. He's an amazing guitar player. He was the one who got Blaine – *Graham* – into music in the first place. They wrote their early songs together but Blaine took them away and left my dad playing pubs while he went off to be famous. My dad should've been the big star, not that jumped-up smackhead.'

Jessica took a large swig of her wine, wishing she'd ordered two. 'Is your dad happy?'

'How do you mean?'

'Is he bitter about whatever happened, or is he happy with you and the life he has?'

Alice turned as the barman started to stack stools. 'He talks about the good ol' days.'

'So would anyone – but that doesn't mean he's unhappy with what he has.'

Alice had a sip of her drink and paused for a few moments. 'I suppose he's happy.'

'Did it occur to you that, if your dad was the rock star you think he should be, then you might not exist?'

'I . . . don't know. He's been married to my mum for, like, ever.'

'What would your dad think if he knew what you'd done?'

'I haven't done anything! I was just messing around.'

'Just because Blaine leaves his hotel room unlocked, it doesn't mean you can sneak in, leave notes, move things around and pretend to be a bloody ghost.'

'They're not crimes, are they?'

'What about tying him up and pouring booze down his throat?'

Alice went quiet, sipping her drink. 'I don't know what you're talking about.'

'I'm sure you don't.'

'He touched my arse! He thinks he can have any girl just because he's famous.'

Jessica downed the rest of her wine. 'So report him. There are ways and means.'

'As if anyone will believe me – he's got a poster the size of a building on Deansgate.'

Jessica nodded, *really* wishing she'd ordered more than one drink.

Alice's voice was a whisper: 'Am I going to prison?'

'I wouldn't have thought so.'

'But I'll get fired. People will think my dad put me up to it.'

She was starting to stand, suddenly sounding worried but Jessica reached forward, touching her on the shoulder and telling her to sit.

'What are you going to do?' Alice whimpered.

'I should report it but everyone thinks Blaine was off his head anyway, which isn't far from the truth. He doesn't seem to think there's much harm done. His stupid manager even tidied up after you, more worried about the bad press. Give me tomorrow to think things over. My head's not right at the moment.'

Alice's chest was rising and falling rapidly. 'Thank you.'

'Don't thank me yet. I'll be back tomorrow – you can buy me a drink.'

Neither of them said anything as the barman continued to stack chairs at the back of the room. He was singing *Threeway* to himself, getting the words wrong.

'Is that one of your dad's?' Jessica asked.

Alice shook her head, smirking, staring at the floor. 'Can I ask you something?'

'Go on.'

'What's tomorrow?'

Jessica sighed, picking up her empty glass. If Hugo was here he could have found a way of magically refilling it. 'I've got to drive to Prestatyn,' she said.

'Why?'

'To scatter my dead fiancé's ashes.'

'Oh.'

Oh, indeed.

47

Jessica stood on the pavement outside the hotel waiting for the taxi. Five sodding minutes, they'd said. Five minutes! Fifteen minutes later, there was no sign of anyone in a cab and if she hung around for too much longer, some dodgy kerb-crawler was going to try to pick her up. Well, that's if she still had *it*.

The air was biting, the breeze vicious. Jessica pulled her jacket tighter, trying to stop her teeth from chattering. She could have waited in the lobby but then bloody Benny would harass her. She'd rather freeze to death.

She wondered if things would feel different in twenty-four hours, whether sprinkling Adam's ashes would finally allow her to accept he was gone. Despite the time that had passed, the coma, Pomeroy and Archie, there was still a part of her that believed he'd return. That he'd walk through the front door as his old self, jabbering on about something Star Wars-related, or some other sciencey thing that she neither understood nor cared about. After tomorrow, she'd surely realise that it was never going to happen.

What then?

Still no sign of the cab. Jessica took out her phone, about to call the taxi company and give someone an earful when it started ringing. 'UNKNOWN' blazed across the front, which usually meant a marketing call.

Surely not at this time of night?

Jessica pressed to answer. 'Hello?'

It was a woman's voice. A young woman's voice. A girl's: 'Jessica?'

'Bex? Is that you?'

There was silence, a plip and then the line went dead.

SOMETHING HIDDEN

Kerry Wilkinson

*The second book featuring private investigator
Andrew Hunter*

Everyone hates Fiona Methodist.

Her war veteran father shot a young couple in broad daylight before killing himself. The engaged pair had witnessed a robbery and were due to give evidence but, with all three now dead, no one knows the true motive.

For Fiona, it's destroyed her life. It's not just those who whisper behind her back or the friends who pretend she doesn't exist; it's the landlords who spot her name and say no, the job agencies who can't find her work.

But Fiona knows her dad didn't do it. He couldn't have – he's her father and he wouldn't do that . . . would he?

Private investigator Andrew Hunter takes pity on the girl and, even with stolen bengal cats to find, plus an ex-wife who's not quite so 'ex', he can't escape the creeping feeling that Fiona might be right after all.

OUT NOW

LOCKED IN

The first in the Jessica Daniel series, Locked In *is the number one bestselling crime thriller from Kerry Wilkinson*

When a body is found in a locked house, Detective Sergeant Jessica Daniel is left to not only find the killer but discover how they got in and out.

With little in the way of leads and a journalist that seems to know more about the case than she does, Jessica is already feeling the pressure – and that's before a second body shows up in identical circumstances to the first.

How can a murderer get to victims in seemingly impossible situations and what, if anything, links the bodies?

extracts reading groups events
competitions books new
discounts extracts extracts
competitions reading groups discounts events
books new extracts reading groups
events books discounts
new books extracts titles reading groups
interviews
events extracts events new
discounts events books
new books events interviews new books extracts
events new reading groups
discounts extracts discounts
www.panmacmillan.com
extracts events reading groups
competitions books extracts new books